Autumn Snow *and* Witch Of Winter

Dr. Robert F. Bollendorf, EdD, CADC

and Donna J. Gluck, MS, LCPC

authorHOUSE®

AuthorHouse™
1663 Liberty Drive
Bloomington, IN 47403
www.authorhouse.com
Phone: 1 (800) 839-8640

Published by AuthorHouse 01/12/2018

ISBN: 978-1-5462-2064-0 (sc)
ISBN: 978-1-5462-2063-3 (e)

Praise for Autumn Snow

"Once again, Dr. Bollendorf, with Donna Gluck, has woven a vivid and entertaining tapestry of dysfunctional family dynamics and the ripples of sadness that drug addiction causes. As the effects of addiction explode the romantic and familial relationships of the well drawn characters, we see the radius of the blast expand to disrupt communities and cultures, particularly the Native American reservations and the tensions of coexistence with the white cities and towns. The themes of addiction, its treatment, and the recovery process are accurate and informative, but rather than simply exposit these valuable lessons, Autumn Snow wraps it all in an entertaining and suspenseful murder mystery.

Dedication

To my Family

This book is affectionately dedicated to Lucille and Linda: one gave me life, one brought me back.

Acknowledgements

This book presented a number of challenges the authors had not faced in previous works. It was our first attempt at collaborating on a novel. The novel was a new genre for us, about a different culture, and introduced new characters joining the cast from Rob Bollendorf's previous two novels, Sober Spring and Flight of the Loon.

We feel fortunate that the right people seem to present themselves when we need them. First we'd like to thank the Menominee people, especially the historical society, members of the tribal police department, and the staff of Maehnowesekiyah.

We also want to say we wouldn't be interested in writing if we didn't have the opportunity to learn new things ourselves. But even in learning as much as we can, we know we won't do justice to a culture as old and complex as the Menominee Nation. Therefore, we apologize in advance for any misrepresentation and we take full responsibility for errors of any kind.

We'd also like to thank the staff of the Keshena library for their help. It was sadly ironic that on the first day we went there to do research, the library was closed because the head of the library had spun out on black ice on Highway VV and was killed. It made us think immediately of a similar incident in the book, but Scott was a fictional character and this person was real, and we're sorry for the loss to her family and to the library staff. All of the characters in this book are fictional, but many of the places are real.

We'd like to thank Father David of St. Michael's Catholic Church who also served, when we interviewed him, on the board of Maehnowesekiyah. Maehnowesekiyah is a real treatment center and we visited it to get information about treatment. It would be impossible in our brief visit to learn all the aspects of treatment; therefore, we do not pretend that what is described in this book is what actually transpires there. Plus, it should be noted that most treatment centers have moved away from the cookie cutter approach of the early days of treatment. Today, patients each receive an individual treatment plan.

Rob would like to thank his friends Bill and Renita Vlasek for their reading, advice, and encouragement, and also his niece Jodi Dabson Bollendorf. Jodi is probably the most prolific consumer of mystery novels ever, and she gave great advice and ideas. Rob would also like to thank Diane Reis and Barbara Frier for early reading and typing. A number of our students read the book at various stages and many were very complimentary, giving us the confidence to continue. At the same time, they offered a number of suggestions that improved the book. We'd like to thank Lisa Hopkins, Bill Makely, Sharon Andersohn, and Eleanor Donlon for editing. Rob would also like to thank his wife, Linda, and daughter, Becky, for their advice and editing.

Donna would like to thank all those—family and friends—who patiently understood and accepted her many absences. With love, thank you to Jamie and Jason for all the encouragement. We would also like to thank Joe for believing in us and April for putting up with all of us so graciously.

Prologue

Scott Brandt was on his way home when it happened. He had not been there in years—not really. Oh, he stopped in, but his heart wasn't there. But now he was excited to be really going home.

Then it happened.

The world before him was dreamlike and unclear—the cars emerging eerily from the snowflakes of an early autumn snow, like wisps of ghosts floating by on their way to haunt someone else.

He remembered trying to avoid the cars that seemed to appear from behind a curtain of snow. He remembered the sensation of sliding on a thin layer of ice. He remembered striking a tree. He had seen the front end of his car collapse as the impact jolted his chest and head against the steering wheel.

Then he must have lost consciousness for a while. Was it his imagination or did he also remember awakening when he felt the needle prick his arm? A hand reached through the broken glass of the window and squeezed the contents of a syringe something that had never happened? He groggily observed the hand searching his pockets and was glad that he had hidden the pictures well.

The accident had not only severely injured his arms, legs, and ribs, making any movement difficult and painful, but it had jammed the doors locked, trapping him inside. A stab of pain shot through his arms as he tried to move them. He felt more than one broken bone—the pain was so intense he could almost hear the grating of bone fragment against bone frag- ment. Had a drug really been administered, or was this just adrenaline and endorphins coursing through his body?

It was hard to stay conscious, but Scott fought to keep his mind awake. He didn't know if the injection had hit a vein. Even with skin-popping, it wouldn't take long to reach the brain. He focused on the idea of the drug, trying to diagnose himself, and to identify the possible concoction: a speedball, perhaps?—that effective combination of heroin and cocaine. It was one he knew well. The heroin would slow down his bodily functions. The cocaine would cause his heart to race, speeding him up. Yes, Scott thought. It might have been a speedball.

Was there someone nearby? He couldn't see any faces. He knew that a number of people wanted to harm him. He wondered if they would kill him or merely disgrace him.

Scott had worked very hard at getting clean and sober. What would happen now?

He didn't have to wait long for his answer. Almost immediately, the pungent odors of gasoline, and then smoke, filled the air. Scott yearned for the sedative effect of the heroin and the numbing effect of the cocaine. The flames, unchecked, began to lick at his body.

Finally, his brain, perhaps even his soul, gave up and fought against him. His mind was blacking out from shock and the drugs—he was now convinced someone had given him drugs—and he felt dissociated from his body, as if he were someone else watching from above. He knew he had to prioritize. He wanted to stay alive, but first he had to protect the pictures, and after all his work to stay sober he wasn't going to give up until his family and friends knew he hadn't caused this overdose.

He moved his head close to the broken window and inhaled the cold, moist, snow-laden air, breathing life back into himself. He beat at the flames now burning his clothes and the resulting sharp pain reminded him of his injuries. He tried slamming his body against the car door, but it was no use.

To stay alert, he began to criticize himself. He was very good at that. He had learned it at an early age from his father, who also excelled at it—at least until he got sober. Like his father, Scott had resisted recovery, and had fought against sobriety. Now, when he had finally taken the chance to recover, this happened. He asked himself, "Why didn't I see this coming? How did I let my guard down? Why is this happening now?" The questions raced through his panicked mind.

If there was one thing cocaine had done for him, it had made him paranoid, and he'd been ready for trouble. It was different this time. Were these the same people—his old "friends"? Could he have made new enemies so quickly?

How had things in his life gone so terribly wrong? He realized that he had begun to feel too safe in his new life without drugs and dealers. He thought of the children he taught and of their innocent faces; how he wanted to protect them from harm, even though many of them had already been damaged by drugs, abuse, and disease.

His mind wandered back to that day a year earlier. It was clear and sunny and started out as one of the best days of his life. He had been running on the football field avoiding tacklers, but by the end of the evening he was running for his life. There had been people then who wanted to kill him, or at least to teach him a lesson he wouldn't soon forget. He thought that was probably the same night he had begun his recovery, but like a camera you take along on vacation and then stick in a drawer, the recovery took a long time to develop after that. The roll of film wasn't finished yet. Still, a picture of that night—the night when he had played his best game—filled his mind. How had he ended up under a pile of leaves?

Scott shook himself again. It was all his imagination, surely. No one wanted to kill him. But he was dying. There couldn't be so much pain without leading to death.

Suddenly, he noticed a new cloud around him even denser than the smoke from the flames. Then another pair of hands reached through the cloud and into the broken window next to him.

The voice echoed hauntingly in his own head, as if he had merely imagined it: "I'm Officer Teller. Lucy Teller. Don't worry. You'll be all right. You're safe now."

That's when Scott fainted.

Chapter 1

Lucy Teller saw the red glow in the sky the moment she turned onto Highway 55 at the edge of Keshena, a small town on the Wolf River and part of the Menominee Indian Reservation. The glow was reflected in the thick clouds, heavy with the first real snow of the season. Lucy winced as she turned on the siren and dome lights on her tribal police patrol car. Highway 55 followed Wolf River, and together they dissected the reservation with all of the twists and turns of a murder mystery. The road was dangerous enough on a sunny day in July, but this was long after dark in late October, and it had been snowing hard for the last forty-five minutes.

From the tire tracks, Lucy could tell that only a few cars had preceded her up 55 since the snow had started. The first few flakes had melted as they hit the highway, but now, as the temperature dipped below freezing, the large flakes were sticking to the road and trees. Already, judging from the tracks, nearly two inches had accumulated. Lucy fixed her gaze on the road ahead, not taking the time to notice the changing could have watched the wet snow stick to the pines and bare branches of trees—trees that, only weeks earlier, were alive with color, but now were caught in winter's icy grip. Near Spirit Rock those trees were silhouetted against the ominous red sky that was the object of Lucy's concern.

Lucy's brain, working with all of the accuracy of a videotape, captured the tire tracks cutting left and right from the slow turn lane on 55 and the fire lane just past Spirit Rock and Wayca Creek, where it intersects with Bear Trap Falls Road. That's when she saw the burning car with its front end wrapped around a large oak tree just off the highway. The car was engulfed in flames, and Lucy was not optimistic as she reached for her fire extinguisher, called for backup, and pulled her car off the road. It was all like a bad dream.

It would only be later, as she replayed it all in her head, that she would remember the footsteps going to and from the car and the burning spots in the snow. At the time, she did not look; she simply hurried to spray her fire extinguisher into the flaming wreckage.

She concentrated on the driver's side door and the man inside. It was the first time she smelled burning flesh. The odor was strong and nauseating. She swallowed hard. She had heard from fellow officers that once she smelled it, she'd never forget it, and now she knew why. She was still frantically spraying the door in an effort to approach and open it when the fire truck arrived. That's when the firemen appeared with the jaws of life.

Within seconds they ripped the door from its hinges. Now there were other faceless men helping to remove the body. In no time at all, the victim was in an ambulance and rushed away to Shawano Hospital. Lucy couldn't even tell if he was alive or dead. She knew he was male and his weight in proportion to his size indicated he was muscular but there was really no way to learn much more than that. Lucy could tell he was young even though he had burns over most of his body—she would guess sixty percent. His clothes and identification were burned, so she couldn't even tell whether he was Indian. Lucy thought he wasn't. The car was already so burned she couldn't tell what make it was. So many things were clear, and so many were impossible to know. But something was already telling her this was not just an accident on a slippery highway.

For the first time, she noticed more vehicles driving down the road. Other officers were arriving. A snowplow approached, clearing the highway, and the officers followed just behind. One car drove up and Lucy, glancing up quickly from her work, saw Ray Waupuse.

It was then that Lucy realized that she had done nothing to secure the area as a crime scene.

The two other cars were from the sheriff's police. The reservation was sparsely populated, but there were three different police departments to patrol it—the tribal police whose jurisdiction included any crimes committed by Native Americans, the sheriff's police who took care of crimes committed by non-Natives, and the county police who patrolled the non-reservation part of Menominee County. A large part of that non-reservation territory was taken up with Legend Lake, a lake and housing development with a number of permanent residents as well as vacation homes owned by people from Green Bay, Milwaukee, and the rest of Wisconsin and northern Illinois. It was not unusual to see three different police cars present at an accident or crime scene.

The officers helped put out the remainder of the fire and secure the area.

Ray Waupuse invited Lucy into his car after the fire was out.

"What do you think we have here?" he asked, as he poured some coffee from his thermos. Ray was kind and generous, with a friendly face. He always looked good in his uniform.

"I don't know," Lucy answered. "I saw the fire as soon as I turned on to 55. I don't think it happened much before that. I'm sure people could have seen the sky lit up from town, and we had no calls that I know of. There wasn't anyone here when I arrived and no houses can see this stretch of road. There were other tire tracks on the new snow heading this way, but they could have preceded the crash. There also were some tire tracks that I don't understand. They headed across the road just about where the car must have lost control."

"Unfortunately, the snowplow would have removed those by now," said Ray.

"I probably should have secured the area first," Lucy said apologetically.

Ray shrugged his shoulders. "Twenty-twenty hindsight," he said. "You didn't know whether the guy was alive or dead. Got to go for the life first."

Lucy smiled. Ray had been a cop for a long time and could have taken the opportunity to criticize Lucy's inexperience, but he didn't. It fit Ray's appearance and personality.

Ray didn't look like a cop. Except for short-cut hair, he looked like a flower child from the sixties. He had a kind and gentle expression, and hair graying ever so slightly at the temples, belying a young-looking face. He'd been a few years ahead of Lucy at the mission school they both attended in Keshena.

Mike Sanipaw stuck his head in the door. "Fire seems to be out, but the car is too hot to go near it."

Mike, like Ray, didn't fit the cop stereotype. He was young and tall with a braided ponytail that ran halfway down his back. He had Hollywood good looks and a friendly smile that came and went easily from his face. He could be very soft or very hard and often moved rapidly from one to the other depending on the situation.

Neither Ray nor Mike had the body types of Menominees. Ray was shorter, perhaps five feet ten inches, while Mike was over six feet tall. Both of them were lean, while most of the rest of the Menominee Nation had thick upper bodies. Without their uniforms and patrol car, these two partners might easily be mistaken for social workers rather than cops.

"Come on in and warm up, Mike," said Ray, offering the back seat of his patrol car. "Anything else you saw that might lead you to believe this was anything more than someone going too fast in bad conditions on a winding road?"

Lucy was about to say no when she remembered the footprints.

"Footprints!" she yelled. "There were footprints in the snow leading to and from the car."

"I don't see any prints now," Mike said softly.

"The heat from the car would have melted the snow along with the prints. Besides, our own prints would be mixed in there now anyway," Ray added.

"The other thing that seems strange is when I was spraying the car, I expected to see gas leaking from the tank to cause such a big fire, but I don't think the tank ruptured, so where did all that fire come from?"

"He might have had a gas can in the trunk or back seat.

Probably a guy heading up to his cabin in Eagle River to take advantage of some early snowmobiling," Ray answered as if he was just thinking aloud. "You know..." He caught himself.

He did not want to share all of his thoughts. If he had been entirely honest, he would have had to admit that he was more interested in figuring out Lucy Teller than the possible crime.

Even after a long shift, she looked good. Very good.

"Lucy," he said, choosing a slightly different subject, "your shift is just about over, and ours is just starting. Why don't you head in? We'll wait for the tow truck and put up the crime scene tape. Chances are, this guy's not Indian, and it won't be our case anyway. And if there is foul play, we'll need to call in the FBI."

Suddenly, the long day and night began to hit her. She was tired to the bone. She felt emotionally bruised and battered. She knew she wouldn't sleep much, but the idea of being at home sounded good. Still, she couldn't let go of the accident. Not just yet. "Let me know if anything else comes up. I think I'll take a quick sweep around with the flashlight before I head in to town."

Near Bear Trap Falls Road, Lucy noticed a rectangular spot in the snow. The snow was at least a half-inch lower in the rectangle with parallel tire tracks—a certain sign of a car, and it had been sitting in the snow for some time. She also found cigarette ash on both sides of the car prints. There were no tracks leading to the print; the plow had eliminated all such evidence. The tracks that still were visible were deep, and snow had spit up from the tires. The car had left in a hurry, Lucy determined.

As she stood there, quietly considering those tracks, a strange thing happened. It was as if her mind was drifting from her body. She could see the top of her head and the ground around her—just as if she were floating above herself. Lucy was confused and perhaps a little frightened. It's not like a drug high, she thought, and anyway I haven't had a drink or used anything stronger than aspirin in three years.

As she stood staring, a voice startled her back into her body.

"We'll check this scene out some more," said Ray. "Wait for the car to cool and see what happens with the victim. Maybe he'll survive at least long enough to talk, and we'll hear what he has to say. This is your first 'up close and personal' with a burned body—that might be part of your bad feeling."

"Well, I know part of it is being tired, so I'm going to take your advice and go home and get some rest."

With a brief smile for goodbye, Lucy got into her squad car and headed back up 55 toward Keshena and to the small brown brick house down the road from Legend Lake that was her home.

Chapter 2

Lucy lived with her mother and her two children. They were all asleep by the time she got home. Even under the best of conditions, Lucy had trouble sleeping. Her AA sponsor kept assuring her that it would get better, but she had been sober now for three years and sleep was still hard to come by. Several of her friends in recovery had told her not to go to bed unless she was ready to sleep. She knew tonight she was not ready.

After looking in on her children, Lucy walked into the kitchen and took some milk from the refrigerator. There was a pan already waiting on the stove; her mother knew of her problems sleeping and routinely put the pan out for Lucy before going to bed.

Lucy used her finger to tell when the milk was just the right temperature to drink. She poured it from the pan and added a little honey to a large mug. Shutting off the light in the kitchen, she walked to the couch in the living room, sat down, picked up a magazine, and tried reading.

After a few moments, she threw the magazine onto the coffee table in front of her and sipped slowly at the warm milk. Too many thoughts and feelings were racing around in her. Added to the queasy feeling of being exhausted to the bone, she couldn't concentrate.

Her mind drifted back to the accident scene. She began to wonder. What if she had seen the glow in the sky a bit sooner or had driven a little faster—could she have improved the chances of life for the driver? She knew "what ifs" were not good for her. They wouldn't help her sleep or recover. In AA, she had learned the acronym "HALT"—avoid getting hungry, angry, lonely, or tired. Right now, she was hungry, lonely, and tired. She wasn't angry—not yet—but she was feeling enough guilt to cover for anger.

She continued to sip the warm milk and it seemed to take the edge off her hunger. Over the last three years, she had learned to be a good mother and a good daughter. She was still learning to be a good cop, and that was the best she could do. Knowing that helped a little with the guilt.

When she finished the warm milk, she set the cup on the coffee table next to the magazine. Even though Lucy was weary from her day, she still wasn't feeling particularly ready to sleep. She decided to stretch out on the couch and at least be comfortable. The next thing she knew, she was dreaming, but it didn't seem like she was asleep.

At the crime scene, she had experienced the sensation of hovering above the scene, but this time the scene was moving and she rode on the back of an eagle. There was a car driving up Highway 55 near Spirit Rock, like the one in the crash. The car seemed in no particular hurry. It was just beginning to snow harder with big wet flakes.

Lucy looked ahead and saw another car waiting at Bear Trap Falls Road. She screamed, trying to warn the driver, but he paid no attention to her. She watched the accident unfold below her, but was helpless to stop it.

Suddenly, she was inside the car—the car now wrapped around a tree. She saw a needle moving toward her, an all-too- familiar sight from her drugging days. She saw flames licking around her and a hand reaching in and grabbing a picture from her lap. She awoke with a start, trembling and covered with sweat.

Lucy had taken several psychology classes at the College of Menominee Nation, and she had learned enough from white men's theories to know that the bizarre dream could have been her unconscious mind's way of unscrambling all the events of the past few hours. Usually, since recovery, she slept so little she didn't remember any dreams. But this seemed very real, and different from dreams she had had in the past.

She looked at her watch. She knew it made no sense to return to the accident scene now or to go to the station. Not all of her Native American brothers and sisters believed in dreams or visions or whatever this was, and it would certainly be laughed out of a court of law. Still, in Lucy's heart, she believed it was evidence.

She hurried to the front door where the children's school backpacks were hanging. She opened one, found a pad and pencil, and wrote down as much of the dream vision as she could remember. As a Menominee, she had been taught that a dream was worthy of attention, and a vision was something to be sought. Lucy still didn't know what she had experienced, but it seemed like the clearest sign that her efforts to rekindle in herself the ways of her ancestors were beginning to pay off.

She wrote for nearly an hour—not just what she remembered from the dream but also how she hoped to follow up the next day, as well as her thoughts and feelings from the accident. She believed more strongly than ever that she was dealing with an attempted murder.

The writing had siphoned off the last bit of energy she had in her body. She tore out the sheets and returned the notebook to the backpack.

She lay back down on the couch and promptly fell asleep. If she dreamed anymore, she didn't remember. The next thing she knew, she heard her children fighting over the prize in a cereal box and her mother shushing them. She got up and stood by the doorway of the kitchen, looking at them and smiling. They were too busy even to notice her.

There was a time when their yelling first thing in the morning would have sent Lucy looking for a drink to calm her nerves. She would have been enraged—consciously or not— that they had the audacity not to be more considerate of her hangover. Now, when she knew how close she had come to losing all of them, she wanted to drink in the moment with every pore. Once again, she told herself silently: "I'm not going to drink or use today."

"Gee, Jerod and Tara, when did they start making cereal box prizes out of solid gold, and aren't you both getting a little old for those anyway?"

"Sorry, Mom, we didn't mean to wake you," they said in unison. Then Tara stuck her tongue out at Jerod.

"Good morning, Mom," Lucy said, as she kissed her mother on the cheek.

"Hey, have you given up on your bed altogether?" her mother asked.

"I just might. Last night was the best I've slept in a long time. You guys aren't going to miss the bus again, are you?"

"No, we're on our way now," the kids said as they dashed from the table. They headed for the front door and their backpacks.

"Put a coat on. It snowed last night." The parental voice followed them to the door. With their long jet-black hair flying behind them, the children ran to meet their friends.

After the kids left, Lucy went to her bedroom and changed out of the clothes she had slept in the night before and into sweatpants and a sweatshirt. From her uniform pants, she took her medicine bundle. At the door, she put on her running shoes, said goodbye to her mother, and stepped out into the warm sunshine. She was anxious to go to the station to see what might have been discovered about John Doe and his accident.

But today was her day off. When she had gone through her drug treatment at Maehnowesekiyah, a treatment center just outside of town, the counselors had preached balance, and she was trying to keep that in her life. Lucy knew a run would be much better for her than going to the station.

She walked and stretched for a block or so on Rabbit Ridge Road. She began running as she took a left on South Branch Road. It was a pleasant day, and the sun was shining brightly. The late fall sun had melted any of the remaining snow through the bare trees.

She ran around the curve of the closely wooded road, changing her direction from north to east. There was an occasional house or trailer on the left, built far back from the road, and on the right side, out of sight, was Legend Lake. The area that was now a large housing development had originally been part of the reservation. The Menominees had sold the land to a developer back in the sixties when they were strongly encouraged by the federal government to drop their reservation status and become a regular county. This effort had ended with a group of Menominees taking over a monastery in Greshem and demanding that their status be reinstated. Much of Legend Lake had already been sold and built on by that time so it remained private. The incident left a bad taste in the mouths of both Natives and Whites and added to the tension between them.

Property values on Legend Lake remained low for a number of years because Whites feared another uprising, but when the casino was built prices rose in a hurry. Legend Lake wasn't a playground for the rich and famous, but the houses were still a contrast to most of the modest reservation homes. On the rez side to her left, three or four cars—some that actually ran— often sat in the yards. On the right, Lucy could see a house through the trees, neat and tidy with a well-trimmed lawn. This time of year, various watercraft might be parked in the yard—a runabout or a pontoon boat or maybe jet skis all removed from their shore stations before the lake froze.

After passing a narrow stretch of road, with the lake on one side and a pond on the other, Lucy ran up and then down into the area where a tornado had ripped through some years earlier, leaving it devastated. The trees had grown back nicely now and little sign of the destruction remained. Lucy had passed by most of the houses on both sides and was now running in an area that was mainly surrounded by trees.

She turned left onto Old South Branch Road—the sand and gravel logging road. She ran a little farther and then slowed to a walk, passing into a clearing and finally sitting down with her back against a large pine tree. Opening her medicine bundle, Lucy took out pinches of tobacco, sage, and sweet grass. She sprinkled the tobacco on the earth as an offering and lit the sweet grass, pulling the smoke toward her face and body. She saved the sage for a later time. Lucy let the sweet-smelling smoke cleanse her. She thanked the Creator for another day and pledged to live it as best she could. Then she sat quietly and took in the sights and sounds of nature. After some time, she closed her bundle and started running back home.

When she entered the house, her mother was in the living room watching TV. "Done practicing being Injun?" she asked. "It seems to help me stay sober, Mom. Would you rather the alternative? I sometimes feel like a cartoon character with the devil on one side and an angel on the other. I have my sponsor on one shoulder telling me to return to the old ways and on the other you're telling me just to be Catholic. I'm doing my best to find my own way."

Before her mother could respond, Lucy decided to change the subject. "Speaking of making my own way, have I told you lately that the kids and I couldn't make it at all without you?" She knew better than to tell her mother about her vision, though she was bursting to tell someone. She also knew her mother was a sucker for a compliment so she complimented her mom even though she felt irritated.

"Now just let me be your sponsor," her mom joked sarcastically, "and things can really begin going smoothly around here. Matter of fact, why don't you see what you can do about getting me appointed as Director of Maehnowesekiyah, chief of police, and how about Chief of the whole damn Menominee Nation? Then everything will run smoother."

"And to think I've been wasting my time trying to get you appointed Director of the Bureau of Indian Affairs, or elected President of the United States! I think you're setting your sights way too low. You have marvelous leadership potential.

If you can straighten out my life, then there is no limit to what you're capable of doing." Lucy knew her mother disliked confrontation as much as she did, and they both used humor to avoid it.

It worked. Her mother just grinned and returned her attention to the TV.

"I'm off to take a shower, Mom."

Lucy showered and dressed quickly in a pair of jeans, a flannel shirt, and cowboy boots. She stopped at the mirror in her bedroom to smooth her wet hair. She looked at the face staring back at her and considered the shoulder-length, jet- black hair. Lucy vowed to let it grow long and not cut it this time.

She was in her early thirties but, even considering the abuse she had put her body through, she didn't look her age.

She sometimes wished she looked a little older and wondered if that would help her to get some respect as a police officer.

Her mother's father was a white man who had been passing through the reservation but the rest of her ancestors were Menominee. She had a clear, bronze complexion and high cheekbones. Many people said she was pretty. She never thought of herself as beautiful, but she did keep a picture on her mirror—the "before" picture they had taken of her when she had entered the treatment center. Since then she had changed from a frumpy, fortyish looking bag lady to a strong, healthy, twentyish woman. Even she had to marvel at the difference.

Next to getting her kids back, the vibrant healthy image she saw in the mirror was her second-best reason for staying sober.

Satisfied, she said goodbye to her mother and drove off in her truck.

Chapter 3

Lucy had many things to do on her day off, but she stopped first at the station to learn if anything new had been discovered.

"Has Scott's car been towed in yet?" she asked the desk clerk.

The desk clerk looked at her strangely. "I just ran the I.D. on the car and found it was registered to a Scott Brandt. I haven't even told anyone yet. How did you know his name was Scott?"

"Did I use a name? I don't know. It was probably written somewhere inside his car, and I didn't register it at the time. You know, one of those subliminal things."

"Well, it must have been super-subliminal to the officers who checked the car out this morning and found no identification."

"I don't know then. Anyway, is this person I don't know still alive?"

"Just barely," the clerk replied. "They're trying to stabilize him enough at Shawano Hospital to transfer him to a burn unit in Green Bay."

"Have any relatives been notified yet?"

"The hospital is doing that as we speak. We figure there would be medical questions."

"I think I'll run down there and see him. If he were to wake up at all, I'd like to be able to ask him some questions."

At the hospital, Lucy waited outside until she saw a tired, stressed-looking doctor leaving.

"How's Scott doing, Doc?" Lucy asked.

He looked at her quizzically.

"I'm the officer who found him. I just stopped by to find out how he's doing."

He shook his head. "I'm surprised he's still alive. He had a heart attack from a cocaine overdose, which might have been what caused the accident, together with burns over sixty-five percent of his body. We're just trying to keep him alive until his family gets here. They live about an hour away and are on their way now."

"Can I see him?" Lucy asked.

"He won't be able to tell you anything. He's not conscious."

"He's the first accident victim I've had where I was the first on the scene. I sort of feel a bond with him."

"Go ahead. It can't hurt," the doctor replied.

Lucy walked into the dimly lit room. Scott was a mass of tubes and bandages. There was no part of his body that didn't look sore, but she wanted to make some sort of contact. She found a spot near his triceps that appeared to be free of burns. She touched there lightly, using only the tips of her fingers. There was no response.

"Scott?"

The body lay still. The only sign of life was slow and weak, scribbled across the monitor screen, but Lucy knew that he was alive and knew that she had to speak to him.

"Please... Scott? Scott... my name is Lucy. I... I'm a friend. You don't know me, but I feel I know you." It was crazy to be talking in this way, and Lucy knew it, but she couldn't help herself.

"Scott? I..." Lucy moistened her lips with her tongue.

When she spoke again, her voice was an earnest whisper. "Scott, I know that you were an addict."

Was it her imagination or did the arm move? It happened again, and she was certain. It was almost imperceptible, but it was movement, repeated over and over.

"Scott, I don't know if you are going to make it, but you have to talk to me. Talk to me, Scott. Let me know if my vision of what happened is accurate. The cocaine could explain the needle I saw. Did you put it there or was it someone else?"

Suddenly the steady beeps on the machine began to speed up. Contrasted with the earlier dull, monotonous tone, this new sound was almost frantic.

By then, Lucy didn't care if she sounded crazy or if anyone heard her. "Scott, just hang on! Just hang on!" Then she used her last persuasive line: "Scott, think of your family. Think of them. Hang on for them!"

The young man's lips did not move, and there was not a sound audible to human ears, but Lucy heard him speak her name. His body seemed to twitch, but he didn't sit up in bed and begin explaining things. She felt his body relax. The racing beeps of the machine slowed to a shrill, endless whine. A flat line appeared on the screen. Scott's heart had stopped beating right in front of her. There was a commotion outside the door. Then the room filled up with doctors and nurses.

Lucy stood back from the bed, allowing the professionals to overwhelm the room. She didn't need to be told to leave. Even from where she stood, far from the whining monitor and the anxious chattering of the doctors, Lucy knew. She left the room quietly. She wanted to run.

As she left the room, she saw a man and woman walking quickly down the hall. Terror was spread across their faces. They looked like they had just seen their little boy take a terrible fall. Scott's parents, she bet, as they raced past her toward his room and disappeared inside.

She thought about the psychology class she was taking at the College of Menominee Nation. A guy there named Rahe listed life-change events and rated them according to how stressful they were. Death of a spouse was the highest at a hundred, followed by divorce in the seventies. She wondered why he didn't include the death of a child. It would have to be number one on any list. Maybe it was even off the charts.

It was painful when Lucy lost her own husband from a drug overdose, but she went right on drinking and drugging. Lucy stayed in denial until the Department of Children and Family Services came and took her children away. Then she entered Maehnowesekiyah and gave drugs up for good. At least up until today. One day at a time, she reminded herself.

A little farther down the hall, she passed two pale young women who walked as if they were in a trance. Lucy later discovered one was Kathy Marks—up until recently, Scott's girlfriend—and the other was Bobbie, his sister. She watched as they made their way down the hall and entered Scott's room.

Then Lucy saw a young man with an intense look on his face who looked to be somewhere between sixteen and twenty— Ryan. The keys he carried made him at least sixteen and the fist in which he held them showed him to be very angry. He was with a younger boy and girl—Paul and Sally. They reminded Lucy of her own strong love toward her children. Once again, she had the horrific thought of what it would be like to lose one of her children. She felt sick to her stomach.

She had stopped in the hall, watching the family pass, and she was still standing there when a cold feeling passed all through her being and she knew it was over. She felt Scott pass by her. She grieved for all the people in his room and swallowed hard to push down her deep sadness. But she still waited, silently, outside the room.

Kathy was the first to come out. She was breathing rapidly. The river of tears had left spots like raindrops on her blouse. Kathy winced as the dark-haired figure with compassionate eyes approached her. Lucy wondered if Kathy thought she was the hospital social worker coming to offer her condolences. Lucy would have dreaded that too.

Kathy's expression changed to surprise as Lucy introduced herself as Officer Lucy Teller.

"I'm Kathy Marks," she said. "I'm… I was Scott's girlfriend."

"I'm sorry for your loss," Lucy said and handed Kathy her card. "I'm the officer who found him. I wish I could have done more." Many unspoken words passed between them as they locked eyes in a moment of silence.

"I'm sure you did your best," Kathy said.

"I'd like to attend the funeral. If you call the number on the card with the time, date, and location, they'll notify me."

"I'll do that," Kathy choked the words out.

Lucy touched her shoulder and said goodbye. It wasn't until later that Kathy wondered how Lucy knew that Scott was dead.

Chapter 4

In the days that followed Scott's death, his family and friends were all bewildered with grief, but memories still emerged. One night in particular stood out—a night when Scott and Kathy had gone out to eat with his parents.

Scott had drunk too much and he cursed himself for it later.

They had eaten at one of the supper clubs in the area after Scott had just played his best football game of the year. Scott's parents still wore the jeans and school sweatshirts they had worn to the game. Scott had to admit, but only to himself, that his parents looked good. His dad had lost the puffiness from his drinking days. Instead of spending time in the bar, Hank was now cross-country skiing and playing basketball with his new AA friends in the winter and canoeing and biking in the summer. Those activities, along with the manual labor he did working for his brother's construction company, left him looking strong for a man in his late forties.

His mom seemed more relaxed. She was always attractive and kept herself in good shape, but in the past, lack of sleep and worry had often showed on her pleasant and kind face. Now the circles under her eyes were gone, and the deep lines in her face had disappeared. Scott's parents even looked happy together, something Scott hadn't seen since he was a boy.

Kathy and Scott had changed out of their uniforms, and Kathy now wore slacks and a sweater instead of her usual jeans and a sweatshirt. Scott knew she wanted to make a good impression since this was her first time going to dinner with his parents. She obviously hadn't considered the possibility that his parents might not be changing clothes since they would be making the two-hour drive back home that night. Now she felt overdressed after changing out of her cheerleader uniform.

Scott's sister, Bobbie, was also at the dinner. Bobbie had transferred to Scott's college in her sophomore year after attending a community college near home her first year.

Scott had three other younger siblings who had not made the trip this time. Ryan had started college this past year. He and his friend Zack attended a school in the southern part of Wisconsin. Ryan was on the swimming team. Paul, his younger brother, was running cross-country and distance events on the varsity high school track team, and he now had a whole group of friends.

Scott's sister Sally, the youngest, was a standout as a high school freshman in both cross-country and track. His mom told him over dinner that Sally's coach fully expected Sally to break records in track if she continued at her current pace.

Sally had the same reserve speed that made Scott a great runner and she probably could make it as a sprinter with her foot speed. But she also had the slow twitch white muscle fiber of a long distance runner. While other girls were struggling to run a four hundred meter race in the sixty-second range, Sally appeared to be gliding along with little effort. On one of his rare visits home after finishing spring football practice, Scott had watched her run in a junior high track meet, and she had moved like poetry on the track as she easily outdistanced the competition.

It was hard for Scott to admit that his father had quit drinking because of an intervention in which he, Scott, had refused to participate. Now the whole family seemed better off. Scott had been using at the time and getting sober was not what he wanted to face. An intervention would have hit too close to home for him then.

Kathy had known Hank and Molly for some time, having gone to the same high school as Scott, but this was the first time she had spent an extended period with them. She and Scott had been friends in high school but had not dated then, so she had never been to their house. She knew them enough to say hello at games. Kathy and Bobbie had gotten to know each other quite well since Bobbie had transferred. They were becoming close friends.

Scott liked seeing his parents at the games but he was uncomfortable sitting down with them, especially where alcohol was available. He would always drink, and now he was the only one in the family who did.

He glanced over at his dad, wondering if the alcohol would be a problem. Scott needn't have worried about his father. The older man appeared to be preoccupied, still reliving Scott's performance on the field. It was as if he had a video in his mind and spent the night on instant replay. Scott could see his father's eyes following every play. Occasionally, Hank would comment to himself, "That was some run," or, "That was some catch." Scott was not sure if his dad even tasted his food.

Kathy had heard that Mr. Brandt drank a lot and looked surprised when he ordered Pepsi with his dinner.

Scott noticed it too. "Pepsi, Dad?" he asked with a touch of sarcasm.

But Hank was oblivious and only smiled abstractedly. He was somewhere in the middle of the game on his private screen. Scott's mother, Molly, on the other hand, was much more present at the table. She was pleasant to Kathy and seemed quite pleased that she and Scott were dating, but Molly stiffened with each drink Scott ordered. She would first look to him and then to Kathy. Kathy only smiled sheepishly.

"Aren't you supposed to be in training?" Molly asked Scott finally.

Scott was irritated. He felt certain her concern was not his football career. Bobbie seemed to want to say something, but her eyes moved back and forth, as if she were watching a tennis match. She wasn't really watching the interaction. Instead, she seemed to be listening to something inside her own head, possibly debating whose side to take, but she said nothing. Scott said little about his mother's reaction, but his drinking increased. At the same time, his irritation became more and more noticeable and he kept complaining that the waitress was not checking back with him often enough.

When they finally left the restaurant, Molly and Hank hugged each of their children and Kathy too so she wouldn't feel left out. Bobbie rode along with Kathy and Scott; they were all going to a fraternity party off campus.

As she sat in the back seat of Scott's car on the way to the party, Bobbie thought about Kathy.

At first glance, Kathy just looked like any attractive college girl. She was about five feet two inches tall and thin, though not with the anorexic pre-pubescent look of some gymnasts. She had a timeless look about her, so classic that she could represent all that was young and pretty throughout the ages. Any person fortunate enough to get closer to her could tell that her limbs were not just shapely but muscular as well. Her legs rippled when she walked, and her back and shoulders had the chiseled look of an athlete. It was difficult, though, to get very close to Kathy. It was not that she was cold or distant. On the surface she was outgoing and friendly, with a cute, contagious laugh, but she gave the impression that getting to know her better would be challenging. Perhaps it was the years of discipline through gymnastics and the self-assurance of being an athlete that had led her to believe that she didn't need relationships.

Bobbie was in her junior year. Every course she had taken at the local community college had transferred, so she was right where she should be as far as course work was concerned. She was happy to be at the larger college, but she missed her family and went home frequently on the weekends. She had spent little time with Scott or Kathy since arriving at the college because they both lived off campus—Kathy at her apartment and Scott at his fraternity.

But when Bobbie thought of the first time she had visited the college, some years ago, she was deeply troubled. During that weekend, she had stayed with Kathy and they spent a good part of the night talking. When she spoke of Scott, Kathy's eyes sparkled and all her feminine beauty rose to the surface. That wasn't that long ago, Bobbie thought. Now, sitting there in the back seat of the car, Bobbie sensed that things were strained.

When they arrived at the party, Scott immediately met up with some of his friends and disappeared for some time. Bobbie's boyfriend, Tom, arrived soon after. He walked in with a group of his friends who were rushing the fraternity along with him. Because Tom struggled academically, he hadn't rushed a fraternity during his freshman or sophomore years. He probably wouldn't have been doing it at all, but Scott had encouraged him.

Scott greeted Tom when he arrived but seemed distracted. Kathy sat on a couch talking with a group of Scott's fraternity brothers and their dates while Scott made his rounds throughout the room like a politician courting votes. He was loud and obnoxious—worse than Bobbie had ever seen. Every half hour or so he would disappear for a while and then return. He spent little time with Kathy, and when he did, there seemed to be friction and a coldness Bobbie had never seen in the four years Scott and Kathy had been together.

The third time Scott disappeared, Bobbie decided to look for him to see if they would have a few minutes to talk privately. When she found him, he wasn't alone, and Bobbie was sorry she had looked for him. It was the first time she had seen him use cocaine.

She slipped out of the room before he saw her, though she found it hard to believe no one heard the gasp she stifled or the pounding of her heart. She couldn't believe what she had just seen. Scott had always done everything right. Still in shock, she went back to the party.

Tom noticed her as soon as she entered the room. "Is there a ghost in the other room?" he asked.

"Why?" she snapped defensively.

"Because you lost your summer tan somewhere on the other side of that door," he said, smiling.

"I'm not feeling well, Tom. Can we leave?" she asked, regaining some of her composure.

"Sure," he said. "I didn't want to be in a fraternity anyway."

Realizing it wouldn't look good for a future pledge to be the first to leave the party, Bobbie told him, "You can stay and I'll go back to Kathy's and lie down." The plan had been for the four of them to meet there after the party.

Tom answered with unusual compassion. "Don't be silly. I'll just tell them my date isn't feeling well. They'll understand. Their punch could make anyone sick!"

Bobbie and Tom left the party. She was quiet on the way back to Kathy's apartment, telling herself all the way there that Scott was probably just experimenting and he was too smart to become dependent on cocaine.

When Kathy got back, Bobbie brought up the subject of Scott's drug use, and she learned what she had known in her heart to be true from the first moment she'd seen Scott at the party.

Chapter 5

Kathy wondered at the party what Scott's mother would have thought of his behavior. If she didn't like his drinking at the restaurant, how would she react to seeing him do a few lines of cocaine? He had been using it for a long time now. The issue was driving a wedge between them. She couldn't persuade him to stop and he kept accusing her of being controlling and rigid.

Once, when they'd been alone at her apartment, she had tried it with him. They'd had a few glasses of wine and both knew where the evening was leading. They were kissing on the couch when he pulled it out.

"How about some snow?" he asked.

Kathy thought at the time what a sharp contrast it was to real snow. When she imagined snow, she recalled how, during recess as a little girl, she would let the first big flakes of late fall land on her eyelids. She remembered noticing how each snowflake was unique. She thought of the special fleeting moments when she would catch the different shapes on her tongue and watch others melt on the faces and tongues of her girlfriends. She compared in her mind the innocence and joy of those moments to this— when she was giving in to an illegal drug for the first time.

Kathy simply smiled and said, "Snow? Sure, why not?" Scott quickly poured a small amount of the white powder onto a mirror. With a razor blade, he divided the small pile into two lines about an eighth of an inch wide and two to three inches long. He stuck a small straw up his nose and put the straw at the beginning of the line. Inhaling through his nose, he sucked in the white powder and swallowed. He then handed the straw to Kathy, and she did the same with the other line.

She didn't really notice that much of an effect. At first, the cocaine burned her nose, and then later it began to feel numb. When they made love later on, everything seemed intensified but she also noticed that she was not as aware of Scott being part of it. It seemed more like the parallel play of two toddlers in the same sandbox. After that, he had urged her several times to try it again, but she had always refused. She watched the cocaine gradually gain power in Scott's life, and she didn't want the same fate for herself. After a while, he quit trying to convince her to try it.

So now when Scott used, he simply disappeared with some of his fraternity brothers and fellow users. He'd return a few minutes later and when he came back, he seemed different. It reminded Kathy of a picture that hangs in your living room for years; the frame is the same, but the picture has changed from a pastoral scene to modern art. He became jittery and demanding. His quiet confidence changed to loud arrogance, sensitivity changed to coldness, and concern for others changed to self-absorption. Kathy had also heard that he had gone from snorting to freebasing. This meant that he was now smoking it to make the high come quicker. She heard that he was mixing it with heroin, smoking or snorting it to get a mellower high. She began to wonder how he could afford these drugs. That question was partially answered on their way home from the fraternity party.

The party was at an old farmhouse outside of town, and when they left, Scott insisted on driving. They had gone a few miles down a two-lane highway and a car was behind them when Kathy noticed that Scott was checking in the rearview mirror every couple of seconds even though the other car wasn't that close. After another mile or so, a second car came up behind and started to pass both cars. When it pulled up even with Scott's car, it matched his speed. Kathy could see that there were at least three men in the car and they were all looking at Scott. The first car was also closer now—tailgating them—and the first was still taking its time passing. With no oncoming traffic, they were penned in.

They say racecar drivers are really good athletes. Kathy couldn't verify that, but what happened next proved that Scott, as an athlete, could be a racecar driver. He suddenly punched the brakes and turned the wheel. The next thing Kathy knew, they were on the shoulder heading in the opposite direction.

Scott accelerated, turned back onto the road, and soon they were screaming down the highway at breakneck speed.

Perhaps the screaming part was Kathy. Usually the last one to be hysterical, Kathy was yelling hysterically at Scott, "What are you doing?"

Scott ignored her and continued to look in the rearview mirror. He soon came to a wooded area where he made another vicious U-turn, stopped the car, and quickly ordered Kathy to drive it to her place. He then vanished into the woods. Kathy called to him, but she heard nothing in response. When she saw the cars approaching, she did as she was told. She drove home, struggling to keep to the speed limit and nervously checking her rearview mirror every few seconds. She tried looking into the oncoming cars that passed her but in the dark she couldn't see anything. At first Kathy thought that the cars were slowing down as they neared the spot where Scott had stopped, but she reasoned to herself that it's not every night you see a man stop his car and run into the woods. Perhaps they were just curious or concerned. Her own mind was racing with questions. Who were those men and what the hell was going on? How could she figure this out?

Kathy lived alone on the second floor of a two-story house that had been converted into a two-flat apartment. She had not known what to think and she spent a sleepless night angry, confused, and scared. Early the next morning, when she heard the doorbell and spotted Scott through the window, relief was only one of her feelings. She was shaking as she grabbed the banister and walked down the wooden steps, her slippers making a scraping sound on the stairs as she descended.

She opened the door and walked back up without saying a word. Scott followed her up the narrow stairs in silence. She left the door open at the top of the stairs. Scott closed it quietly behind him and went with her into the living room. It was neat and clean and decorated simply with a couch and an armchair. The styles of the upholstery were widely different, but somehow it looked well enough. An old trunk for a coffee table was in the middle of the room and a bookshelf made of bricks and boards sat against the far wall.

Kathy sat down on the couch but Scott remained standing.

He began immediately: "I guess my imagination got the best of me last night."

Kathy sat quietly for a moment. "I don't know if it was real or your imagination, but either way, you've got problems."

"What do you mean by that?" Scott shot back defensively. "Oh, I don't know," Kathy answered sarcastically. "Perhaps most guys race from their cars into the woods at two in the morning and show up at their girlfriends' houses the next morning with their clothes all ripped."

Scott looked down as if noticing for the first time that his pants were shredded. It must have happened when he ran through the bushes, he thought.

"You know I had kind of a rough night. I really don't need this right now," he said angrily.

"Oh, you had a rough night! It's all about you, isn't it?" "I was trying to protect you."

"Always the hero, aren't you, Scotty?"

Scott was hurt and angry, and not in the mood to deal with either. "Well, right now, for some reason, this hero is tired and needs some sleep."

His keys were on the trunk in front of Kathy. Scott held out his hand for them, but Kathy leaned forward and grabbed them before he could. She held them for a moment and sat looking at Scott, waiting. He stood motionless with his hand still out. With a flick of her wrist, she threw the keys to him, and he caught them.

"Go ahead, run away again!"

Scott went. He slammed the door on his way out.

Kathy wanted to cry but she wouldn't let herself. She moved around the apartment, trying to pretend nothing was wrong.

A few minutes later, there was a knock on the door. Kathy assumed it was Scott, so she took her time answering.

She took a deep breath and opened the door wide, ready to say, "What?" in an annoyed voice.

A startled sound came out of her mouth instead. Three men stood in front of her. The one in the middle was the smallest but he looked the meanest. These were not men from campus. They were too old for students and too young for faculty. If they taught anything, it would be a course on street survival. The middle one—the small mean one—had a scar by his eye that had been badly stitched, if at all. He had long dark hair that was corn-rolled and dirty, and his dark eyes stared out angry and intimidating, starting at her feet and slowly working their way up Kathy's body. She stifled the urge to shiver.

"Hello, Kathy. Where's your boyfriend?" he asked with a smirk.

"Do I know you?" she asked, knowing full well she didn't. "You don't know me, but maybe we can do something about that. My friends call me Kane." He looked her over again.

Kane's real name was Richard Harkness. He had started school several years earlier on an athletic scholarship as a middle linebacker. His idol in music was Bob Marley and in football it was Marley's son who started for the Miami Hurricanes as middle linebacker during one of their championship runs.

Kane had hoped to follow in Marley's footsteps at Miami, but they never offered him a scholarship. Instead, he settled for a Division 1A school in central Wisconsin that did offer him money. Because of a combination of steroid use and poor grades, he lasted only through the first semester, but he still lurked around the school. His connections with drug dealers in the city and college students eager to experiment made it worthwhile for him to hang around and party.

The two with him were Lou and Vince, neither of whom had even made it through high school. The drug business was profitable enough for Kane to pay them well as bodyguards, not to mention what they received in free drugs.

"Your boyfriend is really protective of you, and I can see why, but he doesn't have to know everything, does he? He owes me lots of money. I told him to bring you around to my place so we could get some pictures of you. Maybe we could even do a video of you and him and me. We could sell them. I make lots of money selling the right pictures to the right people. You see, I like to diversify my financial assets, if you know what I mean." The overemphasis was crudely obvious.

Kathy's body tightened and her stomach wrenched with nausea. "Scott and I broke up," she said flatly.

"Good, that leaves the door open for me. I don't score touchdowns, but I score in a lot of other ways." He reached up and rubbed her cheek with his knuckle.

Kathy winced. She reached for the door, knowing she had little chance of closing it if they didn't want her to.

"I'm down here, Kane." Scott's voice startled her and relieved her at the same time. Kane turned and glared down to the bottom of the stairs where Scott was standing.

"I've been looking for you," Kane replied. Then, turning to Kathy with his hand still at her cheek, he ran it down her neck and over her breasts. "We'll have to finish this later," he said.

Her fear finally and completely turned to disgust. "We'll continue it at the police station if anything happens to him," she said.

Kane moved his face an inch from hers so she could feel his breath. "I like my women with fire, but I always break them in the end."

Kathy closed her eyes and pulled back. When she opened them, he was halfway down the steps, and the two bookends were now staring and grinning. She closed the door, locking it firmly, and they didn't stop her. She immediately went in the bathroom and vomited.

Scott didn't return to her apartment that day, but he called her and told her not to worry. Everything was fine. She hung up. The next day, she saw him at school and was relieved to see no bruises, but she still had little to say.

She began to notice that Scott was without his car for long periods of time. One day she saw him waiting at a gas station. He was pacing and the veins stood out in his neck. She asked him if his car was being serviced. He said yes, but just then Kane drove up, laughing, with some of his friends—in Scott's car. Scott asked her to leave and she didn't hesitate. One run-in with Kane and his thugs was enough. If Scott chose to continue his association, that was his affair.

She later learned that "Kane" was his code name, and Scott had lent him his car as part of what he owed him. Kane always kept the car longer than agreed to, just so Scott would know who was in charge. She also heard that Scott had begun to sell to his fraternity brothers. She wondered what else she would find out.

Chapter 6

It was a few days later. Kathy was lost deep in thought when Brad Albert approached her in the student cafeteria. Brad had been Scott's friend since grade school. Scott and Brad were both intelligent with an interest in math and science but that is where their similarities ended. Scott was athletic and very popular but Brad was considered a geek. Brad was large but looked more like a teddy bear than a grizzly. He wore dark-rimmed glasses, and his fair complexion made them stand out even more on his face. He had been a lineman on the high school football team and might have been good enough to play in college, but he attended on an academic scholarship and had to work hard to make the grades to keep it. Scott often said that he missed Brad blocking for him. Brad continued to work out but now he did it mostly as a break from studying. He wasn't fat, but his stomach protruded like those of the men who participate in the World's Strongest Men competitions.

Over the years, people were surprised that the two guys remained friends. Some thought that Scott felt sorry for Brad. Kathy liked Brad because neither she nor Scott ever felt the need for pretense around him. Scott once commented that being with Brad was like wearing old sneakers.

"Hey, Kathy, how's it going?" Brad asked cheerfully. Kathy didn't respond. Her mind was far away. "Earth to Kathy. Earth to Kathy. Come in, Kathy," Brad said mockingly, as if speaking through a megaphone.

Startled, Kathy said, "Oh, hello, Brad."

Brad teased her, "I thought only academic types are supposed to have their heads in the clouds, but you jocks seem to be able to space out yourselves."

Kathy laughed. "At least I don't make a lifestyle out of it the way you do. You were made for astrophysics, the way you're always on a space trip."

Brad pretended to look hurt. "Take it easy on me, Kathy.

You and your boyfriend may have bodies conditioned to ignore pain, but I still bleed easily. Speaking of your boyfriend, he missed his eight o'clock class again today. I don't mind copying my notes, but I'm now paying some top executive's salary in the Xerox Corporation. What happened to him this time?"

Sounding depressed, Kathy explained that she thought Scott had been out late the night before. Brad listened. Then his eyes clouded as if his thoughts were going far away.

"Now there you go, fading off," Kathy said, with a little bit of triumph showing through the depression in her voice. "You're worried about him too, aren't you, Brad?" she asked.

"I'm supposed to worry about some jock with a rock hard body and genius IQ who travels in social circles that won't give me the time of day?"

"You can kid around if you want to, Brad, but I know you're worried about him."

Sounding hopeless, Brad said, "Yeah, I really am worried about him. But what can we do?"

"I'm not sure, Brad. But it's nice to know I'm not alone with my concerns," Kathy said, taking his arm.

As they were talking, Sue, a mutual friend, approached them. She and Brad had dated occasionally. They weren't very serious, but she liked to pretend that they were, mostly as a joke. Then again, it was hard to tell with her what was real.

Sue was a likable girl who vacillated between the punk look of an art student and the conservative look of a business major. She still wasn't sure which subject would be her major. Some people teased her about not being sure whether she should get out of bed in the morning. Her flightiness added to her cute and funny personality and made her fun to be around. Trying to sound stern, Sue said, "Okay, try to explain this one. I knew you two had eyes for each other, but, Brad, I thought you had more sense than to be seen with this brazen hussy."

Kathy laughed, "Sue, I admit I want him desperately, so you might as well just give up. You know you're no competition for me."

Sounding depressed, Sue said, "I might as well go get that chocolate sundae I've been eyeing all week and drown my sorrows. I know when I'm beat."

"Do you think the soaps we've been watching for the last four years have finally turned our brains to mush?" Brad asked with a smile.

"Speaking of soap operas, what were you two talking about that got Kathy grabbing at you like that?" Sue asked more seriously.

Brad looked at Kathy. "Can I tell her?" he asked.

"What do you mean can you tell? Do you want to see another sunrise?" Sue asked in a mock-threatening tone.

"I guess we have no choice, but be gentle," Kathy said.

"We're both worried about Scott," Brad said, becoming suddenly serious.

"Oh, me too—Mr. All American. Is his problem where he'll get his first million?" Sue kidded.

"No, seriously," said Kathy. "He's gotten pretty heavy into coke and comes down on alcohol, maybe even heroin. He's been missing most of his classes, and if this goes on, I'm not sure he'll graduate. If his education teachers get wind of this, they may not let him student teach next fall. His faculty advisor already doesn't like him much. His dreams could go up in smoke, or, should I say, down the drain like his alcohol should."

"No wonder I hardly ever see him anymore," Sue commented with surprise. "Have you talked to our S.A.P. about your concerns?"

Brad and Kathy looked at each other. "What's S.A.P.?" they asked simultaneously.

"Student Assistance Program counselor in the Drug Education Office," Sue answered with a know-it-all air.

"I can't believe I'm asking you questions, but what and where is that?" Brad asked.

"Well, if you'd get your nose out of the physics lab and take some psych classes, you'd learn about these things. It's right here in the student center. It's for students who want information about drugs for papers and stuff. It's also for students whose grades are suffering because of their drug use, or family or friends' drug use. Someone from the center visited one of my classes once."

Kathy asked, "Can I talk to them confidentially?"

"That depends, Miss Brutae. Are you going to talk about your boyfriend or mine?" Sue said, pretending to grab Brad's shoulders protectively.

"Come on, Sue. Be serious. Besides, who is Brutae?" Brad asked.

"A female Brutus. You know, Caesar's friend," Sue said, pretending to stab herself in the heart with a butter knife. "The one who stabbed him in the heart, or was it the back?"

"I'll talk about my boyfriend, I promise. In fact, why don't you go with me to be sure? I'll need the support. But would it be confidential?"

"Yes, it's confidential. I guess I can go now, if I can tear you away from this two-timing rat."

"I need some time to think about this. Could we go tomorrow?"

"Sure, but you're not going to chicken out, are you?" Sue challenged.

"Well, I guess it won't hurt to talk, as long as Scott doesn't find out. Our relationship is rocky at best, and this would kill it for sure. But I do need to talk with someone. I can't believe that he's the one taking drugs. Why is this bothering me so much?" Kathy wondered more to herself than Brad and Sue.

"I'll meet you here tomorrow at this time, and we'll go over there together," Sue said with genuine reassurance.

"Okay. Well, I've got to go to class. I'll leave you to patch up your relationship. See you, lover," Kathy said as she patted Brad's shoulder and whispered in his ear loud enough for Sue to hear, "Let her down easy."

The next day, Kathy and Sue met in the cafeteria as planned. After some more encouragement from Sue, they went together to the Drug Education Center. Sue babbled most of the way there, hoping to relax Kathy, but Kathy heard little of what was said.

A short, pleasant-looking woman greeted them at the Center.

"Hello, my name is May," she said, extending her hand.

"How can I help you?" Sue explained that she had heard May speak in her class and hesitantly tried to explain Kathy's concerns.

May turned to Kathy and said, "Kathy, why don't you tell me what's bothering you."

"What if I had a friend who took drugs—illegal drugs— and I told you about it?" Kathy spoke rapidly. "Would you have to tell anyone, like the Dean or a professor? Would my friend be kicked out of school?"

In a calm and reassuring manner, May explained,"Assuming that no one's life is in immediate danger, I don't have to tell anyone. For now, let's just use a first name, if you like. My first concern right now is for you. Then we can do what we call an assessment to see just how serious the person's problem is at this point. The policy at this school is that we make every attempt to treat the problem, not punish the person."

Kathy looked relieved. "Okay. My friend, Scott, has been doing a lot of coke. He hasn't been doing it very long, but it seemed from the very first time he tried it, he couldn't get enough. Two weekends ago, he stayed high almost all weekend.

When he finally came down, it was only by drinking beer. He slept most of Monday and seemed very depressed all week. He ended up missing most of his classes. Then on Friday, he started it all over again. He's using up money like it's going out of style.

Scott even started smoking the coke so he could get a better high. All he and I do is fight. I can't even mention beer or coke without him having a fit."

"This sounds pretty serious, Kathy. Does anyone else in his family have a problem with drugs or alcohol?"

"Yes, his dad went into treatment for alcoholism during Scott's freshman year. It really depressed Scott. Although everyone else in his family seemed to accept that his dad had a drinking problem, Scott never thought so."

May continued to ask questions concerning Scott's schoolwork. She explained that she felt that there was a definite problem because his life had become unmanageable. His drug use was having a negative effect on their relationship and his schoolwork, and he was using increasing amounts of cocaine, in addition to using another drug to bring him down. May asked Kathy if she had ever heard of an intervention, and Kathy told her that that was how Scott's dad had gotten into treatment. Scott had been bitter against the family ever since because he didn't think his dad needed treatment and thought what they did was cruel. Then Kathy quickly added that she didn't want to involve his family. May patiently explained that because of Scott's age, his friends' participation in the intervention would have a greater impact than his family's anyway. Kathy listened attentively while May continued.

"Try to get some of his friends together and I'll explain the whole process in detail. Here is some literature you can read that may answer any of your questions. Are you interested?"

Kathy hesitated. "I'm just not sure. Everyone is busy with midterms, and…"

Sue jumped in. "We'll both ask, Kathy. I saw a movie in one of my classes about the intervention process. I'll tell them about it. We can meet next week, after midterms."

Kathy looked relieved. "Well, there will be nothing left of our relationship if he continues this way. Let's set something up next week."

With that, they made a date for the following week. Kathy decided to go home for the weekend to see her father. She didn't think she'd talk with him about it, but it always did her good to see him.

Chapter 7

It was a Saturday, the third week in October. A high-pressure system had made its way down from Canada a few days earlier, and frost remained on the shadows of rooftops where the morning sun still hadn't visited.

Kathy's hazel eyes opened slowly. Her eyes and her short, light brown hair were the only things visible outside the heavy quilt pulled over her. She slowly drifted into consciousness and felt like stretching, but she didn't want to take her arms out from under the warmth of the covers. She finally braved it, and as her hands passed across the window, she noticed the sun trying to work its way through the parallel lines of the blinds. Forgetting the cold, she hopped out of bed and opened the blinds for a better look. The sky was clear, without a single cloud on the horizon to darken her day. She glanced at the tops of the trees and noticed just the slightest breeze dancing with them. She laughed, jumped in the air, tucked her knees to her chest, and did a forward flip back into her bed. She loved running in the woods near her house, especially on crisp fall days.

Kathy smiled brightly as she pulled the covers back over her body. She lay and listened to her father pretending to be quiet in the kitchen. Her smile brightened further as she pictured him struggling with himself to let her sleep, yet desperately wanting to wake her and share the beauty of the day with her. However, she knew that he probably wouldn't say more than a hundred words to her all day.

It had just been the two of them since her mother died of cancer when she was in junior high school. Though it had been nine years since her mom died, as Kathy knew, he never dated. It wasn't just because he loved her mother very much. He was such a quiet man she doubted that he could ever make enough conversation with a woman for her to realize what a kind and gentle man he really was.

The sun streaming through the open blinds was doing its work. Soon Kathy felt sufficiently warm to be brave enough to venture out again from her bed. It helped that she knew that her running clothes were waiting for her at the side of the bed. In seconds, she was out of her nightclothes and into her first layer of gear.

Her next stop was the bathroom just outside her room. She paused at the mirror just long enough to run a brush through her hair and make sure no last-minute blemishes had marred her pretty freckled face. As usual, her face was as clear as the sky outside.

Kathy would have said the face in the mirror was just okay, but if it had been Snow White's magic mirror, he would have told her there was no one fairer. Had he been in a talkative mood, he might have gone on to say there were plenty of women who fussed more over themselves. There were many women who knew more about hairstyles and makeup. There were women who looked and acted more feminine. But Kathy didn't care much about those things. Her efforts tended to be toward her body—not to make it beautiful, but instead to make it healthy and able to do the things she demanded of it. And Kathy demanded a great deal.

After a brief stint in the bathroom, it was a walk down the short hall of their one-story brick ranch to the kitchen. Her father was seated at the breakfast table and smiled when she entered the room.

"G'morning, honey. Have you looked out the window yet?"

Kathy smiled back as she crossed the room and kissed him on the bald spot on the top of his head.

"Yes," she said, "though you'd never know it from in here. Dad, without me or Mom here to tell you to turn on the pilot light to the furnace, I'm afraid I'll stop in some winter day and find you a block of ice."

"Darn it!" he said in his soft voice. "I meant to do that last weekend, but don't you worry. If it gets cold enough, I'll light it. I did it when you were away at college last year."

"Yes, but I also called and reminded you."

Kathy's orange juice and a coffee cup were already waiting for her on a placemat kitty-cornered from her father's place. She took the cup and poured herself some coffee from the electric pot on the counter. She still hadn't decided if she liked coffee, but she didn't want to drink her juice before she ran because it would coat the stomach and keep fluids from moving through. She wanted to keep her father company, though she was quite sure he'd already used more than his quota of words for the morning. After pouring the cup, she sat down in her place and they sat in the comfortable silence, saving words for the people who needed them. After taking a few sips and letting the rest get cold, she pushed away from the table and announced that she was off for her morning run in the woods. She put her arms around his neck and kissed his head again. He responded by placing his hand above hers and closing his eyes—as if savoring a fine wine he didn't want to swallow.

As she walked from the porch into the sunlight, Kathy could feel that the day was already warming. She looked at the sky, still blue between each horizon and the vast colors of autumn trees. She wondered when it was that she had stopped taking the wonders of nature for granted. She remembered her boredom on those Sunday afternoons in the fall when her parents would take her for a ride to look at the colors. Back then, she figured she and everyone she loved would live forever, so why savor the moments? Now she knew differently. She knew this was special. She would never get these moments back, and she was aware that those she loved would not live forever.

Frost is often depicted as an artist, but as she stretched on the front steps, she thought to herself that this year, he must also be considered a conductor. She pictured him holding a baton in one hand. With the other hand turned out and down, she imagined him muting the wind's trumpets and quieting the drumming rains so that the burgundy oaks, brilliant orange- red maples, and yellow birches and poplars had time to catch up with the sleepy sumacs ready to shed their bright red leaves and begin their winter slumber. He had to blend summer with just enough warmth and moisture to bring out the music of the colors and mix them into the rich symphony of autumn. This year, he was truly a maestro.

As she started her run, her body groaned as it gradually became aware that night was over and a serious run was ahead. She decided to go easy in order to avoid running out of energy. She knew she and her father would be covering this same ground later in the day on a walk. She ran toward the edge of town and the fire lanes that cut through the woods and meadows. She watched a yellow butterfly sucking the final drops of nectar out of the wildflowers and noticed how the gold of the meadow complemented the myriad colors of the trees.

As Kathy ran through the woods, she thought of all that had happened. She wondered if she and Scott would make it through this. She remembered hearing in her marriage and family class that there were three things that were essential to a relationship: each person needed to feel trust, health, and safety.

Lately, she didn't trust Scott. She couldn't imagine any relationship being bad enough for her to neglect her health, but some of the characters, like this Kane, who entered her life because of Scott's drug use, sure made her question her safety. She knew no matter what, she would proceed with the intervention. Scott was a good person, and she'd help anyone who was going down the road where Scott was headed.

Kathy shook her head to dismiss her worries and concentrated on her running.

Later that day when she was walking down that same path with her father, Kathy was sure that he was just enjoying her being home and the beauty of the day and the woods.

Then he asked, "What's going on with you and Scott?" Kathy had forgotten, since it had been so long that she had relationship problems, that somehow her father always knew when she was troubled. At first, she tried to act as if she did not know what he meant.

"What do you mean?" she asked.

Her father didn't answer. He had a way of confronting her that was so kind and gentle but worked better than an interrogator with a hot lamp. When she was being dishonest, he just waited for the truth. In his silence, he seemed to say, "I believe in you and in your values. I believe in your desire to keep our relationship honest, and I believe in your integrity."

But the other side was there too. It wasn't just the silence, but more than human. He was rarely critical of her performance in school and athletics, and if he was, it was usually about Kathy's own expectations of herself. "You're only human," he would say to her when she was angry or down on herself. "If you expect perfection, you'll always be disappointed." It always worked.

This time he continued in silence for some time before he spoke again. "I don't want you to be mad or disappointed in Scott. Everyone makes mistakes, and young ones are more prone to them. As for you, just like in gymnastics, I never expected you not to fall, just to get up again."

Kathy took a deep breath. "Scott has gotten in trouble with drugs and alcohol. Brad, his sister, and I are trying to work with a counselor on campus to help him. I'm afraid of losing him either way. If he continues with the drugs, I'll end it. If I meddle with him too much, he'll end it."

Her father took several steps in silence. He picked up a stone and threw it in the stream that wound beside the path. "Well, I'm proud of you for caring enough to help him through this, but of course, as your father I don't want you to destroy your life trying to save his."

Kathy was happy with his response. She detected no judgment of her or Scott, just concern for both of them. "I know, Dad. I'm worried about the same thing. From everything I've read, addiction isn't something that goes away. If I stay involved with Scott, I know he'll never be more than one bad choice away from being back at it."

Her father shook his head. "You know, as a parent I know I can't protect you or your friends from this stuff, but what are drug pushers doing up on a small campus in central Wisconsin? How does someone even get started with drugs?" It was a question more to the air than to Kathy.

"Dad, I've talked to friends from schools all over the country, and I don't know of any place where there aren't drugs." Kathy had a tear in her eye. "If you watch the commercials on TV or listen to the public that doesn't know any better, they all say to be careful of the wrong people. But really it's your friends that introduce you to drugs and even sell them to you. I'm beginning to believe that most of the pain in a person's life comes from the ones you love the most."

Kathy could see that her father understood that. The last thing her mother ever wanted for either of them was pain, but even she had caused them pain by dying. She explained to her father what she would be doing in the intervention. He asked questions about the process but never questioned her for doing it. Kathy walked in silence after that, enjoying the winding road and hearing the bubbling stream. She let nature, her father, and being home restore her for what she knew was coming.

Chapter 8

Kathy had asked to meet in the cafeteria with two of Scott's friends, Tim and Eric. They were standing at the right spot and on time, engaging in their favorite pastime—watching and commenting on girls. Tim was the more conservative of the two, but that was just enough to keep them out of jail. Eric was ogling a new freshman girl who still had that lost and overwhelmed look. She was tall, blonde, and very thin.

"You're just about panting. Wipe the drool off your mouth, Eric."

Eric ignored his friend. "Christ sake, look at her," he said, pointing his finger and raising his voice.

"Settle down, Eric, we're here to meet Kathy," Tim said. "You don't understand. This is the moment I've waited for all my life. I'm in love," Eric gushed.

"You've said that at least a thousand times since I've known you," Tim said in a bored tone.

"I know, but this time it's for real. If I let her go, I may never see her again, and my destiny will be altered. See you later," Eric said, moving away, as he walked confidently toward his latest prey.

"Your destiny is ruled by your genitals. Anyway, you'll be back in five minutes," said Tim.

"You're just jealous because you know she'll like me better," Eric said as he walked away.

Just then, Kathy came along. "Where's Eric going, Tim?" she asked.

"Off to meet his destiny. Don't worry. It's just a short detour. He'll be back in five minutes. What was it that you wanted to see us about anyway?"

"I'd rather wait until everyone is here, so I only have to explain it one time. It's kind of complicated." Seeing Brad and Sue arrive, Kathy breathed a sigh of relief. "Oh good, Eric is coming back," she said.

"Why didn't you tell me she talked like Minnie Mouse, Tim?" Eric asked sounding depressed.

"You would have told me I said it because she rejected me.

So much for destiny," Tim laughed.

"Hi, guys," Jake said, as he joined the group.

"Hi, Jake," everyone answered.

"How's everything in the TKE house?" Eric asked.

"Fine," Jake said.

"When are you going to join a good fraternity?" Eric quipped.

"I did. One without you two clowns," Jake shot back. Kathy took a deep breath and interrupted. She had thought long and hard about what to say and decided just to blurt it out. "I asked you all here because I'm concerned about Scott and his drug use lately. Sue and I went to talk with the S.A.P. counselor here on campus, and she said maybe if we got a group of his friends together and confronted him in the right way, he might be willing to get help." When she finished speaking, the lump left her throat, and she felt relieved.

Eric was the first to respond. "Oh great, you and hippy girl here went and blabbed to some counselor," he shot at her. "Thanks a lot. You're going to get our whole house placed on probation."

"No, I checked on that. The counselor is only interested in getting him help."

"What makes you think Scott has a problem? Everybody drinks and uses. He's young, for God's sake, let him have some fun."

Tim joined in. "Whaddya want? He's twenty-one. Well, almost twenty-one. What business is it of ours if he does have a problem?"

"I thought you were brothers," Brad said sarcastically, "and you cared about each other."

"Stay out of this, dweeb," Eric said.

"You guys have been around Scott more than I have. You know he's changed and that his alcohol and cocaine use is not like everybody else's," Jake chimed in.

"Jake is right. And since you guys do spend a lot of time with him, and you are brothers, he respects you and might listen. Will you help?" Kathy pleaded.

"I don't know," Tim said.

"What if you saw a bump forming on the back of Scottie's neck," Sue asked, "—one he couldn't see or feel—would you tell him about it?"

"What's that got to do with it?" Eric asked.

"I think Scott has an illness that he doesn't know he has."

"Oh, is that some cute thing you learned in a psych class, Sue? Now you're saying he's an alcoholic or something?"

"We don't have to decide that. All we want to do is to tell him our concerns," Kathy said.

"Well, I'll have to think about it. I've just discovered a new destiny. I'll have to get back to you," Eric said as he left the table.

"I'd better go with him to be sure his destiny is over twelve," said Tim.

After they left, Brad said, "To think those two will someday probably hold responsible positions in the world. It's scary.

Well, you can count me in, Kathy."

"Me too," said Sue.

"I'll do it too," said Jake solemnly.

"Good. Thanks. Scott's sister Bobbie is coming too. I talked to her this weekend when I saw her. She's been through one of these before with her dad."

"Yeah, and I know it helped him even though Scott hates to admit that," Brad said.

"Okay, we need to meet at the counselor's office tomorrow night at eight p.m.," Kathy said. "Bobbie will be joining us there."

"What do we tell Scott if we see him?" Jake asked.

"The counselor said to invite him along, but I know he won't come, and I'd rather he didn't know you're all involved," said Kathy.

"Well, I'll go catch up with Tim and Eric and tell them to keep it quiet. They'll at least do that, I think," said Jake.

"Better bring visual aids and make sure you use small words," said Brad.

The following evening, they met at the counselor's office. "Well, Kathy," said May, "it looks like you were quite successful in gathering a fine group here."

"Yes, I was hoping for two others, but they decided not to join us," said Kathy.

"Have any of you done an intervention before?" May asked.

Bobbie spoke up. "I have, with my father. My greatest nightmare is that before I die, I'll be in one of these with every member of my family, and then they'll turn around and do one on me."

"It's really sad how the problem of addiction seems to run in families. Do your parents know that Scott has a problem?" May asked.

"They suspect, but they don't know. Scott would be really mad if we brought them here. Things have really been strained since my father went through treatment."

"Well, I think we can proceed with what we have here. I've gotten enough information from my initial talk with Kathy to believe there is a problem, so we can continue as far as I'm concerned. Do you guys have any doubts?" May asked.

"Yes. I know in my head he's got a problem, but in my heart I've spent so long admiring him, I just don't want to believe this of my friend," Brad responded.

"Okay. It will probably take all of our efforts just to convince him there's a problem, because he probably feels like you at some level. He knows he's out of control, but a big part of him says, 'This couldn't happen to me.' Remember—he's still not convinced his father ever had a problem. Any questions?"

"Yes, how exactly does this work?" Jake asked.

May took a deep breath and began to explain the process of intervention. She told them each to write Scott a letter and to include specific instances when they had been with Scott while he was using. She also told them to describe how they felt during those times and to address their relationship with Scott and the reasons they valued his friendship. "This letter will also help you to be more convinced that there is a problem," May added. "It makes a difference when you see your own experiences and feelings in black and white."

"You want to confront him," May continued. "So tell him why you feel you've earned the right. Open and close the letter with the fact that you love or care about him. Then bring the letters back to me, and we'll review them. Understand?"

Sue asked, "Why are we sending letters? Aren't we going to talk to Scott?"

"You won't send the letters. You'll read them, but it will be better than just saying it, because I'll know better what you're going to say. You won't have to make eye contact, and believe me, you'll be really anxious when you do this. You'll be happy to have the letters to rely on, and it will help you to organize what you want to say. A letter is a personal way of saying what you want," May answered.

"I know I've been doing some of that in my mind anyway. When can we bring them back?" Kathy asked.

"It's unusual to have someone so ready. Can the rest of you be ready in a week?"

"Yeah, I guess so," said Brad. The rest nodded in agreement.

"I hope so," Kathy said with a sigh.

Chapter 9

The next week, the group returned with their letters. May commented on how unusual it was that they had all finished them. Then she helped revise the letters. She asked them what they wanted Scott to do if he agreed to get help. After much discussion, they finally decided. It was the middle of the fall semester and the football season. Because of financial limitations, football, and Scott's social life, he still experienced long periods of sobriety. They thought he could get help by attending the Cocaine Anonymous and Narcotics Anonymous meetings that were held on campus. They also wanted him to agree to attend outpatient counseling at the treatment center, go home and tell his family, and then attend the family counseling sessions whenever possible.

In addition, the group thought it would be good if he agreed to move in with Brad instead of living at the fraternity house. May asked what they would do if Scott didn't agree to get help. Kathy decided she would have to end their relationship. She said, "I can't continue a relationship with him if he doesn't quit. We've been serious for a long time and have talked about marriage, but I don't want to marry someone addicted to coke."

Bobbie's eyes started to well up with tears as she answered. "If he refuses to get help, my parents will want to get involved. Scott may have to look forward to still another intervention with the family. They'll know he has a problem because I'll tell them. They realize they're not very influential at the moment, but I know there isn't any length to which my parents won't go to get him help. We've lived long enough with addiction in my family."

"I'd still be his friend," said Brad, "but if he doesn't get to class, I'm not copying my notes for him anymore."

"What about the rest of you?" May asked.

"I don't think I could tell the coach," said Jake, "but the last week or two his attitude has taken a nosedive, and Coach is really big on positive attitude. I don't think he'll be on the starting team long if he doesn't do something."

"Well," said Sue, "Scott doesn't care whether I live or die, but I sure would try to keep my friends at a distance from him, and I know he cares a lot for his friends. I just don't want to see them hurt."

May wanted to know how and where they could present their letters to Scott.

"I tried to get him to come here, but he won't," Kathy said.

"Well, let's go to him then," May quickly decided. "Is there someplace private on or off campus where we could talk with him?"

"What if we just went to his fraternity?" Brad asked. "That's not good," May countered. "People tend to be more defensive on their own turf, and recently there have been some lawsuits when people have done that. What about one of your places?"

Kathy took a deep breath. "I'll be seeing him Friday night, and I know he'll want to stay over at my place." She looked at Bobbie, but she didn't seem shocked. Kathy felt relieved.

"Friday night is no good," May replied. "He probably uses more then, and if he comes down with alcohol, he might still be drunk on Saturday morning. We need to do this on a weekday morning if we can."

It took awhile to arrange, and it ended up being almost two weeks later before everyone could do it in the middle of the week, and at a time when Kathy knew they'd be staying together.

They did a dress rehearsal the afternoon before. At the end, May confirmed the time. "If we met at your place at, say, seven-thirty in the morning, would Scott still be sleeping?"

"Count on it," Brad said. "Even when he's not hung over, Scott hates to get up in the morning."

Sue invited Bobbie to stay with her. She thought having Bobbie might help her to get up early in the morning, and then she, Brad, and Bobbie could all ride over together.

Bobbie was the first one awake the next morning. In fact, she had never slept. The intervention on her father in some ways had been easier, because she hadn't thought she would be a part of it until the very end. This time, she knew all the way that she'd be a part, and she realized how much she wanted it to work.

Tom had been supportive all along and even volunteered to be involved in the intervention, but Scott didn't know Tom very well. Besides, Bobbie thought, she needed to do this alone. Tom often complained to her that she tried too hard to control things—including him. He pointed out several times when she complained about the snags in the intervention, and that this was another example of her need to control. She knew that she did it, because she was so insecure and even less trusting. She smiled as she thought, "I'll quit tomorrow." She said aloud, "But first, I have to get everyone through the intervention."

She awakened Sue, which took some doing. Sue was hard to wake up and harder to get up. Even then, she moved slowly. Brad had been waiting ten minutes before she was ready. They met the others outside of Kathy's apartment and walked quietly up the stairs to her second floor flat. Kathy greeted them at the door so they wouldn't have to knock. When they were all seated in the living room, Kathy woke Scott and asked him to dress before going in the living room since there were some people there to see him.

It was the beginning of November and it was cold and raining outside. The beautiful color of the trees had gone, and the branches that remained looked like exposed nerve bundles against the gray sky.

"What is this, a convention?" Scott quipped as he entered the room. There was just one chair left for him to take. He had dark circles under his puffy eyes, but he walked with a cocky and arrogant strut towards the only empty chair.

May started: "Hi, Scott. My name is May. I believe you know the rest of these people. They're here because they care about you and are concerned with your drug use. They've prepared some things they want to say to you. Will you hear them out?"

"I know I've heard it all before, but if they want to waste their time, it's okay with me," Scott said, as he scowled and slumped down in his chair. Scott's strong shoulders seemed to weaken under the weight of unknown concerns.

"Good!" said May.

As they had already agreed, Jake started:

Dear Scott,

I have known and admired you for a long time. Being a year behind you in school, I was afraid I'd never get the chance to play on the same starting team as you, but this year I reached that goal at the first game. Part of the thrill of starting was, honest to God, walking onto the same field as you and being introduced at the same time. I felt so proud, and it made all the hard work worthwhile.

But my image of you really sank when I saw you using at parties after the games. It wasn't just that you took drugs, but the way your personality changed. I remember the night I decided I'd ask you why you were using, and you told me it was none of my business and to get out of your face. When I remember all of the questions I'd asked you before about school and sports, you had always answered so patiently, and then—that. I was shocked and disappointed. I felt like a child who had just been spanked by his favorite teacher. I care about you, Scott, and I want you to get help.

Sue went next:

Dear Scott,

I know you don't know me that well, but I feel I know you. It is no surprise to me that Brad feels deeply for you, but I'll let him tell you that. I got to know you through Brad's eyes long before I met you. I thought that no one could be the person Brad had built you up to be. Then I met you, and I honestly believed Brad wasn't exaggerating. You were friendly, warm, funny, and intelligent, but in spite of all those characteristics, you were kind of shy.

Then the other night I saw you after you had used cocaine. I was sad and embarrassed for you. You acted loud and very conceited.

Where before you acted friendly toward me, now you made crude sexual comments that embarrassed me and hurt me. When I asked you to stop, you said, "Who wants you around anyway, bitch?" Scott, I'm here because I care, and I want you to get help.

By this time, Kathy was already crying. She was next to read her letter:

Dearest Scott,

I love you, and I have for a long time—not just because you are smart and a jock but also because you acted like you were neither. Being in sports myself, I grew up with guys who were full of themselves and treated women like pieces of meat, but you didn't.

When you asked me out, I was so thrilled that I thought I might not be able to utter the word "yes." That first year we dated is a blur to me because I felt like I floated through, just barely touching the ground.

I was shocked at myself because sports had made me so disciplined.

But lately, things have changed. When we are out together, you act distant from me and preoccupied. When we make love, you aren't tender and sensitive like you used to be. What I'm most afraid of is the people you associate with to get the drugs. We fight all the time about your drug use. Please get help, Scott, because I want back the man I fell so madly in love with.

Bobbie was next. Stoically, she read:

Dear Scott,

I'm here because I care about you. Some people may think that's trite because I'm your sister and I have to care, but you know that, except for all the times you protected me, I never felt like your sister.

We were like friends. We had to be sometimes, with Mom and Dad so preoccupied. But lately, things have changed. I remember how you and I both vowed that we'd never get like Mom and Dad, Dad with his drinking, and Mom being so obsessed with it.

But the last time you were home, I walked into your room, and you were snorting coke. I confronted you, and before I knew it, we sounded just like Mom and Dad. Scott, I'm afraid that before my life is over, I'm going to be involved in one of these with every member of our family. But I love you all too much to let our lives be destroyed by a substance. Please get help, Scott.

Brad went last:

Dear Scott,

This is very painful for me to be here, not only because I care so much about you, but because I owe you so much, and I'm afraid of losing your friendship. I don't know why you ever chose me as a friend way back in grade school. Maybe you felt sorry for me.

Because I was your friend, I became somebody special. It wasn't just the other kids liking me that made me feel that way; it was because you helped me to feel that way. You helped me to have confidence in myself. The other day, I stopped by to see you after you had been using cocaine the night before. It was only ten in the morning, and you were drinking a beer. While I was with you, you cried and talked about how meaningless life seemed. I know that wasn't you, but how you feel when you come down from the drug. Scott, it scares me to death that you will destroy yourself with drugs and alcohol.

Please get help.

May explained, "Scott, what your friends want you to do is join Cocaine Anonymous, attend individual counseling, and go to family counseling on the weekends. Will you do that?"

"You know, maybe you guys have a point. I guess I've been a little carried away lately, but I can handle it. I don't need all that counseling and meeting stuff," Scott responded defensively.

"Scott, you've told me that before," said Kathy, "but the next weekend, you're right back at it. I don't believe you can do it alone."

"Well, I won't do what you're asking," Scott replied. "Maybe we should read the letters again," May said.

"No, I sat through those once. I'm not listening to them again. I think I should leave now."

"Okay, Scott," said Kathy, "but if you won't get help, I'm afraid it's over between us. I love you, and I probably always will, but I can't live with you married to cocaine."

"Oh come off it, Kathy."

"I mean it, Scott," Kathy said, trying to sound convincing though she was visibly trembling.

Bobbie spoke up. "Scott, your problem is not a secret from the family anymore. I don't want to hurt you, but my life has been a lie for too long, and since Dad's got help, I don't feel I need to lie anymore, and I won't go back to living that way. If they ask me about you, I'll tell them the truth."

"Oh, now the truth comes out. 'You won't do what we want, Scott, so now we punish you'," Scott mocked defiantly.

"Scott, no one wants to punish you," said Brad, "but it is very painful to be your friend right now because you keep rejecting us for the drug. We have to take care of ourselves too. Three times in the last week I've copied my notes for you because you missed class. Scott, you're my friend. I'd copy the entire library if I thought it would help you, but I can't keep copying my notes knowing I'm making it easier for you to destroy yourself with chemicals."

"I don't need any of you!" Scott spat out. "If that's the way you feel, I'll just have to go it alone." With that, Scott stomped to the door, knocking over his chair in the process.

With their heads bowed, the group sat quietly for a while.

Kathy was the first to break the silence. "Oh, May, I didn't want it to end this way."

May hugged her as she answered. "None of us did, but let's give it time."

The holidays came and went. Scott went home only when he had to be there. He used the excuse that he had gotten behind in his classes because of football. He vacillated between periods of sobriety to prove his friends wrong and increasingly heavier use to quiet the inner turmoil. Unfortunately, Scott was becoming accustomed to medicating and silencing that inner turmoil.

Chapter 10

Bobbie had told Scott she would tell the family about his drug use—if she was asked. But she didn't bring the subject up. She thought she'd wait for the right moment or maybe for Scott to change his mind. The family was used to living in denial and it was easy for them to fall back into the pattern of "don't ask, don't tell." Finally, one night at dinner, Bobbie could wait no longer.

Meals had changed considerably in the Brandt house. They were certainly different from the days of Hank's drinking when Hank would come home late and angry and everyone was afraid of him.

Dinners were different too from the icy silence of the first year of recovery when Hank and Molly were barely speaking to one another—and when they did, it was usually harshly. Dinnertime now, at least when they could all get together between school, practices, and jobs, was filled with catching up with each other's lives and lots of laughter. The mood was always one of caring and support.

On a weekend just before Easter, everyone but Scott was home. Scott's sister and brother, Sally and Paul, were running in an indoor track meet that day and everyone wanted to see them. There was a lovely lake next to the track. It was a large spring-fed refuge for a wide variety of wildlife. The ice had disappeared from the lake, and Paul and some of his friends were already getting buoys in place to protect the loons.

Sally had recently wrestled with bulimia, a secret self-torture on which she had relied when overwhelmed by racing thoughts and feelings. Binging had been Sally's way to quiet the thoughts. After succumbing to massive caloric intake, her powerful feelings would cause her to purge. A calm, almost euphoric feeling would wash over Sally after self-induced vomiting. But almost immediately shame and guilt would begin to build again.

Sally still fought to break the vicious cycle of bulimia. But it was becoming easier because she felt such freedom after stopping the self-destructive purging behavior. She was back to her usual funny self.

Paul and his loons—he still fretted over them each spring and summer when the birds returned from their winter home in Florida—often bore the brunt of her jokes. Tonight, she was merciless in her attack. "So Paul, how do you know where your loons go in the winter when the lake freezes?"

Paul just smiled, knowing there was more to come.

"You know, I was watching a show about a guy who led a group of cranes to Florida with an ultra-light plane. Maybe you could do that with the loons, and that way you could be sure they're somewhere safe."

"Loons have been around since the dinosaurs and they'll be around long after humans the way we're going. I think they know how to take care of themselves. I worry a lot more about how you'll survive after I leave for college next year," Paul said.

After taking up the cause of the loons, helping to develop a nesting site for them, and designating a part of the lake outside of town as a protected area for them, Paul had become interested in a number of environmental issues. He had joined Sierra Club and planned to major in Environmental Biology in college.

"Please, Sally, don't get him started, or we'll have to listen to the latest appointment to the EPA and how it's another example of the fox guarding the henhouse," their older brother, Ryan, chimed in.

"Hey, at least he has an interest and a potential major," Hank added his two cents. "That's more than I can say for you, Ryan. Though you've managed to pull yourself away from girls long enough to get good grades and win some swimming events, you know you'll be starting your sophomore year soon and a major would be nice."

"You mean I can't major in girls, Dad?" Ryan answered with a disappointed look on his face that quickly turned into a large wide smile.

"Hank, you've just broken the kid's heart. Now we'll have to deal with his sulking and depression until he leaves for school, and the first girl he sees will make him forget everything you said," Molly said, as she smiled and rubbed Ryan's closely cropped hair.

"Mom, if you keep messing up my hair like that, I won't be able to get them to look back at me."

"Oh, they'll look as soon as you strip down to those disgusting Speedos you guys wear," Bobbie added to the mix, winking at her brother.

There was laughter as the quips continued, and no one was immune.

Though playful hostility continued to be a major form of communication, it was no longer used to cover up what couldn't be talked about. Scott was like an elephant in the living room that everyone tried to ignore, but couldn't. It wasn't because they didn't want to talk about Scott, but the discussion always seemed to end in confusion and sadness. Not one of them knew what to do. It was easier to ignore the subject.

This time, Hank broke through the light air with a mixture of joy and regret. "You know, I'm sure that you guys, like me, wondered whether there would ever be a time when dinner would be this much fun again. I didn't think there would ever be anything I'd look forward to more than a drink after work, but I can honestly say I look forward to dinner with my family more than drinking. I think it's because by the end there were so many negatives to my drinking and with this it's just good stuff. My only regret is that Scott's still not a part of it. Bobbie, I know you know more about Scott than you're saying. What's happening with him?"

Bobbie had just taken her last swallow of milk and she choked on it. After recovering, she took a deep breath. "Before the semester ended, we did an intervention on Scott, but it didn't work." Silence fell upon the dinner table. Bobbie looked at all the blank faces surrounding it. A sad heaviness filled the room.

Molly was the first to recover. "Well, let me see if I can sort though the five hundred questions I have in my mind. One: who's 'we'? Two: what does 'it didn't work' mean? Three: when in the unholy hell did you plan to tell us about this? Four: what's Scott up to now? Five: should I go on, or is that enough for you to think about for the moment?"

Bobbie took another deep breath. "The people involved were me, Kathy, Brad, a friend of theirs named Sue, and a guy named Jake who plays football with Scott. We did it through an organization at school called the Student Assistance Program. A woman named May helped us. She did a fine job and we all did our best but Scott wasn't ready. I was hoping by now he'd have come around and I wouldn't have to tell you all this, but as of now he's still using cocaine and alcohol as far as I know. Since I've been home, I know no more about him than you do. I've talked with Kathy and he hasn't talked to her or Brad either."

"So right now, he's shut off from his family, his friends, and his girlfriend?" Molly asked with a noticeable loss of color in her face. She stood abruptly. "I'm calling him."

Hank got up immediately. He had become the sensitive man with whom she had fallen in love, but that didn't mean he always agreed with her. He stood in front of her and gently put his hands on her shoulders. Towering over her, he said, "I know you want to reach out to your son who's lonely and in pain right now, but that pain may be exactly what gets him to seek help." "Hank, the last thing I need right now is you or one of my AA friends lecturing me on enabling. If he does come to a moment of clarity, I want him to know we're there if he chooses to reach out." Roughly, she removed his hands from her shoulders and went to the phone in the bedroom.

Hank sank back down in a heap. He looked sadly at Bobbie. "Haven't we had enough secrets around here?"

"Daddy, I just wanted to give him some time to work it out, and all it can do is upset the rest of you."

"I hear some pretty scary stories from cocaine users at meetings about the characters they get their drugs from. How does Scott get his, and how does he afford it? He never asks us for money."

"I don't know too much about that. I know he's too smart and too proud to ask you for money. I heard Kathy talk about some guy named Kane, who's a former teammate of Scott's."

Molly came back slowly in the room. "I got his voicemail.

I just said we love him and miss him and hope he's doing well.

I asked him to call but I know he'll wait for the next time he thinks we're all out and leave a message. Bobbie, do you know what his drug and alcohol use has been like since the intervention?"

Bobbie started to cry. "No, every time I see him, he just gives me this look of 'how dare you betray me' and walks away. Now I feel like you guys think I betrayed you too. I can't win." Sally and Paul jumped up and put their arms around her.

"We all know how painful these interventions are, and we've only been involved in successful ones. We need to go easy on Bobbie. She did her best," Sally said angrily. Sally was always very protective of her sister and now she was filled with many different emotions. She felt that she needed to save someone.

"I was involved in a peer intervention at school with a kid in the dorm. He was mad at us at first, but he came around," Ryan added.

"Don't get me wrong, honey. I appreciate the risk you took in doing it and thank you for it. I just spent too much of my own life in the dark about my own addiction. I don't want to do the same with my kids," Hank said.

"Well, let's pray that he comes to his senses," Molly said, holding out her hands. The Brandts joined hands and asked God to help Scott stop using drugs.

Chapter 11

In the beginning, just the opposite seemed to be the case. Scott increased his use and his involvement with others who used. He continued to use through the winter and spring. When the football season was over, Scott's drug use increased even more. Scott even got a job so he could pay his debts and continue to support his habit. Still his family hoped and prayed that he had been more deeply affected by the intervention than he had let on.

When summer came, Kathy went home to spend time with her dad. She worked as a lifeguard at the beach during the day and as a waitress at the local restaurant in the evening. She stayed very busy but still spent a great deal of time thinking of Scott. She longed for his touch.

Scott stayed at school to finish the classes he needed to be ready for student teaching in the fall—his last requirement before receiving his degree and teaching certificate. Unfortunately, he did not get any of his first three choices for teaching. Though his advisor had no proof of his drug use, he strongly suspected Scott of it and told him so.

Scott was given an assignment in a special needs classroom outside the Menominee Indian Reservation about forty miles from Green Bay. He would be working at a junior high school with developmentally delayed and learning disabled adolescents and pre-adolescents.

Scott ran into Kathy when he came back to the college for the first football game of the fall. He told her that he had been upset with the assignment at first but he was really enjoying the students. Kathy wasn't surprised. Scott got angry easily at most adults, but kids brought out a whole different side of him. He was extremely patient and kind—even loving—to little kids.

They seemed to recognize his gift and followed him eagerly and trustingly.

She felt that familiar ache when she saw him, though she tried not to let on how much it hurt to see him and not hold him. She searched his face longingly for any sign of old feelings, but she saw nothing to give her hope. He seemed cold, distant, and resentful. With profound sadness, Kathy feared she had lost the Scott she loved.

After the game, she went to a party where she saw Bobbie.

Neither girl was much in the party mood. Bobbie had also talked to Scott and gotten a similar reaction. Soon Bobbie was crying and she pledged never to do another intervention.

"I'd rather lose my brother to drugs than have him live like this. I can't stand that betrayed look he gives me every time I see him. He's like a ghost who appears every once in a while to remind me of my sins, but in every other way he's dead to me. He didn't come home once over the summer. It's like he resents the whole family and is punishing us for what I did. I hate this!"

After doing her best to console Bobbie, Kathy left for her own apartment. She was barely in the door when she heard a knock. Thinking it was one of her friends or perhaps Bobbie wanting to talk some more, she opened the door quickly. Too quickly. When she saw who was on the other side, her breath left even more quickly. A flash of bright light blinded her.

"Smile," said Kane. There was another flash as he took her picture with a digital camera.

He was alone this time.

"Scott's not here," said Kathy shortly. "Thanks to you and your merchandise, I don't see him anymore." She knew he sensed her fear. Knowing Kane, he probably smelled it. She tried to slam the door in his face, but with surprising quickness, he was on her side of the door before it closed.

"I didn't come to see him," he said, "and I told you I'd be back to finish our conversation." His look froze Kathy's blood.

"We have no conversation to finish! Now get out of here."

Her words were surprisingly forceful, but her backpedaling belied them.

"That's okay. I don't want to talk either."

Kathy was again surprised how quickly he made up the distance she had established between them. In no time, he had his arms around her and pushed her to the floor. Surprises work both ways. Either he didn't know she was a gymnast or he didn't consider the possibility that a girl might have that much strength and agility. When they hit the floor, she kept on rolling, head over heels, and when they stopped, it was Kathy on top. She was poised to shove the heel of her hand to the tip of his nose when she felt the cold hard knife at her throat.

The intervention had more of an impact on Scott than his cold and distant exterior indicated. He went from heavy use to periods of abstinence. He felt depressed—without cocaine and without Kathy and his other friends. He avoided Kathy totally and his relationship with Brad was strained to say the least. He began attending class regularly and he sat next to Brad but had little to say to him. His performance in football improved but it made little difference; the team lost most of its games anyway. Scott felt persistently lonely and isolated.

The team was much improved the next year with a new coach and a talented group of freshmen. Young and inexperienced, the team did manage to win their first game and Scott snorted a little cocaine to celebrate. The old familiar rush was exciting and he looked for someone with whom he could reminisce about past games but all his buddies either had graduated or seemed more interested in their girlfriends at the moment. He walked out of the house and down the block to the stadium. He sat in the bleachers for a few minutes and realized, in a flash, that his whole career was now over. So many things in Scott's life were over. He felt empty.

He'd miss the cheering crowds, but most of all, the high he'd get from making that big play when the pressure was on and those few moments when he really believed in himself. Alone, he wandered down to the field and paused in the end zone. Scott could hear his heart pounding in his ears. He heard the public address announcer: "Waiting to receive the kick, Scott Brandt." He heard the crowd roar as he received the kick and his excitement mounted as he dodged one tackle after another. As he reached the other end zone, he collapsed.

He didn't know how long he lay there sobbing when he decided to go visit Kathy. He heard a voice that seemed to come from both inside and out telling him to get up and get moving.

He thought he'd knock gingerly on the door of her apartment, not knowing if he wanted her to be there or not. When he got to the door, he heard a familiar voice—a mean voice that had reached a new octave of evil. Then he heard Kathy's muffled sobs. He tried the door, and it was unlocked. With every ounce of energy restraining him from barging through the door, he opened it quietly. When he entered, the first thing he saw was Kathy's face filled with shame and terror and flowing with tears. Kane had his back to him and was too intent on his work to pay attention to Scott. Kane was cutting off all of the buttons off her blouse and working to snap the lower band of her bra. He pulled the knife back for a moment, and Scott lunged, savagely grabbing Kane's wrist. Even on a normal day, Kane was no match for Scott without his bodyguards. This time Scott had four friends on his side: rage, the memory of all the times Kane had humiliated him, Kane's out-of-shape condition, and Kane's alarm.

Scott pulled on the wrist he was holding and lifted Kane in the air. He swung his free hand around and landed it squarely in Kane's gut. He heard the groan and the rush of air that whistled from his adversary's body. With his next punch he heard a rib crack. The knife fell from Kane's hand, and Kathy grabbed it as it hit the floor. With Kane bent over in pain, Scott kneed him in the face. Blood covered Kane's face and shirt. He staggered blindly and then Scott rushed him once more, pressing him against the door.

"Kathy, call the cops, and we'll have this prick describe his activities for the night."

"Do that and I'll describe yours for the last several years," Kane spat out bloodily.

"Just get him out of here," Kathy sobbed.

With a knee to the groin that Kane would long remember and fire coming from his eyes, Scott said, "If I ever catch you near her again, I'll kill you."

"Who you going to get your next hit from? You'll never get it from me again," Kane said, with a spray of red.

Scott smiled. "I've been trying to quit, you moron. You've just given me all the motivation I need." With that, he kicked Kane again and watched him roll down the steps. Kane got up with a groan and headed out the door, leaving a trail of blood behind him.

Scott turned to Kathy. With her shirt still torn open, she ran to him and he held her. Breathlessly she sobbed, "What made you come just at this moment?"

"I don't know," he said. "I just know I don't want to be without you and the people I love for even one minute more. But this isn't a time to be talking about me. How are you?"

"Well, I'm mostly numb," she said, "but I'm also afraid. What if he gets those thugs of his and comes back?"

"I think his next stop will be the hospital. Why don't you change? Then I'll take you out of here."

Kathy went to her bedroom taking off what was left of her clothing as quickly as she could peel it from her body. With shaking hands, she took all of it, walked past the hamper, and threw it in a wastebasket in the bathroom. She jumped in the shower and let the warm water run over her for a long time. She took soap and scrubbed hard as if to rub the memory of the event from her body. She dressed quickly, not wanting to stay in her apartment or alone any longer. For the first time in her adult life, Kathy felt weak and vulnerable. Her legs felt like rubber, and her stomach was tied in knots.

When she saw Scott waiting patiently in her living room, his look of concern and warm, shy smile melted her.

"Thanks for waiting," she said, sounding more like a little girl than she wanted. "I'm not one for long showers, but I've never had to wash off that kind of filth before—that dirty bastard," she said, trying to regain her composure.

Usually she was able to tell right away if Scott had been using, but tonight it was hard for her to read. She thought as she came back to the living room that she probably should have asked, but then he might not be honest with her anyway. Besides, she felt safe with him and she did not want to scare him away.

They went out to a restaurant. After what she had been through, Kathy had no interest in food so they stopped at a coffee house near campus. They ordered drinks and sat for a few minutes in silence. Kathy spoke first. "Scott, I don't want to talk about what happened at my apartment other than to say thank you for saving me from that animal, but I'm also mad at you for even bringing him into my life. Tell me again how you happened to be there?"

"I've missed you, Kathy," he said softly, leaning toward her across the table. She moved away slightly. "I came because I didn't want to be away from you anymore."

With a deep breath and in as cool a tone as possible, Kathy said, "I've missed you too, Scott, but not the cocaine."

He reached over and put his hand over hers. She didn't move hers away. "I know my timing isn't good here, but I miss you and I miss the loving. I just really need to hold you, Kathy," he said.

She pulled her hand away. "It took a lot for me to have sex with you. I never had it with anyone before you, but I loved you, and you were so patient, understanding, and gentle, that I never regretted my decision. When you started using cocaine, it was as if you were making love alone. You were no longer sensitive. You thought it was great, but it wasn't for me. I'm not sure you even knew I was there." Kathy began to cry.

The look on Scott's face said it all. He was hurt. He could not hide the deep-seated sadness in his eyes. He knew he needed both her and his friends too.

"Okay, okay. What is it that you want me to do?" he finally asked.

He agreed to go to meetings and counseling. He didn't agree to family counseling, but Kathy didn't push it.

"We can be friends, and I'll support you, but I'm not willing to get romantically involved until I'm convinced you're straight," she said. "I don't want to spend the rest of my life wondering if you've relapsed every time you're five minutes late." They continued to talk long into the night. Kathy couldn't sleep anyway, and it felt so good to see him again and even better to touch him again—even just his hand.

When they finally left the coffee shop, he took her to Bobbie's dorm room and walked her in to be sure she was safe. She entered as the first sliver of light cracked the horizon. She woke Bobbie to tell her that Scott had agreed to get help, and the two talked until the sun was high in the sky.

They agreed to wait a few days to tell the others, and Bobbie decided to wait to tell her family until they could determine if Scott would follow through on his promises. Kathy kept the incident with Kane to herself. She was excited about Scott and besides, she didn't feel ready to share her hurt and humiliation. She knew she had to share it and soon, but not yet.

When she finally went to sleep, she slept only a couple of hours and woke with a jolt—she wasn't sure why, but she decided not to try and remember the dreams that might have startled her because she didn't want to know. She noticed Bobbie had left the room and decided to find her. Kathy did not want to be alone.

Chapter 12

Weeks passed. Kathy still struggled with nightmares and Scott still struggled with breaking away from cocaine. But they no longer struggled alone. Kathy had meant what she said when she told Scott she would not become romantically involved again—not yet. Still, they kept in close touch.

When Scott returned to his student teaching assignment, he called Kathy daily to find out how she was doing and to let her know he was living up to his agreement. He had found a treatment center on the reservation and began doing individual counseling and attending meetings there. He told her he was enjoying the meetings and was starting to get into some of the Native American rituals he was learning about. He preferred the meeting on the rez to other meetings.

One day when he called, his voice was full of excitement. Some of the people he was meeting had invited him to a sweat lodge. He told Kathy that this was a big compliment—some Indians do not welcome white people.

"When I left the sweat lodge, it was as if I was crawling humbly out into the world for the first time—like being born as someone different. When the lodge was finished, we all got together and ate an enormous feast. You should try the fry bread, Kathy—I practically made an entire meal of it! You know, when I was playing football, I always tried to eat healthy. It didn't matter that I was stuffing my body with drugs and alcohol, but I thought I should eat right. What insanity! Now that I'm done and no longer doing drugs and alcohol, my diet has gone to hell. I hope it's just a phase."

Kathy was excited to hear him so enthusiastic. It had been a long time since she had heard that in his voice. Still, she knew she was holding back. She didn't trust this yet, and she was afraid she never would.

He told her there was something else he wanted to talk to her about. He wanted his family's advice about it but he didn't trust the phone to discuss it. He told her he would talk with her when he saw her.

"I tried to pursue it," Kathy later told Bobbie, but Scott held firm. He kept his secret hidden.

Scott also called Bobbie shortly after he stopped using and asked her if she could allow him to tell the family when he was ready. She agreed. There was still a distance between them that they both could sense, but there would be time for that to change. She tried to be patient and continued to pray.

It wasn't just his recovery that Scott began to embrace. He knew the less idle time he had, the less time he had to think about cocaine. When he wasn't at counseling or a meeting, he threw himself into teaching. On the weekends, he would prepare for the week's lessons or he would help out with the Special Olympics. Each day, Scott surprised himself. He was a perfectionist in everything he did. He had demanded the best from his football teammates, but even more from himself. In his last year of college football, he spent the whole time frustrated because the team was so bad. The more he tried, the more he screamed at his teammates, the worse they got. It was different with these Special Olympics kids. When he saw the sheer joy they got from running or swimming and competing, he caught their enthusiasm and simply enjoyed coaching by laughing, hugging, relating, and sharing. He never once yelled, though he did a lot explaining—sometimes over and over again. Still, he never lost patience. He told Kathy that it was because the kids never lost patience with him.

It was after a practice on a Monday that he picked up the phone. He wasn't sure whether he was disappointed or relieved when the phone kept ringing with no answer. The answering machine picked up and he struggled, trying to decide whether or not to leave a message.

Scott's father, Hank, was reveling in his good fortune. The Packers had a Monday night game and no one was home but him. He had lined up his snacks and a soft drink. He would enjoy them if the Packers played well early and developed a big lead. If the game was close or they played lousy football, he would be too nervous or too upset to eat.

Sometime back, he and Molly had gone to Green Bay to watch a one-man play called "Defending the Cave Man". They had both enjoyed it and laughed often, but the part that Molly still kidded Hank about was the line: "Women watch TV, men become the TV." This was always true for Hank, even during commercials, but during the Packers games, it wasn't strong enough.

Hank not only became the TV, he became the Packers. It was great if they were winning, hell if they lost. He moved with every play and felt every hit. So the fact that no one was there—not even his friends to distract him and break his concentration—was a little bit of heaven for Hank.

The Packers received the kickoff and for a change were actually driving forward on their first possession. Then the phone rang.

None of his friends would call during a Packers game. He thought about just letting the answering machine get it, but what if one of the kids was having car trouble? By the time he grudgingly got off his recliner and reached the phone, the machine was rattling off its greeting.

"Hello?"

"Hi, Dad. It's Scott."

At first, Hank couldn't believe his ears, but he swallowed surprise and tried to sound normal. "Hi, Son. How's everything?"

Hank knew immediately that something was different. Scott was not anxious to get off the phone the way he normally was.

"I don't know where to start, Dad. Student teaching is good. I love teaching. The kids are great. They are so innocent, gentle, and accepting. You know what it's like to get unconditional acceptance. I just got home from coaching practice for the Special Olympics, and I've never enjoyed anything so much in my life. I've got some serious problems with my supervisor, but I'll tell you about those when I see you."

"What kind of problems?"

"I'd like to come home next weekend if that's okay. I can talk with you and Mom about it then. I need your advice."

Hank thought his heart would beat through his chest; he was so relieved and pleased to talk to his son. A rush of excited cheering came from the TV but Hank didn't listen. He actually turned away so he could hear better on the phone. The Packers scored a touchdown in his living room, and he didn't even notice. Even when Scott was little, he had kept his own counsel. Now not only was he coming home, he wanted to talk and listen.

"That sounds wonderful, Scott. Your mother—well, hell, everybody will be thrilled to hear that."

"But what I really want to tell you is I'm in a recovery program, and I'd like to talk with you about what works for you. I've been incorporating some Native American spirituality stuff into mine, and it seems to work for me." Scott went on to discuss some of what he'd been doing both in teaching and in recovery, but Hank didn't hear it all. Inside, he was a child learning that his very best friend who had moved away was moving back right next door.

The Packers kicked off, recovered a fumble, and scored again, but it was all lost on Hank. He thought he'd been feeling good before this. There was silence on the other end, while Hank choked back tears. Not since his own intervention and treatment had he been this touched.

"Dad, are you there?"

The Packers kicked off again this time. The other team ran it back to the Green Bay 20 yard line, but on the first play from scrimmage, their quarterback threw an interception, and the Packers cornerback ran it all the way back for still another touchdown. The Packers led 21-0 and less than five minutes had expired in the game. His friends would be talking about this game for years, but he would never be disappointed that he didn't see it.

"I'm here, Son. I just don't know how much I can talk. The whole family has been praying for this every day for a couple of months now." Pause, swallow, and swallow. "I just wish they were here. I'm sure they'd all like to talk with you. That would give me time to compose myself. I'm sorry, Son."

"Don't apologize, Dad. I've been doing my share of crying too lately."

On the next possession, the Packers defense sacked the quarterback twice and stuffed a run for a loss. Hank always watched the game, but turned down the volume and listened to the Packers play by play on the radio. The announcers were going crazy, saying, "This is the way we knew they were capable of playing." But all the announcers' enthusiasm did not register with Hank.

"I'll be glad to tell you about my recovery, Scott, but I'm happy to hear you're finding your own way."

"This has been a long time coming, Dad. I was in denial not only about me but even about you. I resented the family for their intervention on you and my friends and Bobbie for the one on me. Now I realize they saved both of our lives."

"You're going to love recovery, Son. When you come home, you'll see how different things are. We spend a lot less time arguing and a lot more time laughing. I'm glad you see through your resentments. It's a big load to let go of. I know it was for me. It took me a long time, though. Maybe I'll have to learn from your recovery," Hank said with a smile. "Speaking of resentments—why didn't you or Bobbie let us know sooner?"

"I called her and asked her not to tell you. I wanted to make sure it took and I wanted to tell you myself."

"Oh, Scott, I sure wish your mother were here. She'll have a million questions, and I won't have answers for any of them."

"I'm glad it was you, Dad. We'll have lots of time to talk now. Speaking of that, I'd better go. I want to hit a meeting, and I hear the game on. You probably want to get back to it."

"What game?" Hank laughed.

There could be no doubt now that his father was happy to hear from him and excited about the news he had to share. In the old days when his father was still drinking and Scott was little, interrupting him during a Packers game would not only lead to a tirade, it would give him an excuse to leave for the bar so he could watch the game in peace.

"The Packers game, Dad," Scott said with a laugh. "From the sound of it, they're doing pretty well. You'd better get back to it."

"Scott, if they were winning the Super Bowl in a blowout, it wouldn't compare to the moments I've just spent with you." His heart felt like it would burst as he blinked back the tears.

"Thanks, Dad. I love you and I'm anxious to see you next weekend."

"Same here, Son." "Bye, Dad."

"Bye, Son."

Hank heard the click on the other end. "Why did I say, 'Same here, Son'? Why didn't I say, 'I love you and miss you too'? Well, maybe that's too much for two guys," he thought.

He glanced up at the game and saw the score in the corner of the screen: 21-0. The Packers running back was fumbling, and the other team recovered. This was the kind of game they could blow. Developing a big lead early, easing off, thinking it's going to be easy. The other team demoralized. Then a momentum shift. This should have put him on the edge of his seat. Hank went over and shut it off.

It was one of those moments that put sports into perspective. Usually, Hank would live and die with the Packers. He would be in a good mood for the rest of the day if they won, and watch it over again with the highlights on TV that night. He would be depressed for three days if they lost, and there were some painful losses to Dallas in the playoffs years ago that he wasn't sure he was over yet. But today, he knew what really mattered to him. He didn't want a victory or a loss to get in the way of how he felt at this very moment. The only thing missing was his family to share it with him. He waited impatiently for them to arrive.

Chapter 13

Molly was the first to come home. The first thing she noticed as she entered the door was the silence. Then she noticed her husband greeting her at the door with a hug. He was hugging her at the door while the Packers were still playing and the TV was turned off. Fear gripped her, but only for a second, because he was smiling.

She said it anyway: "Who died?" But she smiled back at him.

"Scott called."

Molly tried to catch herself before becoming too excited.

"Did he talk, or was it one of those obligation calls?"

"He talked."

"Hank, don't do this to me. What did he say?"

"Well, in order of importance: he's having some problems with his supervisor; he's coming home next weekend to talk with us about it; he's been in recovery for about a month now and seems to be doing well."

Molly raised her eyes to heaven. "Thank God." She rushed over and hugged Hank again.

"Well, come in the living room and sit down. I want to hear all about it. Wait, maybe I should call him back first."

"I don't think you'll catch him. He was going to go out to a meeting."

"Damn, I wish I had been home." She pulled Hank to the living room and sat him on the couch. She sat next to him and turned toward him so she could drink in his words with her entire body. "Now talk to me. What did you two talk about?"

"Well, I pretty much told you the highlights."

"I don't want the highlights. I want the details."

Hank closed his eyes. Molly could see his pupils moving from side to side as he reconstructed the conversation. Little by little, with a few prompts from Molly, he filled her in on everything. A few times, they both had tears in their eyes.

When he finished, Molly looked at him with great admiration while at the same time shaking her head. "You are a great dad and a great man, and I'm lucky to have you in my life, but as an information gatherer, you suck."

Hank laughed. "That's something else I said to Scott. I said, 'I wish your mother were here, because she's going to have a million questions that I'm not going to be able to answer.'"

"That may be an underestimate. Let's just start to list some of them. What is this problem with his supervisor?"

"I did ask him that. He said he'd talk about that when he got home."

"Where is he going for counseling?" Hank shrugged.

"Have he and Kathy gotten back together?" Hank shrugged.

"You're useless!" Molly cried in mock disgust.

"Hey, what's happening?" Paul asked. He had entered the house and the room without either of them noticing. He sat down on the chair next to the couch.

"Well, Scott called with major news. He's in recovery, and he's coming home to see us next weekend."

"Major cool! Who'd he talk to?"

Molly sighed. "Unfortunately, he talked to your father in the middle of the Packers game."

"Packers game? Dad, are you sure it was Scott and not a wrong number?"

"Yes, he knew who I was, and we talked for quite a while in spite of what your mother says."

"It could have been a telemarketer," he teased his father.

"You know, sometimes I liked you better when you just faded into the woodwork around here."

"Oh, Dad, I know you don't mean that. I've gotta call Donna and let her know the good news." Paul rubbed his hand through his dad's thinning hair as he left the room.

"Who's Donna?" Molly called after him.

"Just one of my girlfriends."

"Girlfriends? How many do you suppose there are?" Hank asked with mock fear.

Molly and Hank continued to speculate about Scott, and all the questions Hank couldn't answer. After Paul got off the phone, Molly called Scott and left a message saying she had heard the good news and couldn't wait to see him. She told him that she had a million questions that (of course) his father couldn't answer.

Sally was dropped off by a friend's mom. She came into the living room and plopped right between Hank and Molly on the couch. "What's up, P's?"

"Is that expression coming back again? Isn't that what we used to call our folks behind their backs?" Hank asked with one eyebrow raised.

Molly ignored his question and told Sally about Scott. "Does this mean he and Kathy are back together?" she asked.

"We don't know. He talked to your father during the Packers game."

"Boy, we're lucky we know this much then."

"I'm tired of getting bashed by this family," said Hank. "I'll have you know we talked more about feelings. We're not all hung up on details like you women are."

"Yes, I feel the Packers are doing really well. What do you feel, Scott?" Sally said in a playful, mocking voice.

Hank laughed in spite of himself. "You know you got that foot speed of yours from your old man, and I bet I could still catch you and give you a good spanking," he said, pretending to take off his belt.

"In your dreams," she said, also rubbing his head as she got up. "I'm going to call Jodi."

"Isn't she the one you just left?" her mother asked.

"A lot's happened since then," she said, as she left the room.

"Is my brat brother Paul home?"

"Yes," her father loudly called after her.

Molly and Hank sat in silence for a while. This had been a long time coming. They held hands and let it all sink in.

Their son, Scott. They had their son back!

Chapter 14

The day after Scott's death, Lucy knew she needed a meeting. She had no urge to drink or use, but she could feel herself getting caught up in something that would not even be her case. Even so, she felt a strong connection to the dead stranger. She knew now Scott wasn't an Indian, so the case would go to the sheriff's office. The coroner might very well rule it an accident, based on the evidence. On the other hand, if it was ruled a murder, the FBI would be called in. Anyway, she was a patrolman and didn't do investigations.

She didn't know of any meeting in the area at the moment, so she went to see her sponsor, Sophie. Lucy was looking for answers.

Sophie was out on her front porch, soaking up the late fall sun on her face when she saw Lucy approaching. She was a woman in her early fifties, but with the energy of a twenty- year-old. She had a round face with an easy smile, and her feelings and opinions came just as quickly as her smile. It was great to be her friend, but you didn't want to be her enemy. Each thought and feeling registered on Sophie's face as she listened intently to Lucy recount the events of the last fourteen hours. She didn't interrupt until Lucy had finished.

"I want to congratulate you on coming here," she said. "You're beginning to know yourself. One of the reasons we all need each other is that addicts don't just lose control with drugs; many of our responses tend to be over the top. I know this is strange coming from me, but I don't know what to tell you. My first instinct is to tell you to let it go. This guy was white and not part of your community. But then, we believe even the animals are our brothers. I'm afraid that this is taking you spinning far away from your center and the things close to it, like your family and your sobriety. But then the vision tells me that perhaps for reasons only he understands, the Great Spirit is using this to teach you of Native ways."

"I know I'm going to the funeral at least," Lucy replied. "I don't know if my reason is to get evidence or to bring some closure to this, but I have to go." Lucy felt her conviction grow even stronger as she said it aloud.

Sophie smiled. "There was a time when I never thought I'd get you into your gut, but I think you're getting there. I imagine it's tough getting all addicts to recognize how they feel, but we Natives culturally are also taught to ignore our feelings—probably because of all the atrocities, prejudice, and hatred toward our ancestors. It was easier to learn to push aside our feelings." Sophie lit a cigarette. "Now if I could just get you back into bringing me tobacco when you come, I'd think you have arrived."

Lucy smiled. "I bring you enough for your morning offering, but I'm not helping you kill yourself. And what does your sponsor think of you still smoking?"

"You were more fun when you smoked too. The worst addict is a reformed addict."

"At least you're admitting that's another addiction, and I'm the only one in this relationship who's truly clean and sober," Lucy said with a playful air of superiority.

"I've noticed that you haven't stopped sucking down coffee by the gallon at meetings with the rest of us," Sophie shot back.

It occurred to Lucy that one of the reasons she had chosen Sophie as a sponsor in the first place was that, even though she could be brutally honest, even when it wasn't called for, she never seemed to say anything judgmental, and in all of her opinions about the faults of human beings, she never excluded herself.

"Coffee's going to be next, and then maybe I'll get some sleep," Lucy said with resolve. "You're hard enough to deal with; I don't need you with a headache too."

The two women rose together and hugged.

"You need some company at this funeral that you're bound and determined to go to?" Sophie asked.

"I'd like it, but if you were there it'd be easy to hang with you rather than talk to some people who might help me understand this thing."

"Fine, but don't be afraid to ask for help when you need it." Sophie's eyes flashed with the concern and compassion she didn't often speak in words.

Lucy walked from the porch. She passed the lawn mower that had been left where either man or machine got tired. The grass behind it was long. The grass in front was longer. She chuckled, shaking her head affectionately at the thought of Sophie.

She wondered why it was that even when, like today, there was no clear answer that emerged from her conversation with Sophie, she always felt better. Sometimes, ironically, recovery was hard to understand but easier to do.

Lucy stopped at the community store at the bottom of the hill where 55 and 47 split. This was the hub of Keshena and housed nearby the tribal police station, sheriff's station, tribal free clinic and the courthouse.

She ran into Ray Waupuse at the store. She filled him in on the fact that Scott had died. He didn't seem surprised. On the other hand, he appeared genuinely pleased to see her. His eyes seemed to light up every time she came into his vision.

Ray looked at her with his kind and gentle eyes. There was no malice in them, yet something about them that made her feel vulnerable. They could somehow see deeper than she wanted them to.

"Let it go," was all he said, but she knew what he meant.

"I know you're right, but I want to go to the funeral. Maybe then I can get this from under my skin."

Ray just smiled as if he somehow knew better, but again he kept his mouth shut. He had many thoughts and shared few.

Lucy finished her shopping and stopped at the station on her way back. There was a message from Kathy saying that the funeral would be on Monday at eleven in the morning, and she left her a number to call for directions.

Lucy was surprised Kathy had remembered to call. Lucy thought some more about Scott and his family. She wondered who they all were and how they got along. She wondered about the events that led to the accident. How many pieces of the puzzle could she put together? She thought of all the different tragedies she had read about in newspapers or seen on TV or heard on the radio, the tragedies of war, violence, and traffic accidents. So many faceless victims without a real story. Just a brief mention. She was determined not to let that happen here.

Lucy picked up the phone and dialed Kathy's number.

Chapter 15

Lucy took a personal day on Monday and drove an hour north. She took the same route Scott had the day he died even though staying on 47 would have been a more direct route. She hoped to get an inkling of why he might have gone that way, but she reached his hometown and the church with no more ideas than she had on starting out.

She took a seat near the back in a pew by herself. She recognized the family and Kathy sitting in the front. Others who appeared to be extended family were sitting behind them. A number of what appeared to be high school or college friends were also in attendance. The church was full.

Just before the service started, there was a little commotion in the back as a large group of junior high students walked into the church. There was some pushing and shoving, but mostly just an air of stifled emotion— perhaps excitement—that showed in their solemn faces as they entered.

At first, Lucy thought the boys at the head of the group had dirty shirts but then she noticed, as they got closer, that each had a handprint over his heart. The handprint seemed to be made from mud and looked as though it was still wet.

There were a number of eulogies that day. A former pastor had returned to the parish at Molly's request to do the funeral. Pastor Brooks assured the family that wherever Scott had been heading on that last evening, God's destination for him had been home. Brad spoke of how great it was to have Scott as a friend and a teammate. Kathy was reminded of his intervention letter when he spoke of how special he always felt being in Scott's company: "It wasn't just that I was friends with the best athlete in school, it's because that's how Scott would make you feel." Kathy was comforted by having Brad there with her. She was glad they had driven together.

Finally, one of the junior highschoolers stood up with the now-dry handprint on his chest.

He walked bravely to the pulpit. He said, "Hi! My name is Chris Fowley, and I have Down Syndrome. But I'm one of the luckier ones with this disorder. I can go to school and even take some regular classes. But for part of the day I was in the special needs class taught by Scott Brandt. He was the student teacher but every other teacher in the school should have been a student of Scott's.

"Our school is expanding, and there is construction going on every day, with a lot of heavy equipment and guys yelling and cussing right outside our building.

"Most of the other teachers just complain about it, but one day while the construction guys were taking a break, Scott took us out in the hole. He told us how the earth marks time and how each step down in the Grand Canyon is walking down a thousand years. He taught us about the different layers and different rocks. We used that day to study different cultures and spiritual beliefs. Some of us are Menominee Indians, and he brought us books that taught us of the great copper bear that entered the world from under the earth and decided to become a man.

"After practice one day, he took us to the College of Menominee Nation to see a large statue of the bear carved from one tree. The Navajos believe that the first man and woman came up through a reed from the earth. The Christians and Jews believe that God made Adam and Eve from the earth and that when we die, we return to the earth.

"After our lesson in the hole, a man in a tractor yelled at Scott to get us retards out of his hole fast. Scott went up to him, grabbed the keys to his tractor and said if he was so smart, he should know just how to find the keys in that hole. Then he threw them in there. The man cursed at him, called him a name, and started running at Scott, but when he saw the look on Scott's face, he changed his mind and went to look for the keys.

"Scott was our hero, and we decided that if Scott was from the earth, and that's where he was going now that he's dead, then we wanted to be a part of the earth too. So we took some of the earth from that hole Scott brought us to and mixed it with water and put it by our hearts. That's all."

As they exited the church with the casket in front of them, Kathy found the bucket the children had used and put her hand to the earth. It was cool, and the mud stuck quickly to her hand as she stuck it to her chest. The mud mixed with the tears that fell from her face.

Brad was next in line, then Hank and Molly. By the time they had reached the gravesite, everyone in the circle around the grave had a handprint on his or her chest. Lucy thought of the medicine wheel that had become so important to her in her recovery. Scott had friends from every race: black, yellow, red, and white. For a brief moment, they were one. They were all together as they were on her wheel.

At the grave site, Pastor Brooks spoke again. "It is at this point in the service that I'm reminded of the choice each of us will make about Scott's role in our lives. He affected each of us, and that's why we are here. But how will he continue to affect us? Will we allow a part of ourselves to die with him? Will a part of each of us be buried in that hole today?

"Perhaps it's appropriate that we return Scott to the earth, and now each of us has a chance to determine how the seeds Scott planted during his life will turn out. Molly and Hank, ninety percent of the marriages that lose a child end in divorce. Is that what you want the seeds that Scott planted to grow into? It is your choice what to make of Scott's life. We can a blessing." There was not a single dry eye.

At the end of the graveside service, Scott's brother, Ryan, stood and thanked everyone for coming and invited them back to the church for refreshments. Everyone accepted the invitation, perhaps feeling that when this group broke up, they would lose Scott a little more.

Lucy in particular knew this was an opportunity to learn about all those people, and all of the different pieces of Scott; yet she also knew this was not the time nor was it her place to interrogate them. Still, she mingled among them and, as unobtrusively as she could, tried to learn what she could. She learned from the students that Scott and his supervisor didn't get along well, but that wasn't unusual.

She learned that Scott didn't get along well with any adults. She learned from Kathy that though Scott had done a lot of experimenting, he never took coke intravenously. And that he had been straight since he promised her that he'd get help several weeks ago. Since then, he had spoken to her nearly every day, and she was confident she would have known if he'd relapsed. Scott was clean and sober; she knew it.

It was with Hank that she felt the strongest connection.

She sensed that he was recovering, and somehow she knew he sensed it in her as well.

"Do you want a drink as bad as I do?" she asked him.

"Worse," he answered.

"Don't drink, and go to a meeting," they both said with pointed fingers and smiles.

"How did you know my son?" Hank asked her.

"I guess I didn't know him, but now that seems hard to believe."

Hank looked at her quizzically.

"I was the officer that found him. I'm sorry I couldn't do more to save him."

She saw the mixed feelings on Hank's face. She read them as relief in finding the last person to see him alive, disappointment and, perhaps, resentment that she couldn't save him. His response was genuine and soothing.

"I wish that you could have too," he said. "I wish that for me as well."

Now it was Lucy's turn for a quizzical look.

"If I had been a better model of recovery instead of addiction, maybe my son wouldn't have been in that situation,"

Hank said. "But as much as I'd like to numb the feelings that I have right now, one promise I made to Scott as I put him in the ground today is that none of my children will ever see me drunk again."

"Promises are dangerous for us, you know," Lucy warned.

"Right now that promise is all I have," Hank said quietly.

"I'd like to tell you one thing, not as a police officer who has evidence but as a spiritual person with kids of her own. I know that God may have wanted Scott home in heaven, but Scott's goal that night was to come home to you. I also know—

not because I have any proof as a police officer but because I believe it in my heart—Scott may have had drugs in his body, but he didn't put them there. My supervisors would fire me for saying this, but I'm not saying it as a cop."

This time, Hank's smile came from deep within. "I know that too," he said. "Will we ever find out how they got there?" "I don't know," Lucy said. "I do know I will not have any official role in the investigation, and I suspect that Scott's death will be ruled an accident."

"So you're here on your own, then?" Hank asked.

"Yes," Lucy said, nodding.

"I appreciate your caring so much about my son. I know this is something I'll never get over," Hank stated with certainty.

"But you, along with everyone I've talked to today, have brought me some peace. I'll be sure to share what I can with my wife.

I know she grieves even more deeply than I do. Did you know what a great athlete he was?"

"I gathered that from the pictures I saw by the casket,"

Lucy answered.

"I wish now I wouldn't have focused so much on that. He always showed great potential. When he was little he used to wait for the kickoff and often I'd watch his eyes. There were times he seemed not even to watch or listen. Instead, he would focus on those stupid yellow butterflies that are so prevalent around here in late summer and early fall. After the game, I'd get on him to pay attention. I wish now I had asked him what he found so interesting about yellow butterflies. There are so many things I want to ask my son."

Hank's eyes filled with tears and Lucy patted him on the shoulder. Then Molly called Hank to speak with some people who were leaving and Lucy moved on to speak with others.

Lucy had two strong feelings as she drove back to the reservation—one positive and the other negative. She felt good about the people she met. She felt good about Scott and the way he was sent to the Creator. As a Menominee, her life was about dying. Her journey was toward dying and being able to say her life was worthwhile because of what she gave to her community. Scott had been through some hard times but those kids and their appreciation of him had made it evident that his life had been a contribution. He had lived a worthwhile life.

On the negative side, she did not feel she was ready to let go. She knew she wouldn't rest—literally or figuratively—until she found out what had happened on the road that night. Was her vision accurate, or was her mind simply trying to make sense of what she had been through?

Chapter 16

The next time Lucy had a day off, she visited the coroner. Marcy was a pleasant- looking woman with a round face and red-framed glasses that matched the many red suits she wore. She was a nurse by training and had won two elections now as coroner. Lucy thought she might have designs on a higher office but wasn't sure which one. Lucy didn't always agree with Marcy's official decisions but at least she did things by the book.

"I was wondering if there had been a cause of death determined in the Scott Brandt case?" she asked.

"The board ruled it an accident."

Lucy looked surprised. "Even with the footprints leading to and from the vehicle?"

"It could have been a Good Samaritan just trying to help who decided to take off when they heard your siren or when they saw the flames."

"What about the intravenous cocaine? Scott had never done that before."

"Addicts are always experimenting with new ways to get high."

"Why were there so many flames when the gas tank hadn't ruptured?"

"We found an open gas can in his back seat."

"Wouldn't it be worth having the FBI at least investigate?"

"I called them. They weren't interested. Terrorism is the name of the game these days."

Lucy left the coroner's office with her problems unsolved but clearer. She knew she owed it to Scott and her own perceptions to continue to investigate. Where would she start?

Her training at the police academy had been as a patrolman, not as an investigator. Even if she was successful in finding Scott's killer and proving the coroner wrong, the case could be dismissed because of improper procedures. But if she didn't investigate, no one else would. Then a murderer would get off

"Scott free." She grimaced at her own bad pun.

She decided to start at the school and hoped that the same construction worker was still there. She waited for school to let out and hoped she'd see one of the students who had come to the funeral.

She was lucky; Chris was one of the last students to leave the building and no one was waiting to pick him up. Lucy took advantage of the opportunity.

A group of boys was gathered around him. Lucy waited until they said their goodbyes and then approached Chris and extended her hand. "Hi, Chris. Lucy Teller. I met you at Scott Brandt's funeral. Do you remember?"

Chris looked irritated at the question, but he responded politely: "Yes, I do."

"I wanted to tell you again that the idea you and your friends came up with was so moving. And the way you presented yourself really impressed me. Have you considered using that gift in some way?"

"I've sent some e-mails to the Down Syndrome organization asking to be a spokesperson, but I haven't heard much back yet—other than form letters saying, 'Thank you for your interest in our organization.'"

"Well, you have a gift, and I hope you are given a chance to make use of it. Remember the guy you mentioned in your speech? The one who had the confrontation with Scott? Is he still working here?"

"Yes, that's him right over there."

Chris pointed toward the construction project. The building was pretty well enclosed and it looked like they'd be able to finish the inside over the winter. A man stood by a still-doorless doorway—a large man with skin browned by a summer out in the sun. His well-toned muscles were rippling in the light a bit self-consciously. He was the sort of guy, Lucy decided, who would spend hours after work defining muscles in his stomach.

Cliff watched Lucy approach up the board that took the place of steps to the doorway. "That board bends a lot more when I walk up it," he commented. "Why do you suppose that is?"

"Muscles weigh more than fat," Lucy said, with a good- natured smile.

"Fat jiggles, and there was nothing jiggling on you when you walked up here. I know; I was watching carefully."

"Aren't you supposed to be working?" Lucy stayed cool and suppressed feelings of disgust.

"I'm on break, but since this is a school, we call it recess. You want to play with me during recess?"

"Do you notice I have a uniform on? Or did you fail to notice that when you undressed me as I walked up the ramp?" "I noticed that you're a tribal cop who has no jurisdiction here, and besides, uniforms turn me on."

"Much as I'd love to continue with recess, I have some questions I'd like to ask you. Did you know Scott Brandt was killed the other night?"

Cliff stood still suddenly and looked more serious. "Two questions, one—who's Scott Brandt; and two—since when do they have patrolmen investigating murders?"

Lucy groaned inside. This guy was obviously more aware of police procedures than she had hoped. "We're short-handed.

He's the guy you had an argument with when this was still a hole in the ground. And I didn't say it was murder. I just said he was killed."

Cliff's face lost some color. "That student teacher? The one who threw my keys in the hole?"

"One and the same," Lucy answered. She was glad to find that Cliff was losing some of his cockiness. Still she didn't expect his answer.

"I've been looking for him. I wondered why I haven't seen him around. How was he killed?"

Lucy was disappointed to realize that she believed his surprise. "His car burst into flame after hitting a tree during a snowstorm on the rez a week or so ago. Why were you looking for him? Did you hope to continue your disagreement?"

Cliff looked embarrassed and was slow to answer. "You know I've got a big mouth, and I'm obnoxious."

Lucy couldn't help herself. "I hadn't noticed." "I deserved that, didn't I?"

Lucy shrugged.

"I was out of line calling those kids retards. I knew it as soon as I said it, and he was right to confront me and defend them. I couldn't admit it at the time, but I was looking for him so I could apologize and buy him a beer. Those kids need people like him. I heard about that crash on the news in my car but never got any details. I'm sorry. Do you suspect it may have been murder?"

"Yes, I do," Lucy answered, wondering why she was beginning to like this guy. Still, she wasn't ready to let him totally off the hook. "Besides you, is there anyone else who might have wanted him dead?"

His calmness surprised Lucy. "I didn't want him dead and I don't know that anyone else did either. One day, though, during recess, I was standing looking toward the building, and I saw Scott talking to his supervisor. I couldn't hear anything they were saying, and I can't say I saw either of them shaking their fists at one another or grabbing each other by the throat, but I just had the feeling it was an intense discussion. Very intense."

"So is his supervisor still here?" Lucy asked.

"You're kidding. He's a teacher; they don't work as hard as us construction types. I saw him leave in his car just before you got here. So, my shift's over. You want to go for a beer?"

Lucy laughed. "Sounds like you construction types go right from recess to quitting time. I must admit, Cliff, you make a better second impression than you do a first, but not that much better, and besides I don't drink."

"Just one beer. Maybe I'll think of something else while we're talking that might help your investigation."

"There is probably a Native American somewhere who can sit down and have one beer. I just never met one. I know I can't. That concept is totally foreign to me. When I used to drink, I drank to get drunk."

"Better yet, let's get drunk together."

Lucy smiled, partly remembering old times, but also noting with pride how easy it was to say no. She handed him her card. "I spent enough time in that state for a number of lifetimes. You go have a beer. If it triggers anything, call me."

She turned and walked down the plank as Cliff stared after her.

"See anything jiggle?"

"No, everything stays right where it's supposed to." Lucy waved but didn't turn around.

Chapter 17

For a week or two after Scott's death, Kathy stayed with Bobbie. They both wanted the companionship in grief. But as the days passed things became increasingly difficult. They didn't argue or even talk about things, but it seemed as if being together made the loss of Scott harder to bear. The sun was low on the morning when Kathy thanked Bobbie and left. Driving back to her own apartment, Kathy watched in her rearview mirror as the setting sun vacated the horizon and passed down over a group of poplars now bare and silhouetted against the red sky. It was a beautiful sunset; she was filled with awe and the raw ache of Scott's death seemed somehow soothed.

Kathy was almost reluctant to go into the house. Walking in the front door, she recalled Kane's face close to hers, and her mood changed. When she remembered the feel of his breath on her face, her spine tingled. Suddenly she could not bear the place. She had nowhere to go, but she could not stand to stay there by herself.

Without hesitating, she picked up the phone and called Brad. She heard the wind whistle from her lips in relief when he answered. She asked him if he could come right over. She didn't want to be alone.

He was there in fifteen minutes.

At first they didn't even talk about Scott—not directly. For the first time, she told him the whole story about the attempted rape, and she told him what had happened with Scott afterward.

As she went on with the story, the impact of how close she had come to being violated, and maybe even dying, began to register, and tears filled her eyes. They had been sitting close to one another on the couch, and

Brad put his arms around her. For the first time since Scott's death, she sobbed openly.

She had put the whole rape thing in a black box inside herself somewhere. The excitement she felt about Scott agreeing to treatment had momentarily overshadowed the reality of the earlier incident. Then the horror of Scott's death had set in.

Grief, fear, and nerves all rushed together.

Brad simply held her for a long time, rocking her gently.

When she finally stopped crying, she looked up at Brad. He had tears in his eyes. Kathy was moved by his compassion but never expected what happened next. Brad moved one of his hands along the side of her face and he kissed her. It was a sweet and gentle kiss, but it was clear that there was much more than friendship behind it. Kathy felt a stirring inside that surprised her. She wanted more. She was all set to kiss him back when Brad stood up and moved from the couch to the chair nearby.

"I'm sorry," he said. "With all that has happened to you, that's the last thing you need to deal with."

"With Kane trying to rape me at knifepoint, a sweet gentle kiss somehow doesn't seem so bad."

Brad smiled. "I'm glad you feel that way."

"Now, why don't you come back over here? Having your arms around me feels comforting and safe."

Brad smiled and closed his eyes and sat back in the chair with a sigh. "Trust me. You're safer with me over here right now."

Kathy felt frustrated and angry, and her response showed it. "What are you talking about? Speaking of the last thing I need, is it for my best friend suddenly to start playing cat and mouse with me?"

Now the fire was in Brad's eyes. "Cat and mouse? Why, because I'm trying to avoid getting into something that's more than you need to deal with after almost being raped and Scott... returning into your life?"

"Scott's dead!" Kathy almost shouted it. "He's dead and I..." The tears threatened to flow again, hot and angry and hurt.

"And you haven't dealt with it yet. Look, I'll come over there and hold you, if you promise to go to sleep. I'll stay with you all night, but just let this go."

"No, no, Brad. I'm calm. I'm all right. After what I've been through, don't you think I can handle whatever it is you are going to throw at me?"

"Of course you can, but do you need to handle it?"

"I don't know what it is you're trying so hard not to tell me, but if it's related to that kiss and my reaction to it, I think this is something I'd like to know. I don't want to waste a moment wondering or worrying. Please tell me, Brad. I want to know your heart."

Brad closed his eyes, as if to pretend that he was just telling this to the back of his dark eyelids. "I've been in love with you since the eighth grade. In high school, I was just too shy and afraid to ask you out. I never even told Scott how I felt about you, and he was my best friend. When you two started to date and became serious, I was sure I had missed my chance forever. Then Scott refused help, and I felt guilty anytime I even thought of any kind of advance or telling you how I felt.

My guilt and shame would hold my feelings in check. You didn't seem interested in anyone else, and I've so enjoyed our friendship, I thought I could give you time. And with Scott dead, the whole thing became more awful. What sort of friend would I be to take advantage of your grief? Forget Scott and move in? I'd sooner forget myself.

"Then today, compassion added to love and for a brief moment they won over the guilt and shame. Maybe if you knew how much you were loved, it could undo all the terrible things you'd been through. But as soon as I kissed you, a voice inside me said, 'Remember what she's already been through. How can you take advantage of the situation? How can you do this to your best friend? How can you think of making a move?'"

Kathy smiled with weary irony. "You know, Brad, I had a crush on you for a long time in high school and there were times I just wanted to shake you because you were so shy. There were times when I thought the feelings were mutual but you were such a good actor I thought I was kidding myself. Then Scott came along. I loved him. But even when I had him I felt so fortunate to have you as part of the package.

"You're right. A lot has happened and I am shocked by what you've told me. I don't know how to respond. I do know that I'm glad you told me. I've got a lot of sorting out to do. I think I'll go back and see May, but I'm glad to know how you feel. I think it's just what I needed to make some of the dark go away. I can honestly say I love you too, I just don't know how yet.

With all that has happened, I'm raw. I need to know if Scott meant what he said about recovery. I need to know if he was going to follow through on what he said. I do know I want and need you in my life, and I don't want anything to screw that up. Brad, I really mean it."

Brad finally opened his eyes. "All along there, I was bracing for something bad. What you said is more than I could have hoped for, and I feel the same way. You know how I feel, and that isn't going to change. I waited eight years to tell you how I feel. I loved Scott too. If you two could have made it together, I would have been happy for you both. I really would have."

"I know that, Brad."

For the first time since the kiss, they made eye contact and both smiled. All the events of the last weeks caught up to Kathy. She began to feel very tired. "I need to go to sleep.

Will you sleep on the couch tonight? I don't think I can stay with Bobbie anymore. Not until things settle, somehow. But if you're here for tonight, I think I will be able to settle back in."

"Sure I will," Brad answered in a way that touched Kathy deeply. There was a sincerity and genuineness about him. He stood slowly as Kathy rose to go to bed. He held her, and they gazed at each other. He did not attempt to kiss her again.

She admired his resolve and discipline, yet with a touch of disappointment. This sweet, gentle giant loved her, and in a moment, an uncomplicated and serene life with him flashed before her. She went off to bed, wishing she could ask him to sleep next to her and just hold her all night. Then she realized even his discipline had its limits. She slept sweetly and soundly until the violent nightmares started again. When she awoke the next morning, she had come to a decision. She called the police station first thing and left a message.

Chapter 18

Lucy fasted and prayed all the day before the sweat lodge. She felt she needed the cleansing healing of the lodge. The stress of past weeks and the increasing tensions of the investigation were beginning to muddle her brain. Depriving the body of food and water—not really depriving, but purifying. She was restraining the physical side of life in the hope that the spiritual side would come into control.

She was there early to help in the preparations. The sweat lodge—round and domelike, made of saplings from the willow tree—was being built by the men. Some of them glanced over and nodded, acknowledging her arrival. The fire keeper was standing by the fire, tending the rocks. Lucy knew they had been heating there for at least four hours. Tobacco had been put down as an offering when the rocks were chosen.

Women were gathered to pound and shape the altar with their hands. Lucy joined them. When they finished, she helped collect and lay the cedar on the altar and in a line leading from the altar to the entrance of the lodge—a line not to be crossed before the sweat began, separating the old life from the new.

As Lucy stepped over the threshold, the voice of an old Menominee echoed soberly, soothingly in her ear: "Going into the sweat lodge, you might have pain, fear, anger, or sadness. Most people feel all the emotions at one time or another. We all have some emotional, physical, or spiritual healing that can take place in a sweat lodge." Lucy hoped the healing would work.

She took her seat with the others in a circle around the shallow pit that represented the womb of Mother Earth.

The first round began. The men brought in seven hot rocks (called Grandfathers) for the seven directions: south, west, north, east, up for the sky, down for the earth, and one for within. Lucy watched them lay down the rocks and considered the significance of each rock.

"North, the direction of wisdom, the inner world of self and soul."

"South, the direction of summer, passion, and creativity." "East, the direction of spirituality and new beginnings." "West, the direction of truth and integrity."

The men poured water on the hot rocks and a thick, hot steam emerged, growing and filling the lodge.

"The four races of man the Creator placed on earth all symbolized by color—red for the South, black for the West, white for the North, and yellow for the East."

"The direction of Father Sky represents the expansive nature of the universe and our past relations."

"The earth direction honors Mother Nature, who gives life and heals the body, soul, and others."

The rocks were in their places.

"Let the door be closed," said the doorman.

The water drum sounded four times and the ceremony began. Each of the rounds passed, and water was poured upon the rocks repeatedly, renewing the steam. The heat became more and more intense, and the steam swirled in the darkness. They invited the spirits to join them in their prayers. They prayed for their intentions, for relatives experiencing difficulty in one way or another. Prayers for addicts abounded.

After the third round, the healing round, and the fourth, devoted to cleansing all negativity away, Lucy began to feel drowsy. The steam wandered, swirled, clouded, and finally cleared. But the scene before her was not the sweat lodge; she was in another vision, but this was of a place she had never seen and a time she couldn't remember. She was in the woods in the night floating in the darkness over a carpet of autumn leaves. She wandered down from the trees and plunged through the leaves.

Suddenly she began to run, and dodging trees, she jumped over a large boulder. She jumped so easily—like an athlete—and, landing, hurried to bury herself under the leaves.

How did I get here? Lucy wondered. Why would she be covered by a pile of leaves under a fallen tree on a clear, late October night? She couldn't see much because only a sliver of moon pierced one small tear in the blackness and dimly lit the woods with a pale silver glow. Here, away from the city lights, the black sky seemed poked with millions of tiny holes where the stars shone through.

Suddenly she wished she could spit and douse the silver light. Maybe a cloud, friendly to his fate, could come and cover the moon. His fate? Who was he?

With a quiet certainty, she knew she was seeing what Scott had seen. She could never have leaped over the boulder like that, but he could. A long time ago—a long time before the accident. Flashlight beams swept over the top of the leaf pile. She was worried; did the leaves look natural enough? Were there any tracks leading to the spot?

The men were persistent. The lights were getting closer and she could hear muffled voices. More frequently now, she saw the flashlight beams sweep directly over and beyond the pile. There were at least four men and they seemed to be walking in a line about fifty feet apart. They kept in voice contact mostly by asking one another if they'd seen anything. Lucy breathed a sigh of relief each time one said no. She felt sure that Scott had left footprints, but as she listened to the men curse as they tripped on rocks or got tangled in vines, she began to hope that these guys were getting discouraged and wanting another drink or hit of cocaine. They were more skilled in street fighting than tracking someone through the woods—she knew that somehow.

"Come on, Scott," she thought. "You just have to survive the night. Just this night."

A shiver ran through her, then suddenly the scene disappeared. Lucy woke up in the sweat lodge as the ceremony came to its close. She woke up hungry and full of questions. Why was Scott hiding in the woods? Who were the people who chased him down? She knew the lengths to which the sort of people who provide drugs to addicts would be willing to go. Were those the people who killed Scott? Yes, she was sure, someone had killed Scott.

Still, most importantly, she was certain that the investigation would have to continue.

That night, which happened to be a Saturday and Halloween, Lucy attended the "ghost Mass" at St. Michael's. It was specifically for families who had lost someone in the past year. Lucy's husband had been dead longer than that, but she went to support Ray Waupuse, who had lost his mother earlier that year. He did not talk much about it, but she knew that he silently grieved.

After the Mass, the families gathered in the hall next door for a meal. Ray was designated by his family to go up and prepare a meal for his mother, consisting of all her favorite foods. He looked pleasantly surprised when Lucy walked up next to him.

"Who are you preparing a meal for?" Ray asked.

"You know!" Lucy said. "Scott, that guy who just died in that car crash. He was white, and they don't believe in feeding their dead. I bet he's hungry." She filled his plate just with fry bread, and set it at the table with the plates of the other deceased.

She returned to the table with Ray. "Don't you think this white guy would like some variety?" Ray asked.

"You know, I was at some sweat lodges with a white guy who filled his plate with nothing but fry bread. Besides, he's not in a place where he has to worry about his diet."

At the table with the others, they ate their fill of their own meals. After everyone was finished, they went out behind the church where a bonfire had been prepared. The meals of the deceased were thrown into the fire. It was cold and rainy, so no one lingered long after both they and the fire had consumed their meals.

Chapter 19

On Monday morning, when Lucy checked in with the station there was a message from Kathy. She didn't bother to call back. Kathy had asked after the accident report, so Lucy knew just where to go. She simply headed up the highway toward the spot where the accident had occurred.

It was a cloudy, gray day, much like when Scott had died. It was near dusk when Kathy knelt to place her wreath by the tree. She knew she was in the right spot because the grass and tree were still charred from the fire.

She was surprised to see that she was not the first to leave flowers. Snow was falling as darkness fell and Kathy finally got up to leave. Tears streamed down her face as she wondered how long it would take truly to bury Scott. That's when she saw the flashing lights approaching.

Lucy pulled up behind Kathy's car. She turned on her dome lights so cars could see them as they rounded the curve. Lucy got out and approached Kathy. Hugging came a lot easier to her since joining AA and it seemed especially natural to give Kathy a hug. Kathy responded as though they'd been friends forever. She leaned into Lucy and held her tightly.

They agreed to go for coffee at the Wild Wolf Inn. It was about a half hour up the road and it was on the way home for Kathy. Lucy called her mother, asked her to get dinner for the kids, and said she'd grab a sandwich at the Wild Wolf.

Darkness had fallen completely by the time they arrived, but occasional glimpses of white water were visible as the rapids twisted their way through the stretch of the Wolf River called Gilmore's Mistake. It had been given the name when a man named Gilmore was offered a logging contract up river, but refused it because he didn't believe the stretch was passable. Another man took the contract, used dynamite, and got the logs through. He became a very rich man.

Both the restaurant and the large bar upstairs were empty when Kathy and Lucy arrived. Rafting season was over and snowmobile and cross-country skiing season had not yet started, so it was a slow time for the Wild Wolf. They were happy to see two customers.

The women sat by one of the larger windows. There was a large bird feeder outside it. In the daytime, the feeders were visited by kingfishers and a number of other colorful birds that remained throughout the entire long, cold winter.

Lucy rubbed the back of Kathy's hand. "How are you holding up?"

Kathy's eyes filled with tears once again. She was surprised at herself. After last night's emotional scene with Brad, she would have thought that all of her tears had been used up. She had endured the death of her mother, and now the loss of Scott. Usually she'd just shrug and change the subject, but there was something about Lucy that left her defenseless and wanting to be open. Still, that wasn't why she had contacted Officer Teller.

"I'm struggling," she said, "but that's not why I called you. Have they decided whether Scott's death was an accident or not?"

"They've decided it was an accident," Lucy said, trying to keep the disappointment from her voice.

"You don't believe that, do you?" "No, I don't."

"I know someone who might want to kill Scott, and the fact that he was injected with a lethal dose of cocaine makes me think it's worth checking into."

Kathy told Lucy of Kane's attack and how Scott interrupted it and beat him severely enough to require a trip to the hospital. She told Lucy that Kane didn't seem like the type of man to let that pass. She was certain he would crave revenge.

"Wait," said Lucy. "You said that when you opened the door, you had trouble seeing?"

"Yes."

"Do you wear glasses or contacts?"

"Neither." Then it hit her. "That jerk took my picture when I opened the door. The flash is what affected my eyes."

"Did he continue to take pictures during the attack?" Lucy asked.

"Not that I remember," said Kathy. "He may have been planning more after he was done having his fun."

Lucy asked more questions about what had happened before and after Scott arrived. When Lucy was confident that she had found out all that she could from Kathy about the incident, she asked how she could locate Kane. She got a description of him and his bodyguards.

She wondered at first what it was about Kathy that made it feel so good to talk with her. Their backgrounds had little in common, yet in this brief meeting, she felt a bond between them—an unusually strong bond forged in a short time.

Perhaps it was the excitement of investigating a crime. She knew instinctively that Kathy felt it too. It wasn't excitement, actually. There was nothing exciting about it for Kathy. She wondered whether it was the fact that she had found someone else who thought Scott's death was murder.

Kathy had a glass of wine with dinner. She sipped it as they talked and ate and left a quarter of the wine in the bottom of the glass. Lucy tried to weigh her feelings about it and found that she didn't really care. And she didn't tackle the waitress when she took it away unfinished. In past years, Lucy would have finished a full bottle by then, and if a waitress had dared to remove her glass before it was empty, she would have been in a sling the next day.

Kathy, too, was surprised at herself. She grew up in an area where prejudice toward Native Americans was rampant. Her family was not biased, but she had gotten plenty of exposure from friends and their families. She had never had much contact with Menominees, and now she felt strangely comfortable with a woman who was older and so different from herself.

They talked a while longer about their lives and their families. Lucy was glad not to be on the clock. If the visit were official, she would have been forced to keep more distance and to stay impersonal.

"I understand you did an intervention on Scott that involved reading him letters you wrote. Do you still have the letters?"

"Yes," Kathy answered. "I wanted to give them to Scott. I thought one day when he had an urge to use, they might help him."

"I'd like to borrow them if I could," Lucy said. "They may help me learn something. Also, I must admit, I'm curious about how that sort of thing goes. Mine was a lot simpler—'If you ever want to see your kids again, get help.'"

Kathy smiled sheepishly. "You'll think this is silly, but I have them in my purse. I'm still waiting to give them to him. In some ways, I don't believe he's dead. I'll be glad to lend them to you." She reached in her purse and handed them over.

"Loss is painful anytime, but what's so sad about Scott is that he seems to have been putting his life back together when it ended. I couldn't judge anything you do to help you heal—as long as it isn't immoral or illegal, of course! You were just beginning to believe in him again."

They sat in silence for a moment. Then Lucy had a thought. "You know, I don't want to make the mistake of focusing just on Kane just because all fingers seem to point to him at the moment. Is there anyone else who might have had a motive to kill Scott?"

"I can't think of anyone offhand," Kathy said, looking puzzled.

"Perhaps someone Scott may have used with or sold to that had problems as a result?"

Kathy considered. "During my second year in college, there was a guy in Scott's fraternity who died of a heart attack unexpectedly. The college and the fraternity kept it quiet. Scott never wanted to talk about it, but I know the guy's parents were pretty bitter."

"Do you know whatever happened to them?"

"No, that didn't affect my world much so I didn't pay that much attention. I guess I understand their pain better now. I understand a lot of things better now." Kathy smiled again, remembering the deep sadness she carried within her. This time it was a sad smile. But she shook her head, raised her shoulders and changed the smile. "I'm going to do my student teaching in the same place as Scott. I was so moved by what he was doing with those kids, I want to continue it if I can. Besides, I want to taste fry bread. Scott said that after sweats, he would fill up just on fry bread."

Lucy's blood ran cold. "Fry bread?" "Yes, why?"

Lucy didn't answer. She knew for certain that she had been with Scott at sweat lodges before he died. But she didn't feel she could talk to Kathy about it. Not yet.

"I'm so glad you'll be close. That's great. It'll mean we'll have more opportunity to talk. I can get the address of those parents from the school."

They said their goodbyes, paid the bill, and left.

On her way home, Lucy thought about how she could pursue these new leads. She questioned the effectiveness of going up to some guy called Kane and asking him if he had killed anybody. She smiled wryly.

Chapter 20

On her next day off, Lucy went back to Shawano to talk with Scott's supervisor.

Mr. Reilly was a smallish man, thin and soft-spoken. He was in his mid-fifties with graying hair and a thin mustache. Lucy watched as he interacted with one of the girls in his class. She wondered why someone who had been in education for thirty years (as it seems he was) had never learned to speak to kids in a way that wasn't patronizing.

When he finished speaking to the young student, Lucy went up to him and introduced herself. "I'd like to talk with you about Scott Brandt," she said.

"Yes, such a tragedy. Why is it a young man with such potential and his whole life in front of him would get mixed up with drugs?" he asked with emotion.

"So you think Scott had a future in education then?" Lucy asked, hoping to warm him up for more direct questions later. "No, actually not. Not only did I learn he had a drug problem, but he seemed incapable of establishing appropriate boundaries with the children. But he was obviously very bright and could have ended up in business somewhere and would have been able to buy and sell teachers or police officers." The final comment was delivered with a self-satisfied smirk.

Lucy smiled back and hoped he couldn't recognize its insincerity. "Neither of us will likely get rich, will we? Did you learn Scott had a problem with intravenous coke even before his accident?"

Another smile crept over Mr. Reilly's face. Lucy could almost hear his thoughts: "Come on, lady, I've been in education too long not to recognize a trick question when I hear one." But he just said, "I knew he used cocaine, but I understand it's one of the confusing things about his accident—most of his friends say he didn't use coke intravenously."

This time Lucy didn't smile back. "How did you learn that Scott used drugs?"

"His college supervisor told me he suspected it from rumors around campus and warned me to keep an eye out.

Then the secretary told me that Scott would get calls while he was in class, and when she asked the caller to identify himself, he would hang up. I thought there were a few times when Scott acted peculiar around the children. I couldn't take a chance with their safety, so I contacted the campus police where Scott went to school and asked if they knew of any students or former students they suspected of selling drugs. They gave me just one name and said they were convinced that he did, but he hadn't been caught. They also gave me an address and phone number so I called the guy. I told him I wasn't interested in getting him arrested, but I needed to protect my students. He, of course, denied any involvement, but he said he was quite sure that Scott used drugs and should be kept away from children."

He smiled and Lucy was sure that he was adding in his head: "You're not the only one who can do police work."

Lucy pretended not to notice the smile. "That's some good police work, Mr. Reilly. Maybe you could moonlight somewhere on weekends so those business people couldn't buy and sell you. Did you think it a bit odd that Scott's pusher would be so willing to turn him in?"

"Even scum have a soft spot where children are concerned. Did you know pedophiles are the most abused group of inmates in prisons?"

"So clearly you thought that Scott was a danger. What was your concern?"

Mr. Reilly gave her a look that demanded: "How stupid are you, lady?"

"We're dealing here with high-risk children who are the most likely to abuse drugs. They don't need their teacher modeling drug use for them. Could we step outside? I need a cigarette."

"Sure," said Lucy. She was pleased to see him ruffled.

They walked down the corridor toward the front of the building. When they reached the front door, Lucy noticed a group of kids waiting outside—the same ones who had attended Scott's funeral. When they saw

Mr. Reilly follow her out the door, they quickly said their goodbyes and dispersed. She also thought she noticed Cliff looking out of a window of the now completely enclosed building.

When Mr. Reilly had lit up and taken a deep drag, she asked, "Had you confronted Scott about his problem?"

"Yes, I had. He admitted he had used, but said he had quit and was getting help."

This might explain the intense conversation that Cliff thought he had seen. Still, Lucy felt like she was reading something that had all of the i's dotted and t's crossed, but with several paragraphs missing.

"Did you believe that?" Lucy asked.

"I believe he was trying to quit, but I don't think he was successful. The statistics on recovery from coke are not very good, and I think Scott was a living and eventually a dead example of that. Now can I ask you a question, officer?"

Lucy nodded.

"If Scott's death was ruled an accident, why are you investigating it?"

Lucy looked Mr. Reilly in the eyes. "I don't believe it was."

Mr. Reilly looked away. "I wish you luck," he said, "but I think you're wasting your time." With that, Mr. Reilly crushed out his cigarette on the sidewalk. "Any more questions?"

"No, not right now," Lucy answered. She was angry and frustrated, but she wasn't quite sure why. She knew two things: that Scott had been killed and that she did not like Mr. Reilly.

"Good. I've got papers to grade." He turned hurriedly and walked back into the building.

If Lucy had not felt discouraged after talking to him, she might not have noticed the message scribbled in chalk on the sidewalk. As it was, she tsked her tongue with annoyance and looked down toward the teacher's crushed cigarette. "DON'T BELIEVE HIM" was written clearly in block letters. Lucy smiled to herself and scraped her foot across the letters in case Mr. Reilly took the same way out of the building.

On the way home, she stopped to pick up her own children before they got on the bus. They were at an age when being picked up by your parents was getting embarrassing, but when they saw her car, they ran to her. As they talked excitedly about their day and fought with each other for her attention, she thought to herself, "This is reason number one for not using." That night, after the kids were in bed, she faced her mother and the questions and comments she knew had been hanging between them.

"Why are you wasting your days off investigating an accident?"

"I'm not sure it was an accident, Mother."

"The coroner thought it was. Isn't that enough? Do you know more than the coroner?"

"The coroner wasn't there."

"Didn't the coroner visit the scene?"

"No. Scott wasn't dead yet then. Besides, even if she had visited, she wasn't there in the beginning like I was. No one was there then."

"Even if that's true, do you think some white cop would use his off time to investigate if the same thing happened to you?"

"I don't know."

"Well, I know they wouldn't," she spat out.

"I do know this particular white man cared a lot for the kids that he taught, even though they were all challenged in some way, even though some of them were Natives."

"Did he do that on his days off?"

"I don't know, Mother."

"Well, I don't like you risking your health and well-being chasing some phantom murderer who, if it does turn out to be real, might kill you too. Then where will your children and I be?

And when is the last time you went to a meeting or a sweat on your day off?"

"I went to a sweat about a week ago. And anyway, do you mean one of those things you always used to complain about me doing?"

Her mother's face turned slightly red. Lucy wasn't sure if it was from embarrassment or anger. "Well, at least when you were doing those things I disapprove of you weren't risking your life and at least you were trying to stay sober. What is this doing to help you?"

"In a strange way, it has added to my commitment to sobriety. It has helped me to see more clearly how drug use— mine in particular—affected you and the children. But even more than that, it may affect people I don't even know in ways I don't even understand."

"Well, I'm glad for that, I guess, though I'm not sure I understand that last part."

"I think Scott died partly because of his drug abuse. Now I'm involved. If something happens to me, though I don't think it will, then it would affect you and the children. They're already being raised without a father because of drug use. My son has no model of a father, and that will influence his ability to be a good father."

"You're way too deep for me sometimes. I'm going to bed and hope that talking to you hasn't given me nightmares. Let me guess—all my talking did is rile you up, and now you're going to follow some lead rather than get some rest." She got up and gave Lucy a kiss on the forehead. "Honey, in spite of my complaining, I'm glad you care, and I love those two kids to death. If something were to happen to you, I'd be there to care for them."

Lucy cursed the tear in her eye. It irritated her that her mother, who seemed so different from her in so many ways, knew her so well. "I know, Mom, and I love you. I just may go out for a while tonight, so don't worry about me."

Her mother just shook her head and wandered off to bed.

Lucy pulled out the letters she received from Kathy and read them again. She tried to focus on anything that might be a clue to explain Scott's death, but her mind kept shifting to what her friends and family might have written to her and all the pain her drug use had caused.

Lucy set the letters aside and went to kiss each of her children.

Chapter 21

Lucy knew she couldn't sleep so she decided to pay Kane a visit. She had gotten his address through the school—and after a great deal of trouble. It made her wonder about how easily Mr. Reilly had been able to obtain that information.

Kane lived on the outskirts of Green Bay in Ashwaubenon, not far from Lambeau Field where the Packers played. The Oneida Gambling Casino and the airport were also close by. He lived in a farmhouse away from other houses, which was good since it was after midnight and music was still blaring.

Lucy thought about the family who probably had lived there before. There was a wide front porch that covered the whole front of the house—they probably sat there, resting after a dinner of home-grown foods prepared by loving hands.

Lucy parked outside at a distance and watched for some time. People would come to the door, stay for no more than ten or fifteen minutes, and then leave.

After a while, Lucy emerged from her car and approached the door. It was a heavy steel door with a tiny peephole. She rang the bell, and though she saw a shadow on the other side of the peephole, the door didn't open immediately. Suddenly, the music was turned way down. Sounds of scurrying inside the house became more audible.

When the door finally opened, Kane stood in the middle of his two bookends, Vince and Lou. "Officer Teller, I've been expecting you, though I must admit, I thought you'd be sleeping with your kids by now."

Lucy was stunned into silence. It unnerved her that he not only knew her name but that she had children. She fumbled in her mind for what to say. "Hi, Kane. May I come in?"

Lucy marveled at her quick wit. Calling him by his drug name was a stroke of genius loaded with professionalism. She felt a nagging at her guts and for the first time since this started, she was afraid. She didn't think Kane was dumb enough to try anything at his own place and with a cop, but she realized how dumb she was to go there alone and with no one knowing where she was.

"We have a few young ladies who need to get decent first."

"I'm not interested in the drug paraphernalia I might see in there anyway. How about if I just ask you a few questions out here?" As soon as she said it, Lucy knew she had made another mistake by appearing indecisive. The smirk on Kane's face and the look he gave his two friends, told her it didn't get by him either. Still, perhaps it was an advantage if he didn't see her as much of a threat. He would have no reason to harm her.

"That's fine, Officer. What can I do for you?" "Did you know Scott Brandt?"

"Yes, I knew him quite well. We used to play football together. After I left school, we stayed in touch."

"Do you know anything about his death?"

"I read he had an accident. The paper said it might have been a heart attack before he hit a tree. Paper said snow might have been a factor."

"Yes, two different kinds of snow. One comes from the sky and the other from Colombia. Do you know how the Colombian kind might have gotten there?"

"I heard that Scott was involved with that stuff. I encouraged him to quit."

"I heard the same thing. Matter of fact, I heard you cut him off after he beat you up for trying to rape his girlfriend."

Kane's two bodyguards smirked at the story. They obviously had been told a different story about the broken ribs.

The playful environment changed. Kane's face and manner developed an edge. Lucy's stomach tightened again as she realized she shouldn't have pushed. Not when no one knew where she was.

"In the first place, if you came inside you'd realize I can have all the women I want without resorting to rape. Secondly, I don't know whose fantasy you've been listening to, but I don't sell drugs or give them to anyone. Third, if Scott Brandt had tried to beat me up, he would not have lasted to die in an accident."

This time, Lucy decided not to push. "Sure. Well, thanks for your time, Mr. Harkness." She turned to leave, but not so far that she would lose sight of Kane or his bodyguards.

"Just a little advice before you go," said Kane. "Scott was involved with some pretty nasty people. If you keep digging around, you could get yourself or even those kids of yours hurt or worse. I'd hate to see anything happen to you."

Lucy got the feeling he wouldn't hate it at all.

"Thanks for the warning," she said, and left the porch.

When she reached her car, she was shaking so badly that she had to use two hands to put the key in the door and then again in the ignition. She wasn't sure whether it was fear or rage that had her so upset. On the way home, she asked herself once again why she was doing this. It was one thing to risk her own life, but to risk the lives of her children and to affect the life of her mother who was already burdened enough—that she had to question. She already knew this was more than she could take on herself. She was thankful to have a community, but she knew they'd be divided. Even worse than division, the community would not even be available until the morning, and that meant another sleepless night. She thought about stopping to see Sophie, who often told her she was available twenty-four hours a day. Lucy drove past the house and decided against it.

The house was dark.

The priest in town and had been a friend of the family for years. Lucy's mother volunteered at the parish. She was constantly baking things for the bake sales and helping out before Mass with the raffles. Lucy didn't go to church every Sunday, but she was more regular than most.

She had a great deal of respect for Father Dan. She often wondered why he stayed at such a small parish when someone with his abilities could be useful at so many larger parishes. But he was somewhat of a rebel, and she suspected he kept a low profile so he could stay there. In the old days, drunks looking for handouts would often awaken him at two in the morning. Since the casino had opened just a few blocks from his parish, that happened less frequently. He had told her he wasn't sure why. He hoped it was because the extra money that the casino brought in and donated to the tribe had helped to ease the alcohol problem in the community. Maehnowesekiyah, the place where Lucy had gotten her treatment, was partially funded by the casino. But with gambling came the rumor that there was more organized crime, and there was no doubt that there were more drugs like heroin and cocaine. Father Dan wasn't sure whether the problem had improved or just changed.

Father Dan's home was just a few steps from the church. As Lucy rang his bell at two in the morning, she thought how like the old days it would be for the priest. His dog barked first, and then she saw a light. A few moments later, she saw him at the door. He had on black pants and a t-shirt. His dark beard was beginning to show some gray. He spoke with a hint of sarcasm as he opened the door, but his voice still had the sound of serenity that she had come to expect and sometimes, like now, need. "It's always a pleasure to see you, Lucy, but I must admit it's more of a pleasure in the daylight."

"Well, the good news is I'm not drunk or high, and this could wait until morning, but I know I can't sleep unless I talk with someone. I could go talk with my sponsor, but I think I know what she'd say. This is a moral dilemma right up your alley."

"Well, let's talk, and then perhaps we can both get some sleep." He opened the door, and she walked to his office. She knew the way; she'd been there before. Father Dan's office was lined with books. An outsider might call it disorganized, but the priest seemed to be able to put his hands quickly on any book from which he wanted to quote. He gave the best sermons she had ever heard. Each one was loaded with wisdom and quotations. She didn't think she'd ever heard him use the same quote twice.

Lucy sat across the desk from him and began to tell him in detail about her suspicions and activities since she had discovered Scott. For the moment, she left out the vision or dream or whatever it was. "I'm convinced that Scott was murdered," she concluded. "I think I know who did it, how, and why. If I stop investigating this, the murderer will go free because the coroner has ruled it an accident, and the FBI isn't interested. I might be able to live with that, because even if I know the murderer will continue to do the kind of things that got Scott killed unless he's stopped."

She paused. "On the other hand, my own life is getting out of balance, and I don't like that. My life and the lives of my children have been threatened if I continue."

"I often marvel at the fact that the Menominee were talking about balance way back when the first missionaries came in the 1600s," said Father Dan. "It's only been in recent years with stress management training that white people have returned to talking about life that way—holistic spirituality was discussed by theologians centuries ago, but a lot of that's neglected now. And yet, the missionaries called the Menominee savages. I applaud you for keeping that a high priority in your life as well as your children. But what has you so convinced that this is murder? I'm a long way from being a cop or a lawyer, but from what you described, there's not a lot of evidence."

Lucy took a deep breath. "Speaking of Menominee history, we were a people who once believed in dreams and visions. I know those beliefs are not very much respected in the white world as sources of information, but I believe in them. The night I found Scott, I had a vision or dream—I'm not sure which—of what happened. I believe his spirit is near and wants resolution of what happened. For whatever reason, he seems to have chosen me to tell the story of what really happened. I know it probably sounds crazy to you."

"I'm sure you can't walk into a court of law with that, but the Bible is loaded with examples of people getting messages in dreams. You don't have to convince me of their importance or validity. Unfortunately, I probably won't be on the jury. Now, what about the other side? Who threatened you and why?"

"This drug dealer who calls himself Kane. He was smart enough to veil it, as if he were concerned about someone else hurting me, but he and I both knew."

"Do you take him seriously?"

"Yes. I believe he'd hurt me or my children, whichever one would give him the best advantage."

"I think I understand your dilemma. If you continue, the ones you love most could be hurt. On the other hand, if you don't continue, you may not know who or when, but you know someone else's pain will continue."

"That's it in a nutshell."

"Can you put the word out that you've given up, just to protect yourself and your family?"

"It might buy me some time, but if I continue, Kane will get the word. I think people like him have eyes and ears everywhere around here."

"As far as whether to continue, if the spirit involvement here is as strong as you say it is, why not let Scott decide?"

"I thought I was weird," Lucy said with a smile.

"Maybe Scott, with divine help, can see things you can't.

If your life is in that much danger, perhaps Scott will 'let go and let God.' Or, maybe he'll give you an approach you haven't thought of yet. Remember, you don't have to do everything yourself." Father Dan smiled. He had many years of experience with Lucy.

Lucy left the rectory feeling more peaceful. She drove straight home, slipped quietly into the house, and went to her room. She lay down on her bed, removing only her shoes. Lucy's spirit guide still had not been revealed clearly to her, but she was hoping it was the eagle. The thought crossed her mind just before she entered the sleep waiting room, the bizarre room of strange pictures, voices, and body jerks.

Soon she found herself running near the Wolf River, where eagles frequently gathered. When she saw one, she flapped her arms, attempting to fly, as she had done in many dreams lately. But as she ran she stepped in mud and, rather than rising with the eagles, she was stuck to the earth. The harder she struggled, the more stuck she became, until she could barely move her legs. She could only watch as the eagle flew away.

She woke with tears in her eyes. "Don't abandon me, spirits," she whispered. She thought for a moment that sleep was behind her for the night, but that was the last thought she remembered until morning. If she dreamt again, she didn't remember.

In the morning, she walked into the kitchen smiling and kissed each of her children on the tops of their heads as they sat at the breakfast table. She even kissed her mother's cheek.

"It's nice to see you found some time to sleep, Officer Sleuth," her mother said.

Lucy just continued to smile. She changed the subject and asked how school was going with her kids. She got about as much information from them as she usually gave to her mother. She told each of them again she was sorry for the pain she caused them. She told them each to write her a letter telling her about the pain her drug use had caused them. She told them she might need those letters sometime to stay sober. They all just rolled their eyes but Lucy was certain that they would do as she asked.

As soon as the children had left, she told her mother she had visited with Father Dan and that she was feeling better about things. Without giving her mother much time to ask questions, she added a light jacket to her sweats since the weather was turning colder and left for her morning ritual. On her way out, she heard her mother singing a George Jones song, one she had heard him sing at a recent casino appearance.

She let a couple of weeks pass without doing much investigating into Scott's death. She did call the college to ask about the young man who had died from the heart attack. She learned that his parents did suspect drug use and had threatened to sue the school. They had not followed through and had since divorced and both moved out of state.

She was hoping for a sign that didn't come, at least not in a way she could recognize. She was sleeping better, but her dreams (if she remembered them) seemed only the reworking of the events of the previous day.

She decided to visit Mr. Reilly's classroom during the week after Thanksgiving. She was taking an education class at the College of Menominee Nation and had to do some observation. She decided since she at least had some knowledge of the teacher and the students, she'd get more out of visiting his classroom. She wasn't sure if he had any more contact with Kane, but it couldn't hurt to tell him she'd decided to accept the wisdom of the coroner and the board.

She found herself fascinated with the children and their projects. Mr. Reilly maintained good classroom discipline and kept them occupied and interested. He had a young female aide to provide some of the nurturing they needed. Lucy took the time to view the classroom for her journal and noticed that the walls were covered less with kids' projects and more with photography. Most of the pictures were nature scenes, but there was at least one picture of each of the kids in the class with one of the child's projects underneath. After class, Mr. Reilly approached her.

"Find any new clues, Officer?"

"No, I'm here as a student today. I decided patrolman, mother, and student are enough hats. I'll leave investigating to the FBI." She complimented him on his teaching and the way the classroom was arranged. "Who's the photographer?"

"Oh, I am," he answered. Lucy could tell he was a sucker for a compliment, and soon he showed her the class newsletter.

It was full of his photographs. She was very careful not to mention Scott or anything remotely related to his death.

That night, Lucy got a letter from her daughter. It said nothing of the pain that she lived through during her mother's abuse, but it did say how happy she was to have her back and sober. Lucy crumpled the letter, held it to her heart, and cried.

Thanksgiving came and went. Lucy, as always, thanked God for her children and especially that they were back with her. She thanked God for her sobriety and for her mother who loved and helped care for the children. She thanked God for the support she had on the rez and especially for Sophie and Father Dan. She thanked God for Ray Waupuse, but she asked Him to remove the strange feeling she had each time she saw Ray. At church, she found herself watching him or trying too hard not to notice everything he did.

She had time to go to a few more meetings and did another sweat lodge the day after Thanksgiving. The weather was colder now and made her shiver each time she stepped from her patrol car. For some reason, it often felt worse than the middle of January. Legend Lake had frozen over, and she hoped no fool would try going out there in a snowmobile yet. If she shivered getting out of her squad, imagine how she'd feel diving into freezing water trying to save some fool who might be doing the world a favor by eliminating himself from the gene pool. The Wolf was also beginning to freeze in the slow- moving parts away from the rapids. Everything was cold, icy, and frozen—but she knew that the investigation would not be any of those things for long.

Chapter 22

In the weeks before Christmas, Lucy's sleeping was beginning to improve. Between her job, school, and preparations for Christmas, she was kept busy. Early one morning she and the kids went out to the woods and cut down a Christmas tree. It was exhausting work, so by the time she slid beneath the covers that night, she fell asleep immediately. She soon began to dream. She was with Ray in a bed in the middle of a field. He was stroking her hair, and she was giggling like a child. There were children running around them and a man in the shadows taking pictures. She was disturbed by the flashes and concerned about the children running around in very little clothing. She called to the children to come in under the covers, and one boy turned to her, but in a grown man's voice the boy said, "Wake up. They're coming for you."

Then the dream stopped, and she lay half-awake until she heard the same voice once more.

"Get up now," the voice said with even more urgency.

She heard a car outside, and it sounded like it was turning into her driveway, but no headlights flashed into her window. She jumped up out of bed and looked out cautiously.

The car was there, visible even in the dark. Two shadows emerged from the car, closing the doors behind them without a sound. Lucy slid on some pants under her nightshirt and ran to her mother's bedroom. She put her hand over her mother's mouth to keep her from screaming and awakened her with a hoarse whisper to follow her to her bedroom. On the way back, Lucy realized she had left her weapon in her truck. Her 40 Glock Kill was of standard issue. Most of the cops she knew did not need anything more powerful than the Glock, but you really had to have it on you for it to be of any help.

Lucy thought to herself that she needed to keep it with her at all times in the future. She hoped the men didn't bring their own guns with them. She hoped that surprise and a house full of women would be enough to put the men at a disadvantage.

Her mother looked at her with fear and curiosity.

"There are two men coming toward the house. They are after me. When the first one comes through the door, he's going to bend over. When he does, lift your knee to his face as hard as you can."

Now her mother looked at her even more strangely. She started to open her mouth, but Lucy anticipated the question and put her finger to her mother's lips. "Trust me; he'll bend over." She placed her mother against the wall just past the doorstop, so the door would clear her body. She moved to the other side of the doorframe and knelt on one knee. She kept the door open just a crack so she would be able to see the men approaching. Lucy's bedroom was the first on the hallway off the living room, and she hoped they would come inside and not continue down the hall toward the kids' room.

She heard glass break in the kitchen and some gravelly noise that meant drawers opening. She felt a little relief. She wondered if she should take her mother and barricade herself with her family inside the kids' room. She would have to wake up Jerrod and take him to her daughter's room. While she wondered if there was time, she heard the same voice from her dream saying, "Don't go there." She listened.

She figured they were looking for knives to use as weapons rather than bringing their own. Lucy knew burglars often do this so if they are caught outside the home they won't have weapons to increase the charges. She wished she had thought to pick something up on her way through the kitchen. Soon she saw the two men walking toward her room. She heard her heart beating in her ears and even felt it in her head. Again, Lucy had to remind herself to breathe. The first man pushed the door open ahead of him and paused.

Lucy stayed crouched next to the doorframe. A moment later, she saw his leg slowly moving into the room. She whirled as fast as she could and planted her fist in his groin. He groaned and bent forward. Just as she was instructed, Lucy's mother raised her knee. You could hear his nose break and he collapsed, curling up on the floor.

Lucy lunged for the knife the first man had dropped, but just as she grabbed it, the second man hit her on the back, knocking the air out of her lungs. He moved toward her quickly before she could regain her footing. Then he lunged toward her awkwardly and she rolled to avoid his weight.

Instead of attacking her, he fell to the ground next to her and didn't move.

She scrambled to her feet expecting him to do the same but he stayed on the floor, unmoving. She looked up and saw her son. Jerrod was standing next to her with his baseball bat ready for another stroke. He was very calm. For the first time, she remembered her cell phone, and tried to remember where she had put it when she came into the house. Her daughter had already found it and was dialing 911.

"When did these kids grow up and become so responsible?" she asked herself, marveling.

The men were taken away in handcuffs. Lucy didn't ask them any questions, afraid she might spoil any case they had against them. When she saw them in the light, she recognized them; they were both addicts who hung out at the casino. She thought back to the conversation she had with Kane in the fall. She wondered if his long, dirty fingers stretched as far as the reservation. She hoped that whoever questioned them would have some answers for her, but she doubted it. She was sure they'd stick to a story of burglary. That not only protected whoever might have sent them but also kept them from being brought up on more serious charges—like attempted murder.

Even so, she was convinced that it would be difficult to prove that their motives were not burglary. Why would they bother with her house if they wanted valuables? There were several cabins on Legend Lake that were unoccupied and had better stuff to fence. The questions that remained were more troubling. Why would they want to kill her? Why were they here?

There was only one thing that could be at the root of the matter, and she knew what it was. Still, whatever she would learn would have to wait until the morning. Her focus now was on her family. She expected a lecture from her mother but instead, in one brief moment, her mother had turned into John Rambo. She was high-fiving Jerrod and Tara in the living room. "I guess they picked the wrong house to break into, wouldn't you say?" she said, pumping her fists in the air.

They had way too much adrenaline to sleep, so they all crammed together on the couch. Lucy tried to apologize to them, but they'd have none of it. "You were incredible," her mother said. "I'll never make fun of all that exercise you do again. You moved like a cat."

"Well, I made lots of mistakes and put you all in danger unnecessarily. I left my gun out in the car, I had no idea where the cell phone was, and I never even thought of it until after it was over anyway. I need to be better prepared."

"I had the phone in my room," Tara said. "I was talking to my friends after you came home. From now on, I'll put it on your nightstand when I'm done."

"How about warm milk all around?" Lucy asked.

"I'll get it," her mom said in a take-charge voice. "You stay with your kids."

The family continued to discuss things that would make them safer.

After they had sipped their milk, Lucy looked at each of them. "I've been thinking that maybe I should quit the police department and go back to school full time. I could finish my teaching degree in a year and get a job as a teacher."

"Mom, if you want to be a teacher, do it," Jerrod said. "But don't do it because of what happened. I'm proud of what you do and I think you're good at it. I'd feel guilty if you stopped doing what you're good at to protect me."

"I agree with Jerrod. Boy, does that sound weird!" Tara said.

"I'm not concerned about my well-being, but I'm your mother, and I am worried about you," Lucy's mother added. "But we'll support you no matter what. Really, I mean that."

All their words ran through her head as Lucy wasted her time trying to sleep later that night. By the time morning came, Lucy was already wishing it were evening so she could sleep again.

Chapter 23

Exhausted, Lucy dragged herself to the station to find out what they had learned from the two "burglars" who had broken into her house. As she had suspected, they claimed they were only there to burglarize and had no intention of harming or even having any contact with the family. The thing that was interesting, the investigator told her, was that the two of them didn't need money for drugs at the moment. The police had found a kilo of heroin in their trunk, and they had brought some with them into the house, as well as a syringe all cooked up and ready to use.

Lucy wondered how much she even wanted to know about the two of them. She thought about trying to find out where they got their drugs and seeing if she could trace it to Kane, but would she want to know how to get access to drugs again? Most of her old sources were in jail or dead. She knew she was better off not knowing who the new people were.

Lucy was convinced that syringe was meant for her arm. This sounded a lot like what had happened to Scott, Lucy thought. Break in and inject her—a recovering addict—with her drug of choice. Hopefully, after a taste, she'll go back for more, but even if she doesn't, you can destroy her credibility if word gets out she's still using. Throw some of the drugs around her house, then an anonymous phone call to the tribal police, and she would have been suspended or maybe even kicked off the force.

The problem was she could now think of several people who might benefit from her dismissal and disgrace, but just one who'd have the connections and only one who'd have the resources at the moment. Lucy shuddered at the thought of having come that close to having heroin in her body again. She wondered whether she would have the strength to quit for a second time. The danger of this work kept mounting. She was not only subjecting her whole family to physical danger, but now there was the threat of losing herself to drugs again.

As she was thinking what to do next, she saw Ray walking into the station. He smiled as soon as he saw her. "How's it going, Night Fighter? I hear one of those men is suing you on behalf of the children he'll never have, and the other is suing your son for the loss of brains he didn't have in the first place. We offered to let them out of jail if they made bail money, but they're afraid of you stalking them."

Lucy smiled, not so much at his dumb jokes but at seeing his face and recognizing the concern behind his attempts at humor. Lucy got close to him and whispered in his ear. "You just remember what I'm capable of if you try sneaking into my bedroom." She punched him lightly in the stomach. "I can hit a lot harder and aim a lot lower."

Ray cringed. "Okay. I get your point."

They looked at each other for a moment. Lucy wanted to take it all back. She wanted to say, "You are invited to my room any time."

That's when Lieutenant Moon walked by them. "Well, Lucy you had an exciting evening last night, didn't you? We're going to have to look at your salary. If people are breaking in and trying to rob you, you must be making too much. Why do you think they were really there?"

"The part about them bringing a syringe into my house has me frightened. Why would they bring that inside? They didn't plan to shoot themselves up in my house. What was in that syringe was meant for me. We should see how much dope was in there. We might have them for attempted murder. Even if it wasn't enough to kill me, if they got me started again, I'd be dead. We could at least charge them with that and see what shakes loose. Maybe they'll give up who sent them."

"If we do that," Ray argued, "we might send whoever sent them further underground. Why not pretend we buy their story and tail them? Maybe we can find out who they buy their dope from."

"Do you have any idea who that might be, Lucy?" the Lieutenant asked.

"I've been thinking about that. I think it's Kane."

The Lieutenant looked over his glasses at her for the first time in a while. "I thought you let go of that."

"That's what has me stumped. I was hoping Kane thought that too. Why would he risk putting me back on his trail? That's the only part that doesn't fit."

"I think Ray's idea makes the most sense. Let's charge them with burglary and possession and let them go. See who they run to or from. If someone sent them, I don't think they'd use those two again, as bad as they bungled it. So I don't think we're putting your life in any greater jeopardy, Lucy. Ray, why don't I put you on keeping tabs on them? If people are trying to kill or discredit my officers, we're going to get to the bottom of this right now. One more thing, Lucy. They said that they were unarmed. Why didn't you draw your weapon and tell them to freeze when they entered your bedroom?"

"That's only partially true. They stopped at my kitchen and got a knife." Then Lucy tried to mumble the last part. "And I left my weapon in my truck."

The Lieutenant rolled his eyes. "You make sure you carry that wherever you go. That's an order."

"Yes, sir." Lucy backed out of his office quickly before he had time to ask her about her cell phone. She was in her car before he thought of it. Ray walked up to her car. "Gun and cell phone with you at all times." He handed her a slip of paper. "I want you to have my number on speed dial. Your kids can do it for you if you can't."

"That's a sneaky way to get me to call you. You're just too smooth, Ray Waupuse."

Ray smiled and shook his head and went to his car.

Chapter 24

The second week in December, Lucy took a day to visit the Brandts. When she drove up to the house, she noticed that theirs was the only house on the block with no decorations. Bobbie answered the door and let her into the house. It was neat and clean, but there was still no indication of the holidays except perhaps for some cardboard boxes piled in a corner that Lucy suspected were filled with decorations. It was after dinner, and she had expected to find more people at home, but Bobbie was the only one.

"Finished for the semester?" "Quarter," Bobbie answered.

"We still have a week to go. I'd like to be done, with Christmas coming and two kids. How do you think your grades are going to be?"

"I don't expect to do that well," Bobbie answered, her voice showing neither anger nor disappointment. "I should have withdrawn when Scott died. My heart just hasn't been place is like a tomb." "Where is everyone?"

"I think Ryan, Sally, and Paul are visiting friends. I don't know where my mother is, and Dad is at a meeting. He's been attending more since Scott died, and he's sponsoring a lot more. I think he's made it his personal responsibility to make sure no one else dies of this disease."

"I could use a meeting myself. Can you tell me how to find it?"

"Sure!" Bobbie answered and gave her directions.

The meeting was just as Bill Wilson, one of the founders of AA, had intended. Not too many more could fit around a kitchen table. Lucy wondered whether the stares were more because she walked in late or because she was Native American.

Some even appreciated her figure, but not in a flattering way Hank was quick to her rescue.

"This is the officer who is trying to find the truth abou Scott's death, and she's recovering. Please make her feel welcome."

Immediately, the facial expressions in the room changed names were exchanged and the discussion continued as if Lucy had always been there. Afterward, Hank invited Lucy for coffee.

"How did you know how to find me?" he asked.

"I stopped by the house, and Bobbie told me where to find you."

"Ah," said Hank slowly, "Bobbie was the only one at home, I presume."

"Yes, she was."

"You know it's like the old days, but now everyone is like me. We all stay away. When I see them, they all make me think of Scott. Then in the back of their eyes I see blame. I imagine them thinking I'm the one who brought this terrible disease to our family."

"I know the feeling. I feel guilty when I look at my mother, but when I ask her, she doesn't seem to feel that way. You know, when you were drinking, no one could talk about it. Now it's Scott that no one can talk about."

"You're right about that. I know no one thinks of much else, but no one utters his name."

"Has anyone in your family thought of anything that might help me find out why Scott died and why he might have cocaine in his system that he didn't put there?"

Hank's eyes shifted downward, but he didn't speak. There was a long period of silence. Out of respect, Lucy also looked down and made no attempt to break the silence. Hank finally looked up, and the feeling uppermost was that he was impressed with Lucy. No one else he knew would have given him the time he needed to get comfortable with what he was about to say.

"You may think what I'm going to say is weird. I don't know why I'm telling you this, but I know I can't tell my family or even my friends." Hank took a deep breath. "I don't think what I'm about to say helps to clear Scott's name. If anything, times since Scott's death, he's come to visit me in my dreams. I know it must sound funny to hear me say it like that, but that's how it feels. It's not like I'm dreaming of Scott. It's like I'm dreaming of something else, and then he flashes in like some of those, what do you call them, subliminal things, but long enough for it to register. He's got an embarrassed, even shamed look on his face, and he's showing me pictures of his students. I can't make the pictures out clearly, but I know they're not right."

"What do you mean not right?"

"I don't know exactly, but the feeling I get is that they're naked. I'm afraid Scott is trying to confess from the grave."

Lucy could see the pain on Hank's face. She admired the courage it must have taken to tell her all of this. "I can't tell how much I appreciate your telling me that. The reason I'm investigating this is because Scott has visited me too. My people have a history of listening to dreams, but I don't get that from your culture. We believe people and powerful messages can come to us in our dreams. It's our responsibility to respect and pay attention to them. I was embarrassed to tell you this before because I was sure you wouldn't respect it. My dreams tell me, though, that Scott is not ashamed but that he's asking for help. I don't know what he's asking of you, but you don't have to be ashamed. Invite him back. Together maybe we can make sense of this."

"Do you have the same dream as I have?"

"No. Mine was about how the accident happened. I've also dreamed of things a long while ago. About the sort of people who might have wanted to kill Scott."

"What did you see?"

"In one dream, I dreamed Scott was under a pile of leaves in the woods, hiding from his drug suppliers. I have talked with Kathy and she told me of a night when she and Scott were followed. He jumped out of the car and ran off into the woods. I think it was that night I saw. In the other dream— the accident dream—there were four cars: Scott's and three others.

Two sat and waited for him, one followed. Just past Spirit Rock, the two lead cars forced him off the road, and he hit the tree. One person—and I only saw the top of his head—went to the car. He seemed to be looking for something he didn't find.

Then I saw a needle that seemed to be coming toward me, and someone was reaching on my lap for pictures. The next I knew there were flames, and I was above the car again."

Lucy took a deep breath then continued. "When I first got to the accident scene, there were footprints moving toward and away from the car. The heat of the flames melted them before anyone else saw them. I also saw a place just in front of the accident scene where cars appear to have been waiting on a road intersecting the one where Scott was driving. In both places, spots exactly the size of a car had a half inch less snow than what surrounded it. But that all disappeared when the snow melted the next day."

with determination in his voice.

"Yes, but all I have is a dream to prove it."

Lucy could see tears filling his eyes. "Well, you may never prove it in a court of law, but you brought justice to my heart.

This is the best I've felt since this whole thing started. You know, through all my drinking days, I never came close to having an affair, but God has protected me lately because if the right woman had come along I don't know what I'd have done. I just know I want to be comforted so badly. I know Molly wants the same, but because we're both so empty we can't seem to give it to one another."

Looking deep into his eyes, Lucy reached over and patted his hand. "You're a good man, Hank Brandt. Did you learn about 'Act as if...' in treatment?"

"No, I can't say I've heard that one. I got the abbreviated version in outpatient."

"I had a counselor who used to say, 'Act as if, and the feelings will follow.' Why not go home and help your family decorate your house and maybe some feelings of Christmas will follow."

"Perhaps with what I've learned from you today, I can do that. Thanks, Lucy."

They said their goodbyes.

Hank returned home and he and Bobbie began to sort through the Christmas boxes they had brought out a week ago.

That night after dinner Hank asked each family member to stay at the table.

He began by saying, "I know we're all hurting about Scott. If you are like me, you are somehow blaming yourself for his death and wondering who else in the family may also blame you. I also know that it is painful to look at each of you because each of you in your own way reminds me of something about Scott. I don't want to bring up his name just in case any of you might be having a brief moment of peace from your thoughts. You need to know that, though I blame myself, I don't blame any of you.

"I think Scott would be the first to tell us that life is for living, and it's time we went about making our lives and the way he may have touched us mean something. I think the healing for us as individuals and as a family will take years—maybe forever. But I'm telling you that mine starts today. Who wants to join me?"

Molly answered immediately. "I'm willing and I'm proud of you for what you're saying, but I have no idea about how or where to go from here."

Hank began to feel as if the large gaping hole from losing his son might heal. He smiled affectionately back at Molly. "I don't know either," he said. "But I know in alcoholism it starts by sharing your powerlessness and by being honest and being open to God."

"I'm with you, Dad," said Ryan.

All the others added their commitment. Hank was right: the healing was long and painful, but it started that night.

Chapter 25

The next day, Lucy went to talk with Kathy at her apartment in Shawano. She asked Kathy about the photos. Kathy swore that no one had ever taken her picture except for Kane that night he tried to rape her, and then only right after she had answered the door.

Lucy took a deep breath. "Is it possible that someone might have taken them without your knowledge? Maybe even of you and Scott together?"

Kathy shivered. "I suppose that's possible, but we hadn't been together in that way since before the intervention. And Scott never told me about it if it happened."

"Scott may have found out that Kane did something on his own."

"How could they do that? I never leave my shades open." "They have tiny cameras they can place in your bedroom or bathroom when you're not home."

Kathy shivered again. "Could they have them here?"

Together, Lucy and Kathy checked the likely places and found nothing.

"Make sure you keep your doors locked when you're not here," Lucy warned her. Then, to soothe Kathy's nerves, she talked about something else. "On another subject, how are your students doing?"

"They seem to be adjusting to Scott being gone, and they relate well to me, but I think they are careful because they are afraid of losing someone again. I don't know what magic Scott weaved with them, but they sure don't seem to have that with anyone at school including me, no matter how hard I try."

"Not even with Mr. Reilly? They've been with him a long time."

"None of the kids seem very close with him. I think it's his personality. He doesn't seem to be that close with anyone at school, even with the other staff. With the kids, he focuses on discipline and seems very worried about any of the kids crossing some imaginary boundary he's set in his mind. He's even warned me about getting too close with them. He doesn't seem to approve of it. I think that's what he and Scott argued about."

"Remember to keep your doors locked," Lucy repeated as she left. "And look for any items that may have been moved while you were away. Keep an eye out for places someone may have hidden a camera."

Kathy shivered again.

In the days that followed, Lucy noticed something odd by the accident site. She had continued to see the fresh flowers by the tree Scott had hit. She knew they weren't put there by Kathy or Scott's parents because they lived too far away. These flowers were not from a florist; they were a collection of goldenrod or other wildflowers. Each day, more flowers were added.

It was on an afternoon shortly after Christmas that Lucy found the answer to the riddle. She was driving along 55 in her squad car. She was totally lost in thought and it was as if the squad was driving itself. It was getting dark before 4:30 now and lights were coming on in the houses and trailers she passed. It was snowing big flakes when she passed Spirit Rock. As she passed the tree she saw a tiny figure kneeling by the tree. As the squad got closer she could tell the figure was a young girl.

The girl started to run away until she saw it was Lucy stepping from the car. Lucy recognized her as one of the girls who attended the funeral—a girl from Scott's class. She was one who stayed in the background and Lucy had never heard speak. Lucy recognized the thin lips and small frame and one withered arm, symptoms of Fetal Alcohol Syndrome or FAS. She was always so thankful that her own children miraculously escaped.

Lucy approached the girl and put out her hand. "Hi, my name is Lucy. I know you were with the group I met at the funeral. I've visited your class a few times but I don't think we've spoken. What's your name?"

"Lisa," was all she said.

Lucy had only read a chapter on special needs in her education class and a little in her psychology class, but she guessed this girl was hearing impaired as well as developmentally delayed and just plain painfully shy.

Lucy looked over at the tree with the flowers then back at the girl. "You really miss him don't you?"

Lisa nodded her head and started to cry. Lucy pulled her toward her to comfort her, but the little girl pulled away. That startled Lucy. "I'm sorry I just…"

Then she stopped. The girl seemed to be somewhere else. It reminded Lucy of the experience she had the night she found Scott in this very spot. As if Lisa's mind was floating above somewhere. This time Lucy was careful not to touch Lisa. She stood right in front of her. "Lisa? Lisa!" she called softly. It worked. She could see the girl's mind return to the back of her eyes. "It's cold, dark, and snowing. Where do you live?"

"Bear Trap Falls," Lisa said and then she pointed.

It was less than a quarter mile from the tree. Lucy decided she would like to speak to Lisa's mother. Perhaps Lisa saw what happened that night and was too traumatized to talk about it. She wondered if she could get her permission to have Lisa talk to the child psychologist at the tribal clinic. "I'll take you home. I'd like to speak with your mother." Lucy immediately saw the panic in Lisa's eyes. "No. Don't take me away from her. Please." She started to cry again.

Again Lucy didn't touch her, but rather went directly in front of her. She stood silent until the girl looked up and saw the tears in Lucy's eyes. "My own children were taken from me once. I wouldn't want to put anyone else through that." For the first time she saw trust. Lisa's home was close by and her mother was so drunk she probably would have signed her into slavery, so getting permission to have Lisa see the psychologist was easy. Lucy arranged it for the following Saturday and agreed to drive Lisa to and from the appointment. The psychologist thought it would take at least three sessions to gain trust. She asked Lisa for permission and then gave her own authority for Lucy to watch through a two-way mirror. Lisa and the psychologist engaged in play therapy.

"It's difficult to get even normal children to talk," the psychologist told Lucy in explanation. "And it's especially hard after a trauma. Often they communicate best through play.

They gain mastery through their play and they tend to focus on the things that traumatize them. If a child has been in a car accident, they'll crash cars together over and over again. If they've been physically abused, they'll take a doll and hit it again and again. If they've been sexually abused, they'll focus on the genitals of the doll."

What Lucy saw through the two-way mirror surprised her. The room was full of toys but the psychologist didn't direct Lisa to the cars.

"That's like leading the witness," the psychologist explained to Lucy later.

Lisa did not go to them on her own. Instead, she went straight to the toy camera and began taking pictures of everything. After a while she focused on the girl dolls. She took off their clothes and began taking close-ups.

A light bulb went off in Lucy's head. She left the observation room and knocked on the door of the room where Lisa was with the psychologist. She asked permission to enter. The psychologist looked slightly confused but nodded.

"I'm new at this so help me if I get stuck, or stop me if you think what I'm saying might hurt Lisa." Then she turned to Lisa. "You know, Lisa, I saw the picture that Mr. Reilly took of you in the classroom a few weeks ago. You looked cute as a button." Lisa smiled and lowered her head.

"Did Mr. Reilly take other pictures of you?"

Lisa's eyes began to glaze over as they had at the accident site. Lucy looked at the psychologist.

The psychologist spoke softly and slowly. "It's okay. Lisa, you're safe now."

Lisa came back and nodded her head.

"Were some of those without your clothes on?"

Lisa started to cry. She paused for a long time and the two women just waited. "He said we could use them for proof."

Lucy stared at the psychologist.

"Proof that your mother never hit you?" the doctor whispered.

Again the girl nodded.

"He said if I told they'd take me from mommy."

"That's not going to happen," Lucy said.

"I think that's enough for today," the psychologist said with a sigh.

Lucy took Lisa back home. When this was all over she'd do what she could to get Lisa's mother to treatment.

Her next stop was the hospital. She found the doctor to whom she'd talked the morning just before Scott died. "Do you remember what happened to the clothes that Scott was wearing when he came into the hospital?"

"I'm sure we disposed of them when we heard it was ruled an accident. We wouldn't have given them to the parents. They were nearly burned off of him."

"Do you remember seeing bits of photographs inside his clothing?"

"Now that you mention it, I do. There were little pieces inside his shirt. Not in a pocket or anything."

"Would you testify to that?"

"Sure, but what would that prove?"

"Maybe just enough," Lucy smiled. "Thanks, Doc."

She then went home and called Kathy. "I know who killed Scott and I know why. I don't know if we can get them for murder but we can try. If you'll testify to what Kane did to you we can at least put them in jail for a while and stop them from doing what they've been doing. Will you testify?"

"You bet I will," said Kathy.

"I'll get back to you. I have to talk with the coroner about reopening the case."

Lucy drove to the coroner's office but her secretary told her she would be out of the office for three weeks. She was in Florida visiting her children and was to be contacted only in an emergency. Lucy didn't think the coroner would think that this was.

But neither the coroner nor Lucy could know what would happen next.

Chapter 26

When she arrived back home she received a call from the station saying a Mr. Reilly had called. He said it was important and to call him back. Lucy felt a strange feeling in the pit of her stomach—she wasn't sure if it was a warning or her own excitement. She took a deep breath, and then called back.

Mr. Reilly said that he thought she should go back to investigating Scott's case. "Come to my classroom and I'll show you some evidence. It might just prove Scott was murdered." He refused to say anything more over the phone except that he wouldn't wait long.

When she arrived the school was dark, but Mr. Reilly was waiting by the door. She went up to him and asked him if he could get into the building.

"We don't have to," he said and pulled a gun from his pocket. He checked her for a gun and laughed when he didn't find one. "You have to be the dumbest cop ever. Now get back in your car."

They got into her car and drove back through the reservation toward Spirit Rock. They were driving past a dirt road on the side when he spoke again. "Go back. Back into it." Then he threw her some handcuffs and told her to cuff herself to the steering wheel. She did as she was told.

"Since I'm going to die anyway I'd like the satisfaction of knowing that I might be a stupid cop but I at least got this thing figured out."

"Go ahead. Amuse yourself. We'll be waiting here for a while anyway."

"Scott found some pictures you'd taken of one of the students. He confronted you with it. You promised you'd resign and get help. He said he'd give you a couple of days. He told you about his plans to go home. You called Kane, who had actually called you first because he wanted to get even with Scott. You told him he could. Neither of you planned to kill him. You were just going to run him off the road, inject him with cocaine, and get the pictures back. That way his credibility would be shot and you'd have the pictures back. But he hit the tree harder than you expected because of the snow and Kane— who wasn't as new to all this as you—wanted him dead anyway so he injected enough cocaine to kill him. He looked for the pictures and couldn't find them, so you figured you'd just burn the car to get rid of the evidence. I'm surprised a perv like you didn't want to search his body first. That's where he hid them." Reilly hit her in the mouth with the barrel of the gun. Her lip started bleeding.

"I never touched any of those students. Of course no one would believe or understand and I'd go to jail. The inmates would treat me like a child molester even though I'm not."

"I know a lot about denial in alcoholics. They define themselves out of the category too."

"Just shut up and wait for Kane."

"It's not too late. I'll testify you didn't mean to kill him.

When will this end? How many more have to die to cover up your problem?"

"Just you and your friend Kathy. No one else can prove we committed a crime."

Lucy's blood froze. "You're going to kill Kathy too."

"Kane's bringing her. Since you mouthed off to him about him trying to rape her, Kane's wanted to protect himself and his reputation. I have a friend at the hospital. We sometimes exchange pictures. He heard you talking to the Doc."

"Baseball cards, huh? Is he going to go along with you murdering someone?"

"I'll hit you again. The marks won't matter. I take pictures along this river all year long. Every season is beautiful. I know a spot up the road where it's deep and close to the highway.

They won't find your bodies until they take rafts down it this summer. By that time I'll be in South America. I'm tired of this cold weather anyway."

Just then Kane pulled into the dirt road. One of his bodyguards was driving. The other was in the back seat with Kane. Kathy was in the passenger seat with a gun to her head.

When she got out of the car, her blouse was torn and Lucy could see dried blood by her mouth. The boys had obviously had some sport with her on the way; they were laughing as they got out of the car.

They quickly rearranged people in each of the cars. Lou drove Lucy's truck and Kane stepped in the back seat. Vince stayed with Kathy in the front and Reilly climbed into the back seat behind her. They set off; Lucy's truck was in the lead.

It was dark now, but a full moon cast shadows of the bare winter trees on the road ahead. Snow had accumulated up to a foot or more on each side of the road. The snowbanks sat up even higher. The moon cast a shadow from the banks so just a silver ribbon lay in front of them. Lucy's mind raced for ideas but nothing came. Lou Holz used to say luck follows speed and she knew if they could just catch a small break she and Kathy could outrun them in the woods. But the cars were moving swiftly and jumping from the car would not work. Kane seemed busy in the back seat, but Lucy couldn't tell what he was up to.

He started laughing. "Hey, Injun cop, I've got a nice surprise for you. I hear you used to be fond of speedballing and I have a nice concoction rigged up for you."

Lucy's blood ran colder than the Wolf. "No," she said, "please kill me if you have to but let me die clean."

"That would be nice if I gave a shit but we don't want to take the chance of you guys swimming away after the car hits the water. We can handle one with a blow on the head but two would look fishy, if you'll excuse the pun. Then there's that credibility thing. If by some miracle you did escape, they won't believe you if you're back on drugs."

Lucy drew back but there was nowhere to go. Kane was rolling up her sleeve when it happened.

First Lou just saw the shadow moving toward them along the ribbon of highway. It was an eagle swooping down toward them like a prehistoric symbol of vengeance. The eagle flew straight at the truck, as if it were playing chicken. All color left Lou's face. At the last moment he swerved into the snowbank on the side of the road. The new snow was powdery and sprayed all over the windshield, blinding them. The older snow was icy from warm days and cold nights. It quickly brought them to a halt. The syringe fell from Kane's hands to the floor in front of Lucy. She saw it and smashed it with her foot. Lou's face hit the steering wheel hard and cut his lip. After that there was cursing and swearing, and the other car pulled behind them. Lucy tried to open her door but it was blocked by the snowbank. She rolled down the window and crawled out into Reilly's waiting arms. She looked up just in time to see Kathy dashing for the woods. Over to her left she saw Kane raising his gun to shoot. With her free arm she hit his gun hand and the shot fired into the snow. By the time he had raised it again Kathy had disappeared in the trees. He swung and hit Lucy in the ribs and she felt the air rush from her lungs as she doubled over in pain. He turned and hit Vince in the face with his gun.

"She was your responsibility, you idiot!" he yelled. "Now go and get her!"

Lucy's heart stopped when she heard a gunshot in the woods. Then she heard a familiar voice: "Hey, Custer, give it up."

Kane and Reilly looked at each other. "Who are you?" Kane yelled.

"The Menominee Tribal Police, Custer. Put your weapons down."

"I don't believe you, and why are you calling me Custer?"

"'Cuz just like him you underestimated your enemy, and you have five seconds to get the faith and start believing."

Reilly immediately dropped his gun and let go of Lucy. Kane grabbed her and put a gun to her head. "Now," he shouted back into the woods, "you drop your gun and come out here or she dies."

Reilly dived for his dropped gun. Lou, who had been nursing his smashed nose, leapt for his. Just then there was an explosion in the woods. Kane's elbow was shattered, and blood splattered across Lou's face. First the gun fell, still clutched in what was left of Kane's arm. Then Kane collapsed at Lucy's feet. Lucy turned, pushed the leaning Reilly to the ground, and kicked the gun from his reach. Reilly looked up from the ground and she kneed him in the face. Lou, standing by the other car, dropped his own gun and held up his hands.

A honking from the road caught Lucy's attention. A car pulled up and four men poured out. It was Cliff with three friends, each toting a hunting rifle. "Looks like we arrived too late," he said disappointedly. "I wanted to shoot the little weasel."

They trained their guns on what was left of the three men. Then Vince emerged from the woods. Ray Waupuse was behind him, pushing him forward with the barrel of his riffle. Kathy came out last and Lucy ran to her and gave her a hug. When they came back an ambulance and squad cars were pulling up.

Kathy looked at all the commotion with even more bewilderment. She turned to Lucy. "You people in AA—don't you say when your day is going bad that you need a 'do over'?"

"Yes," Lucy said with a smile.

"I think I need a do over. But first how did all this happen?"

"Well, I think Kane had your phone bugged. In any case, he knew I called you and what we were planning. Then Reilly called me and said he had some new information for me. For a change I thought like a cop and called Ray to tell him where I was going. I left my cell phone on so he got to hear Reilly admit to killing Scott. How Cliff—that's Cliff," she said pointing to him as he tipped his camouflage cap, "—got here I haven't a clue."

Cliff was only too happy to provide an answer. "I was over at the school picking up some tools when I saw you pull up.

Then I saw that little prick leading you to your truck with a gun. I followed you and called the police department and they patched me into Ray here. When he figured out where you were, I picked up my friends. We were just getting ready to go hunting but we decided to follow in case you needed help."

"Thanks, Cliff," Lucy said. "You're alright."

"Great," he said turning to Lucy, "does that mean we can have that beer now?"

Lucy was just about to make an excuse when that same rescuing voice she heard earlier said, "She can't. She's having coffee with me. We have to make a report from all of this somehow."

Lucy smiled at Ray. "I have to take Kathy home first. She came here with Kane, but I don't think she wants to go home with him, even if he would be capable of driving."

Ray walked them to the car. "By the way," she asked, "how did you learn to shoot like that?"

"I was a sharpshooter in Desert Storm."

"I never knew that," Lucy said, surprised.

"It's not what I'm about anymore," Ray answered softly.

Lucy thought to herself it was one more among so many other things she liked so much about him.

Kathy decided to go home to her father's. Though the ride home was nearly an hour, Lucy and Kathy talked little. Words just seemed inadequate with what they had been through.

They were exchanging something that was more powerful than words. They both knew this would be a relationship that would continue.

It was some hours later when Lucy and Ray finally met up and even later when Lucy arrived back home. For once she thought she would sleep soundly, dreamlessly, and even well.

Chapter 27

New Year's morning was cold and dark. Lucy woke up early and looked out the window to watch the heavy snow-laden clouds moving slowly across the sky. Then she got up quickly and dressed. It was going to be a busy day and there was a visit she wanted to make before the snow came and before the day really began.

Not many people were on the roads and Lucy made her way quickly but cautiously up Highway 55 to the place near Spirit Rock where Scott had died. She got out of the car and walked over to the tree. Then she stood, puzzled. It was not the right place. Lucy got back in her car and drove again, this time to the graveyard where Scott was buried. She wasn't surprised to see other cars there. Of course Hank and Molly would visit their son on the first day of a new year. Of course all the other Brandts would come too. And of course Kathy was there.

The Brandts looked up as Lucy walked toward them. They nodded hello but did not say anything. Lucy laid her offering of flowers beside those Molly had brought. Then they simply stood silently together over Scott's grave.

After a long time, Hank spoke. "What are your plans for the day?" he asked Lucy.

"Family dinner. And with a friend. And you?"

"Family dinner for us too. A real family dinner. Something we have not enjoyed for a very long time."

"And, Lucy," said Molly, "you know you are always welcome to our house. You gave us Scott back, so you are really a part of our family now too."

There were tears in Lucy's eyes as she thanked Molly. They hugged.

The others hugged Lucy too, and Kathy gave her an extra hard squeeze. "Are you going with the Brandts?" Lucy asked.

"No," said Kathy, "not today. I'm going home to see my father. Brad's coming too." She said this with a quiet, thoughtful smile. Then she left.

Bobbie stayed last. Her face was pale and her eyes were red. She looked at Lucy and smiled weakly. "I guess I'm not as good at recovery as everyone else," she said.

Lucy hugged her. "One day at a time," she said.

Bobbie hugged back, then turned, brushing the tears from her eyes and ran back to join the rest of her family in the car.

The Brandts drove off and Lucy was left alone. She sat beside the grave and closed her eyes. In a moment, she was, once again, with Scott in a car driving up Highway 55 on a colorful fall day. The road dipped and turned, following the contour of the land as well as the Wolf. It was fun to drive, and Lucy knew Scott had enjoyed it.

Then it started to snow. The big wet flakes stuck immediately to the pavement. The flakes were also sticking to the trees. Soon it looked like a winter wonderland. The car slowed down, as if they were there simply to enjoy the sights Scott was going home. It was good to be going home.

Another car pulled up beside the graveyard but Lucy only sensed it vaguely through the haze of her vision. One man got out and another man remained in the car and drove away.

The dream lifted and Lucy was sitting on the ground beside Scott's grave with the Brandts' cheery goodbyes and eagerly repeated invitations to return for family dinner sometime soon echoing in her ears. A shadow passed over her and a noise from the skies made her look up. It was an enormous bird—an eagle—flying directly over her head. She watched as the eagle flapped its majestic wings and glided off into the far distance. She felt strangely lightened. At that moment, a new stage of her own recovery was born.

"Well, Officer Teller," said a voice beside her, "are you ready?"

Lucy looked up at Ray with a smile breaking like the dawn across her face. "Yes," she said. "Yes, I am."

Other Books of Interest
by Robert Bollendorf
From AuthorHouse

Sober Spring

Sober Spring tells the compelling story of the Brandt family's struggle with the tragic uncertainties of alcoholism. The book brings to life the torment of a father's addiction, the pain of a family's recovery, and the healing of a community's deep inner trauma.

Flight of the Loon

This sequel to Robert Bollendorf's Sober Spring chronicles the rebuilding of the wounded Brandt family, and shows how events, even tragic ones, can hasten the family's healing.

Witch of Winter

Witch of Winter, written with Donna Gluck, is the fourth novel in Robert Bollendorf's addiction and recovery series. It con tinues the story of the Brandt family and Officer Lucy Teller. Involved in a harrowing investigation set in deep Wisconsin winter, Lucy learns a great deal about relationships, recovery, and the true meaning of love.

Summer Heat

The Challenger

A Rose by Any Other Name

Family Dynamics of Addictions

Rob Bollendorf Ed.D. CADC, Rob Castillo LCSW, ICAADC, MISSA II

In the following chapters, we will discuss the dynamics of how alcohol and other drugs (AOD) impact the family system. We will also review several assessment tools that will help the counselor or even a family member to assess the addicted family.

First, let's discuss why we refer to the entire system as an "addicted family" if only one member is addicted. This is because even if there is only one person with the illness, it is very rare that other family members have not been impacted by the individual who has been using, often called the identified patient (IP) (Steinglass 1987).

Two examples of this are the family rules and the family roles. In any family, there are usually two different kinds of rules. The first are spoken rules, which include things like times for meals, bedtime, and curfews. There may be spoken rules that include conduct in and out of the home, such as how a child should relate to adults as well as other expectations.

The other kinds of rules are those that are unspoken. As strange as in may seem, even though these are never said out loud, they are often more closely followed. In the alcoholic/dysfunctional situation, there are three basic rules. Author Claudia Black (1982) described these three rules – don't talk, don't trust and don't feel – in her groundbreaking book It Will Never Happen to Me.

The first rule is don't talk about the problem. This is often referred to as the elephant in the room. The metaphor is an obvious one: even though the problem is clear to each person in the family, no one talks about it. Two additional rules in an alcoholic/dysfunctional family include don't trust and don't feel. It is not just the addiction that members in the family don't discuss, it is any meaningful or significant issues. Since members of the family see bizarre things happening and other members of the family act like they don't see it, members begin to question what they see, how they feel and how they should react to those events, especially younger members.

In Sober Spring (Bollendorf, 2016), when Hank shoves Ryan's head in the toilet, but the next day doesn't remember it happening, it leads everyone to wonder "was that a dream?" It seemed so real and so important at the time, but then the next day it doesn't exist. Since no one can talk about it, members of the family have no feedback about their perceptions or feelings. They begin to question what is "normal." They wonder if they can trust what they feel.

Another important characteristic of the alcoholic family is the roles each family member plays. An important aspect of continuing the persistence of any behavior is what each of us does to support that behavior. In addictions, we call that support enabling. Some of these roles may not sound like support initially, but the explanations should make them clear.

Three therapists were instrumental in identifying family roles: Virginia Satir, Sharon Wegscheider-Cruse, and Claudia Black. Virginia Satir (1964) was the first and developed Roles of Communication. Her roles were more flexible and could be played by different family members depending on who they were with and what the situation was. The important thing about these roles is they all blocked communication. Her four roles were as follows: the blamer, the placater, the distractor or irrelevant, and the computer or super reasonable.

The blamer blocks communication by looking for fault, usually in someone else.

In Sober Spring (Bollendorf, 2016), Hank played this role. The blamer usually likes to take the offense in an argument. Physically, they like to point their finger, often all five fingers. They lean forward, and often have a red face and other physical characteristics of being angry or righteously indignant. In The Structure of Magic (1976), Bandler and Grinder later also identified them as being visually oriented and using visual language (i.e. look, see, read, colorful, etc.).

Both Molly and Bobbie were placaters in the family, looking to please others. Physically, they gesture with their palms up, often have slumped shoulders, and a soft voice. Bandler and Grinder identified placaters as kinesthetically oriented, using words like feel, hard, soft, grasp etc.

The reader may wonder why someone who is trying to please is difficult to communicate with. The answer is they share little or nothing of themselves and are only interested in what the other person wants.

Sally, particularly in the first and second books, was a distractor or irrelevant. Both terms do a good job of describing this behavior. The distractor plays the role of changing the subject when what is being discussed is uncomfortable. They also usually change it to an irrelevant topic. The person playing this role is not only all over the place in conversation, but also physically. Rarely does their posture line up. Hands and arms move in all directions while their upper body does not line up in a straight line with their legs. Their speech may change from visual to kinesthetic, or to auditory (i.e. hear, sound, loud, song, etc.).

Paul probably is the best example of the computer or super reasonable. Physically the person playing this role is still from the neck down. They use little or no hand movements or gestures. They not aware of their feelings, and have no desire to be aware of them. They are most comfortable when conversations are intellectual. They use big words, and not necessarily correctly. Think of the professor who uses old yellow notes and reads directly from the page, in a monotone voice.

While Virginia Satir spoke of roles of communication in her book Peoplemaking (1964), it is possible to play different roles – for example, one role with your boss (perhaps placater) and another with your wife (like blamer), while the family roles that Sharon Wegscheider-Cruse describes in the book Another Chance (1989) are often more consistent. For instance, the person who is the scapegoat in the family will also play that role at school. Her roles consist of the alcoholic, the hero, the scapegoat, the lost child, and the mascot. The alcoholic is the one who has a problem with a substance or process. The other roles enable this person to continue their addiction. Each of these roles take a large toll on the person playing the role both in terms of severely limiting their personality as well as taking an emotional toll.

The hero enables the alcoholic to deny he has a problem because he can point to the hero and ask "how can I have a problem when I've raised a kid like that?" The hero puts tremendous pressure on himself to succeed at everything he does. Often, it is not just to succeed, but to be the best. It doesn't matter whether it is academics, sports, music, or theater, the hero must not only be good, but be the star.

The scapegoat is the exact opposite of the hero. The alcoholic points to the scapegoat and says "If you had a kid like that, you would drink, too." The scapegoat gives up their life and even their freedom playing their role. It is their fate not only to fail, but do it to the point that causes them problems.

The mascot enables by reducing stress, usually with humor. Frequently, the class clown will often be the mascot from an alcoholic family or the person you work with who cracks a joke and gets everyone laughing during stressful times. The mascot has a hard time even taking himself seriously.

The last role is that of the lost child. The lost child reduces stress by disappearing. This child played by Paul, especially in the first book, is someone who has an uncanny ability not to be noticed. If you are a classroom teacher and at the end of the day you wonder if a particular student was in class today, there is a good chance that child plays the role of lost child in their family. This is particularly true in stressful situations. The danger for the lost child is an inability to interact socially. They tend to be quiet and shy. They do not learn to assert themselves or ask for what they need.

One of the most satisfying things for us as writers – and we hope for you as readers – is watching Paul break out of the lost child role in Flight of the Loon and subsequent books, as did Hank, Molly, Ryan, Bobbie, Sally, and even Scott in Autumn Snow (2017).

Finally, Claudia Black developed roles in her book It Will Never Happen to Me (1982). She also talked about the hero, the scapegoat, the lost child and the mascot, but she added strengths and deficits for each role. She also added the people pleaser or placater, which Bobbie fit best in during the beginning of the Sober Spring. We see evidence of her breaking out of her role already in the first book.

Another issue in the alcoholic family is what Virginia Satir referred to as pot. Pot is similar in many respects to self-esteem, but Satir's problem with self-esteem is that people tend to think of it as a constant. One's self-esteem is either high or low and doesn't change much, but Satir believed while there usually wouldn't be huge swings, pot could change daily. High pot would mean someone felt all filled up and could offer much to the world, like a cooking pot that could feed several people. Low pot, on the other hand, meant the person felt empty and needed to be filled herself. Often in an alcoholic family, most members, even the hero, feel low pot.

Another assessment tool has to do with links to society. This can be thought of in two different ways. One way we may think of this is the face the family presents to the world around them. Is the face genuine and similar to what you might see if you were a mouse in their house, or is the face a mask? Does the smile hide the frown that is the real true picture of the family? Or does the pleasant look hide the anger and resentment that seethes underneath the surface?

Another way of looking at this is asking who are the other people and systems that the family relates to outside of themselves. There may be some systems that the entire family connects with, such as church, family counseling, or extended family. On the other hand, there may be systems that only individuals relate to, such as school for the children, or work for the adults in the family.

There also maybe a variety of relationships with these systems. The relationship may be weak, such as the family that attends church on Sunday but has no other contact with the church or its members. Or it may be strong, where the family members are part of smaller systems within the church, such as teens in teen club, parents in men's and women's clubs, or bible study. Perhaps a number of their friendships are with church members. If we were to represent this, we would start with a large circle, and a simple genogram of the family on the inside of the circle lines would connect family and members to the various outside systems, and these lines would vary depending on the relationship. A line with dashes would indicate a weak relationship, and a double line would indicate a very strong relationship. Arrows going both ways next to the line indicate the involvement with the system.

For instance, if the arrows only go out, it is an indication that the family member puts a lot of effort into the system but gets little in return (think of a father who works very hard at his job but is regularly passed over for promotions and raises). On the other hand, if the arrows go in but not out, it may mean that the family member puts little in but get much out.

This may be a child who does little in school but gets good grades anyway (see diagram for examples).

Another important assessment tool is the genogram developed by systems theory (McGoldrick & Gerson, 1987). In the genogram, we can chart not only what the relationships are with both nuclear and extended families, but also the history of the family. We can learn about parents and grandparents, aunts, uncles, and cousins. We can learn about divorces and remarriage, step-siblings.

Diagraming all of this (see diagram) makes all of this information manageable and often highlights issues the counselor may wish to explore in future sessions. The genograms can also highlight diseases that run in the family as well as disorders, such as depression – which we know has a genetic link.

There are specific abbreviations for these issues (see diagram), or the counselor can develop his own. Again we often see a pattern for things like eating disorders and addictions in the genogram. For instance. in eating disorders, we often find other out-of-control issues in the family history such as gambling, eating or addiction. Often in addicted families, we will find a history of accidents as well as repressed grief issues.

We can sometimes notice illnesses such as cirrhosis and pancreatitis that may indicate an undiagnosed addiction in relatives who may have died before addiction was readily recognized. In short, the completed genogram is a storehouse of useful information for assessment and treatment. See the diagrams for a simple genogram, or a much more complicated thorough approach provided by Genpro.

Still another assessment tool is the structural map, which is a piece of what Salvador Minuchin does in Structural Family Therapy (1974). This tool is utilized by systems, structural, and strategic family therapies, to name just a few. In a family one, of the most important skills is establishing and maintaining boundaries. Though the genogram requires skill in asking questions about history, structural requires the counselor to be skilled in assessing relationships within the family.

The first important boundary is the family boundary. In describing this boundary, we can illustrate something that is true of all the boundaries we will talk about, and that is a boundary is different than a line in the sand that no one is allowed to cross. The skill in establishing boundaries is clear rules about when they can be penetrated, when they can't and by whom.

To establish these rules. we must first know the kind of system with which we are dealing. For example, the boundaries for Grand Central Station will be much more flexible than the Pentagon. In the case of families, there is a lot of flexibility with the external boundary, however, an external boundary that allows too many people in and out or too much information in and out becomes chaotic, while a family that allows too few people and information in and out becomes rigid. We can see these examples in nature. A sponge is an example of an open system, while a rock is an example of a closed system.

A family also has what we call subsystem boundaries. We often refer to these as the grandparent subsystem, the sibling subsystem and finally the most important, because it is the hub of the family, is referred to as the parental subsystem, marital subsystem, or executive subsystem. The grandparent subsystem houses the parents and or step-parents of both the husband and wife.

Like the family boundary, it is important that appropriate boundaries are established, and there is no easy answer for what is appropriate. There are definite unfortunate circumstances when a grown or even growing son or daughter may need to sever all ties with their parents and other circumstances when that relationship may need to be closer than ideal. For instance, when, due to financial emergencies, a couple may need to move back in with one of their parents. There are also cultures when this relationship is closer than it might be in others. It is important for the counselor to know these factors before intervening in the boundaries or lack of them. There are few examples in military history where an army has fought a two-front war and has been successful, and yet a married couple with children and parents must do this every day.

The third type of boundary focuses on the relationships between family members. The first type is called an engaged relationship. In Gestalt Therapy (Pearls 1969), one of the ways of describing a functional relationship is when two people are able to make contact with each other and also to withdraw from that contact. Non-verbally, one might consider a simple handshake as an example. Verbally, when one person moves toward another by asking "How are you today?" and the other person responds

"I'm fine. How are you?" as they walk down a hallway and then continue on their way. Both are examples of making contact and withdrawing from that contact in the most basic way.

In a family relationship, we do this over and over again and on a variety of verbal and non-verbal levels. Engaging in sexual relations, for instance, goes way beyond the handshake non-verbally, and a serious discussion about where the relationship is headed in a dating couple goes way beyond the "How are you?" in the hall.

Another type of relationship is the disengaged relationship. This happens when two people are unable or choose not to make contact with one another. One may say "How are you?" in an effort to make contact, but the other responds, "None of your business. Get out of my face." If this continues, the one attempting to make contact gives up and no further effort is made by either party to make contact.

A third type of relationship is the over-engaged relationship. In this case the individuals lack individuality. This is also referred to in the field as an enmeshed relationship. These are two people who are unable to withdraw from the relationship. Many times, it is as if they operate with one nervous system. A mother my say to a son, "It's cold – don't you want a sweater?" and the son will respond "Do I need one?" In other words, you must tell me if I'm cold or not because as Sal Minuchin would say to some of his clients, "You see, she's got your nervous system."

Still another form of over-engaged relationships is the alliance. Just as is true with countries, individuals form alliances to protect themselves from another relationship they find threatening, or as a way to affirm herself. Following an argument with her husband in which he refers to her as "crazy," a mother may turn to her daughter and ask, "You don't think I'm crazy, do you?" In doing so, the mother is also saying, "Take my side, not dad's." Again, a diagram of these relationships makes it easier for the counselor to keep all this straight. (See diagrams).

Finally, from Strategic Family therapy comes the symptom-maintaining sequence. In laymen's terms, this may be thought of as a vicious cycle. This may be a series of behaviors that repeats itself daily, weekly, or even yearly. We all may have had times in our lives when we have asked ourselves, "How did I end up here again when I swore I wouldn't be back in this position?"

Assignment

In these diagrams, we have included an example of an abusive relationship. See if you can understand how this might occur with an alcoholic relationship.

Appendixes

APPENDIX A

Family roles as described by Claudia Black (2001) in "*It Will Never Happen to Me: Growing Up with Addiction as Youngsters, Adolescents, Adults*" (2nd edition, revised).

FAMILY HERO + RESPONSIBLE ONE		PLACATER + PEOPLE PLEASER {often referred to as the "co-dependent" or chief enabler}	
STRENGTHS	*DEFICITS*	*STRENGTHS*	*DEFICITS*
Successful	Perfectionist	Caring/ compassionate	Inability to receive
Organized	Difficulty listening	Empathic	Denies personal needs
Leadership skills	Inability to follow	Good listener	High tolerance for inappropriate behavior
Decisive	Inability to relax	Sensitive to others	Strong fear of anger or conflict
Initiator	Lack of spontaneity	Gives well	False guilt
Self-disciplined	Inflexible	Nice smile	Anxious
Goal-oriented	Unwilling to ask for help		Highly fearful
	High fear of mistakes		Hypervigilant
	Inability to play		
	Severe need to be in control		

SCAPEGOAT + ACTING OUT ONE		LOST CHILD + ADJUSTER	
STRENGTHS	*DEFICITS*	*STRENGTHS*	*DEFICITS*
Creative	Inappropriate expression of anger	Independent	Unable to initiate
Less denial, greater honesty	Inability to follow direction	Flexible	Withdraws
Sense of humor	Self-destructive	Ability to follow	Fearful of making decisions
Close to own feelings	Intrusive	Easygoing attitude	Lack of direction
Ability to lead (*just leads in wrong direction*)	Irresponsible	Quiet	Ignored, forgotten
	Social problems at young ages (i.e.) truancy, teenage pregnancy, high school dropout, addiction		Follows without questioning
	Underachiever		Difficulty perceiving choices and options
	Defiant/rebel		
		MASCOT	
		STRENGTHS	*DEFICITS*
		Sense of humor	Attention seeker
		Flexible	Distracting
		Able to relieve stress and pain	Immature
			Difficulty focusing
			Poor decision making ability

Links To Society

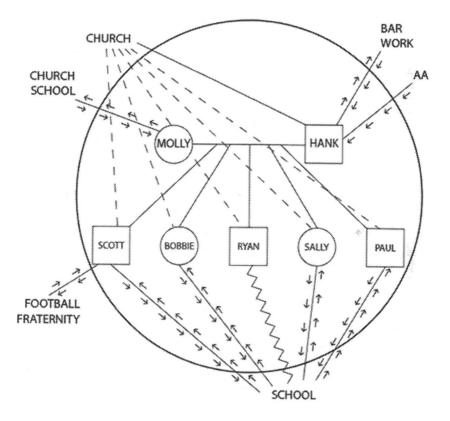

Structural Map

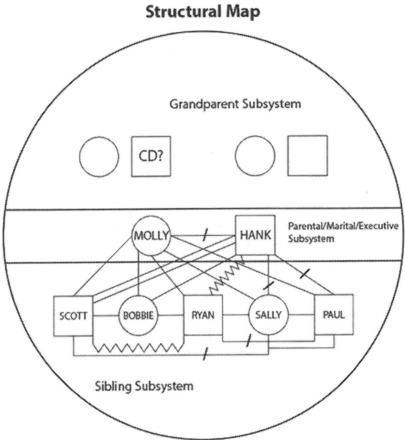

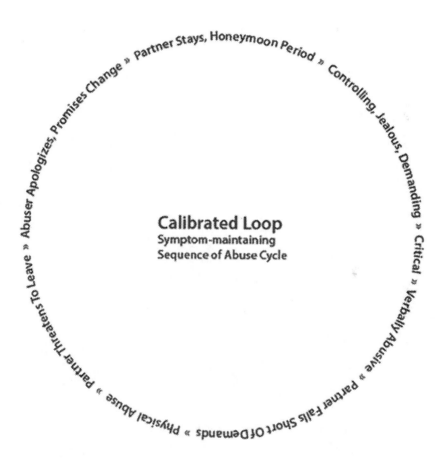

Calibrated Loop
Symptom-maintaining
Sequence of Abuse Cycle

Partner Stays, Honeymoon Period » Controlling, Jealous, Demanding » Critical » Verbally Abusive » Partner Falls Short Of Demands » Physical Abuse » Partner Threatens To Leave » Abuser Apologizes, Promises Change »

Simple Genogram

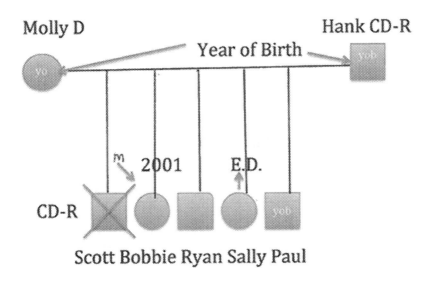

Molly D   Hank CD-R

Year of Birth

2001   E.D.

CD-R

Scott Bobbie Ryan Sally Paul

Legend:
CD-R= Chemical Dependence Recovering
M. =Murder
D= Depression
E.D.= Eating Disorders

Legend Cont.

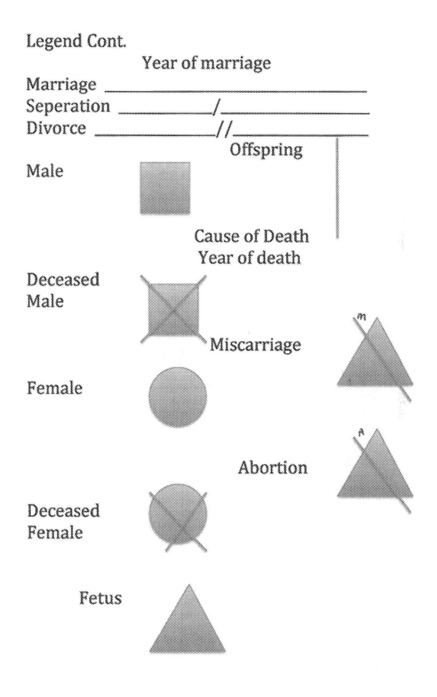

Year of marriage

Marriage _____

Seperation _____/_____

Divorce _____//_____

Offspring

Male

Cause of Death
Year of death

Deceased
Male

Miscarriage

Female

Abortion

Deceased
Female

Fetus

Bibliography

Steinglass, Peter (1987-1212-20) "The Alcoholic Family" – Amazon.co http://www.amazon.com/Alcoholic-Family-Peter-Steinglass-1987-12.../ BO1FIZDY18.

Black, Claudia. "It Will Never Happen to Me" – Official Site www. amazon.com/books

Satir, Virginia. Peoplemaking. (1971) Science and Behavior Books

Grinder, John and Bandler, Richard. The Structure of Magic II: A Book About Communication and Change. Amazon.com: Books

Goldenberg & Goldenberg Family Therapy: An overview (2017) Cengage Learning

Wegscheider-Cruse, Sharon. Another Chance: Hope and Health for the Alcoholic Family. (1989) Amazon.com

McGoldrick & Gerson. Genograms in Family Assessment (1987). Amazon.com

Minuchin, Salvador. Structural Family Therapy (1974) Harvard University Press

Pearls, Fredrich. Gestalt Therapy Verbatim (1969). ISBN 0-553-20253-7

Haley, Jay. Learning and Teaching Therapy (1969). Guilford Press

Eating Disorders

In the second book, Flight of the Loon, Sally suffers from an eating disorder – an unhealthy relationship with food – and she is not alone in our culture. Some 50 percent of teenage girls and 33 percent of teenage boys admit to unhealthy methods of controlling their weight, including smoking, vomiting, and laxatives. Anorexia, from which Sally suffers, is 12 times higher than any other cause of death for preteens. Three-quarters of women in college diet to maintain or lose weight (Jacobovits et al, 1987).

Recall a statement made earlier in this article regarding addicted families often suffering from other out-of-control issues; eating disorders may be one such issue an addicted family experiences. Another possibility, as in Sally's case, is that Hank's drinking and early involvement with AA may have left her starving for a relationship with her father, a concept explored in Margo Maine's book Father Hunger: Fathers, Daughters, and the Pursuit of Thinness (2004).

The DSM lists three different types of disorders: anorexia, bulimia and binge eating. With anorexia, a person uses abstention from food as a means of controlling weight. In all eating disorders, there is usually a distortion of body image, but this is perhaps most obvious in anorexia. It is not unusual for the anorexic to look like a concentration camp victim, where every bone in their body is visible and yet they still see themselves as fat.

Bulimia is another disorder listed in the DSM. This usually is a part of a binge-purge cycle in which a person consumes large quantities of food, particularly carbohydrates, and then uses some method of purging the food such as vomiting, laxatives or exercise. There may be a number of reasons for this. It may be that the bulimic does not have the willpower to be anorexic, or in Sally's case, when she was forced to eat by her parents, she would use vomiting as a substitute for not eating.

Another term often used in eating disorders is bulimarexia, in which a person will starve themselves for as long as they can, but when they give into eating, they overeat, feel guilty and then purge. Bulimics may not be underweight, but it is still a very dangerous disorder because the combination of binging and purging often leads to an electrolyte imbalance. One of the many functions of electrolytes in the body is to keep the heart in rhythm, and if they are out of balance, the heart may stop beating. If vomiting is involved as a method of purging, the counselor can sometimes recognize the problem if the enamel is missing from the teeth, and frequently, the teeth are discolored, due to the repeated corrosive nature of stomach acid.

A third type of eating disorder is binge eating. Like bulimia, binge eating involves binging but without the purge cycle. In each case, food is used as a way of dealing with a character flaw. In anorexia, it is often an obsession with being perfect. Sometimes the anorexic is so afraid of disappointing her parents that she uses not eating (often seen as a good thing in adolescence) as her only way of rebelling. Anorexics are often good students, with no disciplinary problems. They may excel in sports or clubs, and cause little or no problems at home.

Bulimics may often use food as a substitute for something missing in their lives, most commonly relationships. Some speculate that females use food to make up for an absent relationship with their fathers. (Father Hunger, Margo Maine)

In binge eating, we may find the same problem with using food to fill holes of some kind or another. However, it may be true that the binge eater may just use food for comfort from a variety of painful experiences. This may be a way of dealing with experiences such as hurt, depression, anger, or disappointment, among others. It is unfair, however, to speak of eating disorders as just a problem with the individual without mentioning the culture as a whole.

There is tremendous pressure from the media and advertising to have the perfect body, yet these same people push food and drink as a way of finding happiness. Lack of exercise and sedentary lifestyles also contribute to the problem. One example: roughly half of all trips by car in the U.S. are three miles or less.

A number of years ago, a poster reminded us that there a five supermodels in the world, and the rest of us are stuck with the bodies we have. No matter how much we diet and exercise, there are things about our bodies we have to accept: you can't make your legs longer, wide hips are a natural part of bone structure, and as we age, we get age spots and looser skin. Gaining weight is as difficult for some as losing it is for others. Yet countless ads continually tell us that if we use a certain product, we can be thinner, more muscular, younger looking, healthier, etc. In many cases, the greatest benefit of these products is the financial benefit to those who sell them.

Another important factor in Sally's case, as with many eating disorders, is that they can be triggered by a comment, particularly from someone loved or respected, but because of the age when eating disorders often start, peers also can have a huge impact. In Sally's case, Roper's comment triggered her eating disorders. Therefore, it is imperative that we educate parents, teachers, counselors and anyone working with young people to be sensitive even to joking comments. We need to be aware that even if the young person is the one commenting, we must not reinforce these statements or think that because they say it, we now have permission to make the same comment.

The treatment of eating disorders is almost as vast as the number of approaches in psychotherapy; therefore, we will limit ourselves to some broad treatments. Since eating disorders often appear in families with other out-of-control issues, as was the case with Sally, family therapy can be a good intervention.

In pointing out the problems of other family members, it can help the eating-disordered client feel less the focus of attention and allow her more room to respond to her problems. If she sees other family members getting better, it may also provide models for a healthier life. She may also be the family scapegoat, and escaping from that role can be useful for her. Body tracing can also help her to recognize the discrepancy between her body image and how she really looks. Cognitive approaches can help her to recognize faulty messages she is telling herself, such as all food makes me fat, by replacing that with "I need a healthy diet to look and feel healthy, to have energy, to think and respond clearly to life situations."

Because her peers can play such an important role in her perceptions of herself and others, group therapy can also be beneficial. Finally, helping with food shopping, meal planning and cooking may help her feel as though she has more control over what she puts into her body.

Classroom assignment: Body tracing: Using butcher block paper and a black felt-tip pen, have one person lie down on the paper and another trace the outline of their body. After finishing, ask the person to get up and look at the outline. Make sure that all of the comments about the outline are from the person themselves. Other students are required only to be encouraging and supportive.

Bibliography

Maine, Margo, "Father Hunger: Fathers, Daughters and the Pursuit of Thinness" (2004) 2nd Addition Gürze Books

Yates, Alayne, Compulsive Exercise and the Eating Disorders: Toward an Integrated Theory of Activity (1991) Brunner/Mazel

Anderson, A.E., "Anorexia nervosa and bulimia in adolescent males" (1984) PedAnnals13:901-907

Beck, A.T., Rush, A.J., Shaw, B.F., and Emery, G., Cognitive Therapy of Depression (1979) New York: Guilford Press

Bell, R., Holy Anorexia (1985) Chicago: Chicago University Press

Bruch, H., Eating Disorders: Obesity and Anorexia Nervosa, and the Person Within (1973) New York: Basic Books

Dally, P., Anorexia Nervosa (1969). London: Heinemann

Garner, D.M., "Cognitive therapy for Bulimia Nervosa." (1985) Annals of Adol. Psychiat.,

13:358-390.

Pyle, R.L., Mitchell, J.E., "Bulimia: A report of 34 Cases." (1981).J. Clin. Psychiat., 42:60-64

The Witch of Winter

Chapter 1

Lisa

It was the middle of February, Lucy Teller wondered at first if she was dreaming when she saw the girl kneeling by a tree in the middle of a foot of new snow. Lucy had been lost in thought as her squad car drove itself along Highway 55. She should have been paying more attention since there had been a major snowstorm the night before, and the roads were still white with snow. It was one of those surprising snowfalls that started gentle and turned into a major snow event. The kind Lucy liked to walk in after dark. The temperature was in the mid twenties, and there was no wind. She expected, when it started, that it would snow an inch or two. It was beginning to taper off, but not before it had dropped nearly a foot on top of the several inches that already existed on the ground.

Lucy, still the new kid in the department, was working the day shift on a Sunday for the Menominee Tribal Police. It was early morning just past dawn, which meant because it was still snowing that the headlights didn't work quite as well. She had just driven past Spirit Rock. The Rock was back in the woods and covered by a blanket of fresh snow.

Lucy wondered about the legend of the Rock. It was said that a group of hunters approached the God, Nanabush, to ask for improved hunting skills. Nanabush was impressed with their courage at approaching him, since he wasn't known for his kindness toward humans, and granted them their wish. Then one of the group members pressed his luck even further and had the audacity to ask for eternal life. This angered Nanabush, and he

165

had turned the man into a rock and pushed him into the ground, saying, "Now you have eternal life."

It is believed among the Menominees that if the rock ever crumbles, the tribe will cease to exist. Lucy wondered if the rock still had the spirit and feeling of a man, and if so, whether he liked the new snow that covered him, giving extra protection from the subzero temperatures that always followed a heavy snow in northern Wisconsin. She was glad, too, that the legend didn't include the rock being covered as leading to the demise of the tribe since that happened every winter for as long as she could remember. She thought though that winter was certainly a good description of the current state of the tribe: It was covered and surrounded by white.

It was estimated that the Menominee tribe had been in existence for ten thousand years, and they originally considered nearly 10 million acres as their land. Since 1634, when the Menominee meet Jean Nicolet, the first white man to visit them, their land had shrunk to 234,000 acres. If it weren't for Chief Oshkosh refusing to move, they would be in Minnesota somewhere, and blended with other tribes.

As it was, they had lost much of their history due to their children attending mission schools and the elders being discouraged from passing on tribal history and tradition to their young. Still, the Menominee has preserved the land in their charge. Ninety-five percent still produces hardwood, pine, and hemlock trees, and Lucy was lost in their beauty as she drove though the large trees in their winter slumber, covered with a fresh coat of white. She was traveling next to the twenty-four miles of Wolf River that still ran through Menominee land, but their brother, the sturgeon, was no longer able to visit Keshena Falls in the spring to spawn, due to the dams that had been built upstream.

Still, it was impossible for Lucy to think what her life might be like had none of that had taken place. Change had come, and the Menominee had to adjust but hopefully keep their culture alive as well. She was near the tree where Scott Brandt had been killed by two men now in jail and hopefully would stay there a long time. She wondered again why she had gotten so caught up in helping a white man she had thought she had never met.

That's when she saw the tiny figure kneeling by the tree that Scott had hit. Because of the deep snow, she couldn't pull her squad car completely off the road. Though she was concerned about startling the girl, she had to turn on her dome lights. The girl immediately turned, looked at the car, and began to run into the woods.

Lucy was able to get a glimpse of the girl as she turned and saw the squad car. Lucy's mind raced. "Lisa" She called to the girl. "Lisa, it's Officer Teller." Lisa had been the girl who had provided a major break in Scott's case and it had started right here at this tree. "You're in no danger or trouble." Lucy saw a tiny Witch of Winter face emerge from behind a tree surrounded by snowflakes. A long breath escaped Lucy's body without her being aware. "Come out. It's OK, Lisa. I just want to talk with you."

Lisa walked slowly from the tree, watching Lucy carefully. As the girl approached, Lucy she stretched out her arms to give Lisa a hug, and the girl backpedaled. Lucy slowly put her arms by her side and made a mental note. Lisa stopped backing away but kept the same distance. Lucy tried a safe smile, showing no teeth.

"What are you doing out on such a snowy morning, Lisa?"

"I came here to ask Scott to help me find my brother."

Now it was Lucy's turn to take a step back. A million questions flooded her mind. She knew from the thin lips, small stature, and withered arm that Lisa had Fetal Alcohol Syndrome, a condition she thanked God daily that her own children were miraculously spared. It was hard to tell how developmentally delayed Lisa was or even how old. Her small stature made her look younger than she probably was. If Lucy had to guess, she'd say ten, but she was sure that mentally and emotionally she was younger. Lucy had to sort out her questions and ask them one at a time, taking care not to overwhelm Lisa.

"I didn't know you had a brother," Lucy said, trying to sound cheerful. "How old is he?"

"Don't know. He hasn't had a birthday yet."

That took care of Lucy's next question. She didn't have to bother asking whether he had just wandered off somewhere. "How were you hoping Scott could help you?"

"I'm not sure, but I know he's the only one that ever has been able to help me. I guess he did it by bringing you. Did he bring you?"

That question made Lucy wonder. Perhaps that was the magical thinking of a little girl, or maybe she was making a connection neither of them fully understood.

"When is the last time you saw your brother?"

"Last night I woke up and saw a witch pick him up and swallow him whole, though a hole in the back of his neck."

This time, Lucy not only stepped back, but she was sure she blinked once or twice also. She didn't even know what to ask next. It's not like she hadn't heard of witches since she was a little girl. Witches were alive and well on the rez, at least as far as rumors were concerned. But they were more likely to be talked about by the elders, the people Lucy referred to as aunt and uncle, even though there was often no blood relation. Lucy was not as likely to hear it from younger people, especially ones that interact regularly with white people. So much of their tradition continued to be lost.

"Besides the fact that he swallowed your brother whole through a hole in the back of his neck, is there another reason you thought he was a witch?"

"Yes, he had square feet, a third eye in the middle of his forehead, and he had a painted face. Then he told me when he saw I was awake that he'd make my mother and me sick if I woke my mother or called the police. He must have put a spell on my mother because I can't wake her up. He was also big and strong but looked to be about a hundred years old."

"Did your brother cry when this man picked him up?"

"No, my brother doesn't cry much. He mostly just lies in his crib. When I try to pick him up or play with him, Mama tells me to let him alone, because he's happiest when he's by himself."

"What season was it when your mother had the baby?"

"It was early spring. I know, because the days were getting longer, more light was out, and the snow was almost gone, but there weren't any leaves on the trees yet."

Molly thought the baby would be about nine months old, too old to be just lying in his crib. Maybe that was just the mother's way of not letting Lisa pick him up. Lucy head was spinning. There were so many questions. "What did you do after the man left?"

"I tried to wake my mother, but I couldn't. She's been taking more of her cooking medicine lately, and it's hard to wake her, but I'm sure the witch did something. Then I went to the window to see where the man had gone, but it was snowing so hard I couldn't see. I went back to bed and talked with Scott. I asked him to help me. At school, he liked it when I brought him flowers, so I tried to gather some to bring him, but mostly all I found was sticks."

"What is your mother doing now?"

"She's still sleeping. I couldn't wake her."

"How about if we both go over and give it a try?"

Lisa looked hesitant. She stood frozen in place.

"Scott sent me to help you, Lisa. Please let me help." Lucy said the magic word. Though Lisa still looked hesitant, Lucy could see her softening.

"O.K.," she said, then a soft smile of relief spread over her face.

Lucy wondered about the power Scott must have had to make such an impression on these kids in such a short time. She felt a wave of sadness flood over her that such a force was removed so prematurely from the world. She would always remember the look of despair and defeat in Scott's father's eyes at the loss of his son's powerful life.

Lucy and Lisa got into Lucy's squad car and drove a short way down Bear Trap Falls Road, which intersected Fifty-five near where the accident took place.

When they entered the house, Lucy felt a shiver run down her spine. It was like re-entering her own life from the past. The house was small like most houses on the rez, and once inside, she could see everything but the two bedrooms, which were down a short hallway. Lisa's mother was lying on the couch. One arm dangled down to the floor, and Lucy could immediately see the tracks of regular intravenous heroin injections. There were old scars running the length of her left arm. Because the mom's skin was dark, the scars were a lighter color.

Scattered randomly in her track marks were fresh-scabbed injection sites. It reminded Lucy of the white lines down the middle of a road. Mainlining drugs was like taking the road to self-destruction. Loved ones are cast aside, so many can be destroyed along the way. It was like car wrecks piled up along the side of the highway. As she approached the woman, Lucy could tell she was barely breathing, and when she took her pulse, it was faint and slow. She looked at a face that reminded her of looking in the mirror five years ago. It was a mixture of old and young. There were few wrinkles, which gave the impression of a young face, but the puffiness and lack of care made her look old beyond her years.

Lucy immediately reached for the radio attached to her belt. "Send an ambulance immediately to Bear Trap Falls Road. Tell the paramedics to bring a dose of Narcan. We will also need a crime scene investigation. There is a little boy approximately 9 months old missing and possibly abducted. I don't know the address, but it is just off 55. I'll turn on my lights in front of the house."

Lucy ran out to her squad andher dome lights still operating. When she turned around, Lisa, whom she had almost forgotten about, was right behind her looking panicked. Lisa was pale.

"What's the matter with my mommy, and what are you doing?"

Lucy started to reach for her and then remembered the reaction the last time she tried that. She also remembered how Lisa referred to the heroin. "Your mommy has taken too much of her medicine, and that's why you can't wake her up. I called some people to give her an antidote that will make her feel better."

"What's an auntie-dote, and will they take me away from her?" Lisa's eyes were as big as saucers.

"It's another kind of medicine that will make her feel better real fast. You'll see. They may have to take your mother to a hospital for a while, but you can stay with me and my kids while she gets better." Lucy could see that her words were making no impact on Lisa, he could see her mind drift somewhere else, somewhere safe. Lucy knew in Lisa's world, perhaps the only safe place she had ever found had been taken from her, and she hoped somehow Lisa could find a piece of Scott to which she could cling. He had become a safety net for Lisa, and she missed him terribly.

With the falling snow, the ambulance was slow to arrive, but once there, the paramedics quickly assessed the situation and gave Lisa's mother an injection of Narcan. Within seconds, her eyes opened, and she was able to speak. Her first question was, "Where's Lisa?" as her eyes darted around the room.

Lucy was amazed about two things. First was how quickly the Narcan worked, and second, that the mother didn't say, "Where are my children?" Just, "Where's Lisa?"

When the paramedics gave the drug to Lisa's mother, her reaction seemed miraculous to Lucy, though she had seen it before. Lisa's eyes opened wide, and for the first time since losing her brother, Lisa saw something to give her hope, and maybe believe in someone again. What Lucy said would happen did happen. She did not understand why this police lady was telling her the truth. That didn't often occur in Lisa's world.

Lucy began to question Lisa's mother and found out that her name was Dawn. She had awakened after Lisa had gone, to find both of her children missing in the midst of a snowstorm. Faced again with her failure as a mother, she took a larger than normal hit of heroin. She told Lucy that was the first time that she had noticed her son was missing. Though the heroin was not able to affect Dawn's nervous system right now, years of abuse still affected her brain. Lucy realized she would get very little relevant information from Dawn at present.

Lucy changed tactics and began to try to convince her to go to treatment. Dawn's first question was, "What will happen to my children?"

Lucy said, "Lisa could stay with me, and at the moment, your son is missing." This seemed to hit Dawn for the first time, but all that registered on her face was a confused look. Dawn was not convinced she needed treatment. Lucy looked her in the eye. "You and I are both addicts. Like you, I also have children. At one point, mine were taken from me. You've already lost one child, because you were too stoned to even hear an intruder enter your house. The police are not going to believe your daughter's story, and right now, you will be the number one suspect in the disappearance of your son. If you don't want help for yourself, damn it, do it for your children." Reluctantly, Dawn finally agreed, and the paramedics took her to the treatment center, Maehnowesekiyah, just outside Keshena.

Lucy decided she and Lisa would just be in the way of the investigators that arrived right after the ambulance left. She answered their questions and asked if she could be of any help. They suggested the most helpful thing would be to remove Lisa from the home. They had asked Lisa the same questions that Lucy had with the same results. Lucy left with Lisa the same way that Lisa said the intruder had left, but the snow had covered any tracks that might have remained. Lisa did not see which way the car had gone, nor was she even sure there was a car. Lucy drove home slowly and dropped Lisa off with her mother and children.

Lucy's mother said little when she brought the child in, but Lucy saw the look. She turned to her children and said, "We have to be nice to Lisa. Her mother is in the hospital, and her little brother is missing."

Then she turned to her mother and noticed that the expression on her face had changed. "I talked her mother into going to Maehnowesekiyah. I hope it helps her as much as it did me. I'll be home as soon as my shift is over to help you with dinner. Lisa can sleep in my room. I'll sleep on the couch. I sleep better there anyway."

Just for a moment, Lisa thought she saw a smile and a look of pride on her mother's face, but she dismissed it in her mind as fast as the smile came and went.

Lucy noticed that Lisa looked uncomfortable as she was leaving to return to the squad car, but Lucy's daughter took Lisa by the hand. "I still have some dolls in my room that I've been saving. Maybe we could dress them up." Lisa smiled. Now it was Lucy's turn to feel proud.

At dinner that night, Lucy noticed the dynamics around the dinner table had changed. Usually the kids fought, and Lucy and her mother would take turns refereeing and trying to change the subject to something more positive. However, that night, everyone seemed on thier best behavior. The kids asked Lisa questions about her school and told her about theirs. Lisa, for her part, seemed to focus at times and then other times seemed to drift away, perhaps to her mother or brother or maybe to Scott. She was missing them all. Her little heart felt like it would burst.

Chapter 2

Karen Fish

The next day, Lucy drove Lisa to school. She tried to engage Lisa in a conversation about school, but Lisa got that far-away look and said little. After dropping her off, Lucy drove to the tribal office of Family Services to speak to Karen Fish. The very thought of Karen had once brought terror and hatred to Lucy. She was the same woman who had taken Lucy's children from her. She was a powerful woman even without the authority of her position. Physically, she looked like many Menominee women. She wore her dark hair long and straight. She was about 5 feet 6 or 8 inches tall. Her legs and hips were slender, but her upper body was large in comparison. She had large breasts and a stomach that stuck out nearly as far as her breasts. She had broad shoulders and long arms.

Her face could look determined and firm, or compassionate and kind, depending on whether she was talking to a child, a judge, or an abusive or neglectful parent. She was a woman whose strong convictions and values were evident in every fiber of her being. She didn't sway from them, nor could anyone in her charge. If you were against her and her values, you had a formidable opponent. If you worked with her, and she knew you loved your children, then you had a powerful advocate who would speak to anyone on your behalf.

Karen Fish was a passionate woman. Lucy still shook with anticipation every time she went through the door of Karen's office. When Karen turned to her with her piercing eyes, Lucy felt as if every sin she had committed was revealed on her face. Still, Karen smiled warmly and inquired, "How's my favorite police officer doing?"

Lucy managed to stutter out that she and her family were doing well. "I'm here to ask you if you ever had occasion to work with Dawn Lake and her daughter, Lisa. They live over on Bear Trap Falls Road. She also has a son."

Lucy panicked. She hated not having her ducks in a row when she talked to Karen. She couldn't remember whether she never gotten the boy's name or just couldn't remember it. When she looked at Karen with embarrassment, she realized it didn't matter, because Karen was already someplace else.

"Michael," she said with a sad look on her face. "I was this close last week from taking those children from her. Now you're going to tell me that something has happened to them, and I will have to add them to the list of things that will haunt me in my old age. That's why I can never retire."

Lucy was shocked. She realized for the first time that as hard as Karen could be on others for their mistakes, it was nothing compared to what she turned onto herself. For all the confidence that she displayed, Karen was not above second-guessing herself.

"Well, sometime either late Saturday night or early Sunday morning, Michael disappeared."

Karen's face registered so many different feelings, Lucy lost track, but she definitely saw confusion and regret.

Karen spoke to the confusion first. "That child was Failure to Thrive; there's no way he got up and walked away. What could have happened?"

"If you talk to Lisa, she will tell you that a witch with three eyes, square feet, and a painted face came in and swallowed the boy in one gulp through the mouth in the back of his neck, then disappeared into a snowstorm. What does 'Failure to Thrive' mean?"

"The boy is not developing the way he should, and there doesn't appear to be any medical reason for it. It usually happens due to a lack of stimulation, particularly tactile stimulation a baby gets from being held and cuddled. Children can actually die from it. A witch? Do you believe her?"

"I believe Lisa believes it happened. I think that Lisa had a dream that, to her, explained the disappearance of her brother. I convinced the mother to go into treatment. I really don't know this for sure, but I suspect she will be the number one suspect. Do you have any idea what she might be capable of doing?"

"If I would have thought she was actually capable of harming either of those children, they would have been out of there, but obviously I had my doubts. The problem is, where do you place children with Failure to Thrive Syndrome and Fetal Alcohol Syndrome? But that also leads to the question: who would abduct children like that either? Karen gazed towards the ceiling.

It dawned on Lucy that she had never heard Karen use the term, kid or kids. "I bet she would say kids are baby goats," she thought. Anyway, it spoke to the respect she had for children.

"Well, that is one reason I haven't totally discounted Lisa's story. I've heard of groups that use ki...children in sacrifices. Perhaps a child like that would bring less concern, and less heat. Maybe police don't look as hard, particularly when the mother is a drug addict. They probably figure she's really responsible for the disappearance."

"Oh, that's awful. Why didn't I remove those children?" Lucy could see the deep regret in Karen's eyes.

Lucy spoke in a firm voice. "Now don't be so hard on yourself. Remember, we don't know anything yet. Is there anything else you can tell me about this case that might give us a clue?"

"Like what?"

"Well, for instance is there a father out there? Might he be interested in Michael?"

Karen shook her head in disgust. "The father is also her supplier. He could be a suspect in the disappearance, but only if he found someone who'd pay him for Michael. I wouldn't even put it past him if he left Michael on a snow bank somewhere. He appears to be a man without a soul. But my guess is, if the baby were disturbing him in any way, he'd just leave. I think if there is any hope for Dawn, she needs to kick that guy to the curb, as the expression goes.

"By the way, I took Lisa home with me last night. Is it O.K. if she stays with us for a while? I think she's doing my kids some good."

Karen smiled. "You are one reason I could retire. I could sit by the river and watch it go by, and think of the families with whom I'd made a difference. Then cases like this one would come up, and I'd jump into the river. Yes, it's fine. I'll note it in her file."

"Don't give up hope; maybe we will find Michael." Even as she said it, Lucy felt little hope herself. She had no idea where to turn. Perhaps the crime scene investigators had turned up something. She decided to walk back to the station. Lucy thought of her own two children as she walked. Suddenly, she was missing them both very much. She even felt a stirring for her mother.

Chapter 3

The station was within walking distance of Karen's office, so Lucy had parked there and walked to Karen's. The sky was now blue, and the snow had moved east, probably somewhere over Detroit by now. The temperature had dropped but not severely, and the high-pressure system must have moved quickly because the winds were calm. The area was blanketed in white, and it looked beautiful. Lucy wished she could get out in the middle of the woods and appreciate the peace that the snow provided, but the snow was so deep, she didn't trust her truck off road.

On her way into the station, she met Ray Waupuse. A smile ran across his face as soon as he saw her, and Lucy's mirrored his. "I hear you're involved in a new mystery now. Don't you think you should retire while you are batting a thousand?" he asked with a smile and a wink.

"Do you still believe in those patron saints they used to teach us about in the mission school? Wasn't there one for hopeless cases? Maybe you could pray to that guy for me."

"Which is the hopeless case that I should pray for? You or the one you are investigating?"

Lucy wrinkled her nose and gave him a disapproving look she didn't mean.

"I'm sure if I leave this new one to the department or the FBI, they are going to pin it on the mother, and she's got enough to worry about right now. Even if she is responsible, I'd like her to think that someone is on her side. I don't think she has anyone."

Lucy clearly remembered what that was like.

Ray shook his head. "I worry about you. I think you may just be too kind to be a cop."

Lucy smiled. "I need to be mean and heartless like you are, right?"

Now it was Ray's turn to give a disapproving look he didn't mean. "I talked to your supervisor. Maybe for this case, you can at least use department time instead of your own. I knew you'd want to pursue it. I also organized a group of my friends to search the area around their houses with snowmobiles this afternoon if you want to join us."

Lucy smiled and gently touched Ray's arm. "I was just going to talk with him about that. Thanks for running interference.

Now that Lisa is living with us, I can't afford to leave my mother with my kids and Lisa too, while I pretend to be a detective."

"I'm not sure I've done you any favors. I talked to one of the investigators, and they found nothing that would indicate any kind of intruder. You know as well as I do, these cases almost always end up being a parent that gets angry and goes too far, then covers it up with an intruder story."

"In this case though, it's not the mother saying that, it's the sister."

"Maybe the sister was playing with him too rough? Ray asked in a confrontational tone.

"In the middle of the night? And besides, would she be smart enough to come up with the kind of story that she did, to cover her own tracks? Lisa would not be able to come up with that story. I'm convinced that she saw what she described. It may have been in a dream, but she didn't make up seeing it."

"Well, all you need to do then, is find a witch with three eyes, square feet, and a very large mouth in the back of his neck. That should be easy," Ray said with an endearing sideways smile.

Lucy was surprised he knew so much detail. "Boy, word sure does travel around here, doesn't it?"

"I'm convinced that if it has anything to do with witches, everybody knows about it in hours. We're like kids during Hallowe'en all year round."

"Thanks for your help with my supervisor. Also promise me you'll let me know if you see the person you just described."

"I'll be sure to do that. You take care of yourself, Lucy."

"I will." Then just like always, Ray walked away, and Lucy felt disappointed. She felt like she was missing something. What was she looking for that she didn't get? She thought to herself, but no answer came.

Lucy took a deep breath and went in to see her supervisor. It's not that Lucy didn't like her supervisor. Or that she thought he didn't like her. It was juts that she seemed caught in a vicious cycle: every time she saw him, she did something stupid. This made her feel self-conscious whenever she saw him. And that increased the likelihood that she would do something stupid. And sure enough, she did.

Lieutenant Moon was sitting behind his desk when Lucy walked into his office. The desk was large, and that added to Lucy's feeling of intimidation. He was a big man, and that didn't help either. He was taller than most Menominee and had the large barrel chest and stomach. His hair was black, as were his eyes. He wore reading glasses and would always peer over them at Lucy, giving her the feeling of being judged.

In her mind, she was already thinking he was cringing inside at the thought of her presenting him with another hair-brained scheme or theory. Back when she was working on the Brandt case he would frequently ask her about any new developments that he could take to the FBI in her case with Scott, and that he knew she was pursuing the case on her own. She always had to say no. Then he'd look over his glasses at her and say "nothing". She would then speak for him, and say that she knew he thought she should give it up, but she wasn't ready to do that yet. She'd then wonder why she assumed that, and the cycle continued.

Lucy started talking. She decided to take a different tack. "I know it's not part of my job description, but I'd like to try to help Lisa and her mom."

"So you believe the little girl's story," Lieutenant Moon said, looking over his glasses.

"I don't know about that," Lucy said quickly. "I just think, as a good detective, you should leave all of your options open."

"So you've promoted yourself to detective now, Officer Teller?" Lieutenant Moon asked. There was a hint of a smile on his face.

"No, it's not that. It's just that I was hoping you'd let me pursue this case. Since none of us seem to have a clue what's going on here."

"So you're assuming the crime scene investigators found nothing?"

"Well, not that, Sir. Well, yes, I guess I did assume that." She could feel her face getting slightly flushed.

"They did find a trace of blood in the child's crib and some on the couch were the mother was lying, but admittedly not enough to assume foul play." For the first time Lucy could remember, Lieutenant Moon smiled. This was the first time that she got the impression that maybe he enjoyed seeing her flustered. "We don't know much about this case, and I think you're the best officer we have to pursue it, given your background. You can take half of your time to investigate. Just keep track of your hours, and keep me abreast of what you find," he said, as he leaned back in his chair.

"Thank you, Sir. I'll need your advice. This is pretty new to me."

"You need to start by organizing a search party. I'll help you with that part. Locking eyes with Lucy, he said, "I'm glad it was you who found the little girl." Then the lieutenant dismissed her.

For a change, Lucy walked out of Lieutenant Moon's office feeling better than when she went into it. Unfortunately, the good feeling lasted only a short time. When she read the report from the crime scene investigators, she realized that she had nothing to go on, particularly nothing that didn't point to Dawn getting rid of her son, Michael. There had to be more. There just had to be more information.

What was she missing?

Chapter 4

Dawn

The next day, Lucy went to visit Dawn at the treatment center. Lucy was reminded of the dark heaviness she had felt as she went into treatment, like most people, she had entered feeling dirty.

Dawn would still be detoxing and probably would be able to provide little information, but Lucy wanted to support her, because this would be a crucial time to keep her in treatment, Her body would be screaming for drugs and she would be begging to leave treatment. Lucy remembered this feeling clearly. The memory of her horrific struggle to get clean was one of the things that helped to keep her sober every day.

Lucy stopped first to visit Dr. Meany. Meany wasn't his real name; it was Wolf, but in detox, everyone is in pain-physical, emotional, and spiritual pain. The medical doctor is in charge of dispensing drugs to help ease the pain, but no matter how much he dispenses, it's less than the patients are used to getting from their own self-medication. They always want more than Dr. Wolf is willing to provide. Hence the patients' nickname: Dr. Meany.

He didn't deserve this term. First, Dr. Wolf had ignored the pressures of the rez in order to do well in school, and left its familiarity for the first time to attend college. Alone and afraid in a strange world, he struggled through college and got into medical school.

There, he had felt an emptiness that was hard to describe. He could not understand it himself. He desperately missed the familiarity of his people and the ways of the reservation. All the while, he avoided the alcohol that had gotten so many of his family members in trouble. He finished medical school and went into residency for neurosurgery. He was well on his way to completing it, when he made what seemed to him a brilliant discovery. He could help relieve all the pressures of residency, and avoid working extra jobs to get through financially and pay off his student loans, by just prescribing himself medication.

"It's hard to believe, he says now in meetings, that a medical student wouldn't realize that by taking minor tranquilizers I was just eating my booze, but it didn't register.:

Soon he became hopelessly addicted. A DUI had helped him to come to his senses before he destroyed his life and his medical career. However, his stint in treatment changed his focus from neurosurgery to addictionology. When he had finished his residency at the Betty Ford Clinic, he he had come back to Keshena, where he'd now been for ten years.

What he is unwilling to dispense in medication, he gives instead through endless hours of time, and the willingness to care, to understand, and to be available through the hard times, for which he is rewarded with endless anger and criticism.

Lucy had been one who was, at first, convinced that this guy was a quack. She thought he had a lot of nerve for someone who didn't know half of what she knew about drugs. But eventually Lucy got it. She was willing to admit that, when it came to drugs, all she knew was getting herself in trouble, and that it was time to trust somebody else. That someone was Dr. Meany and the team at Maenoysachiah. They saved her life and gave her kids back their mother.

She now tried never to let an opportunity pass to atone for all the abuse she had given him in those first few weeks. She was eternally grateful and had a deep respect for him. When she stopped at his office, he wasn't there. She asked at the nurses' station where Dawn Lake's room was, and if she could visit. The nurse was friendly and recognized Lucy as a regular volunteer. She told her the room number.

"The Doctor is down there now and probably could use some reinforcements," the nurse stated, as she smiled and rolled her eyes toward the ceiling.

As Lucy walked down the hall, she could hear Dawn using a variety of skills to persuade Dr. Wolf to increase her meds. The skills ranged from being semi-seductive, to whining, to questioning his skills as a physician.

Dr. Wolf's response Witch of Winter was always the same: "I understand you're in pain and not sleeping well. All of that is your body's response to learning to live without heroin and alcohol. I'm giving you as much medication as I can responsibly give you. Part of your recovery is learning to trust, and giving control of your drug use over to some being other than yourself. You can help yourself by beginning to go to group therapy and learning to connect with people again. Try to get out of yourself and the pain you are in, and focus on others. It is about time you got out of your own way and started looking outside of this disease."

Since nothing else had worked, and Dawn was getting frustrated, the anger came next. "I don't need no damn group. I need rest. I need to stop being in pain. I thought this place was supposed to help you, not hurt you. Since I've been here, all I do is get worse. I can't stand the way I'm feeling. You've got to help me," she pleaded and began to cry gut-wrenching sobs.

Dr. Wolf continued with his same soft and kind approach. "If you had a malignant tumor and went in to have it removed, you may go in to the hospital pain free, but after the surgery was performed, you'd probably hurt like hell. The same is true here. Sometimes you have to feel worse before you feel better, but if you stick with us for a while, you're going to feel better than you have in years. You've got to trust me," he stated in a firm, fatherly voice.

Lucy knocked softly on the door. "You still using those same tired lines, Doc?"

Lucy walked in slowly and gave the doctor an encouraging pat. She touched his shoulder, but did it so it was out of Dawn's view. Since Dawn was already mad at him, Lucy didn't want to be guilty by association. However, since she was the one who had talked her into coming here, she probably already was.

"I know it feels like they aren't doing enough for you, and I don't blame you for feeling that way, but I was where you were several years ago. These people saved my life and gave my kids their mother back. You need to trust them."

"What are you doing here? Why aren't you out looking for my boy?" Dawn spat.

"I have a group of snowmobilers mobilized to begin searching for him this afternoon. I came here to ask you some questions that might help in our search, and to tell you we'll do all we can to find your son."

Sneering, Dawn turned to Dr. Wolf. "See? Besides all physical pain that I'm in, I have a son out there lost in the snow. I need something to help me sleep."

"Just like you have to learn to cope with physical pain without drugs, you need to learn to cope with emotional pain without them also," he answered in his same patient and calm style.

"Is there anything you thought of since I last talked with you that might help us to find your son?"

"I thought that was your job. Just find him." Dawn's eyes sparked with anger, and her eyes appeared to be shooting darts.

Lucy marveled at Dr. Wolfs patience- She was there ten minutes, and she wanted to wring Dawn's neck. "You know Dr. Wolf can help you get better, but if it happens, it'll eventually be up to you. I can help find your son, but if you want him found, you have to do your part, too. That's another reason you need to go to group; the other patients won't put up with your crap the way he does. Quit biting the hands that are trying to feed you."

If Dawn heard any of that, she gave no indication. "I need to rest now." Dismissing them from her room, Dawn went to her bed and began gently rocking with her arms wrapped around her legs, and knees tucked under her chin.

Dr. Wolf motioned with his head for Lucy to follow him into the hall. As they walked down the hall, Lucy asked, "What do you think, Doc?"

"She's got to be willing to trust and to let other people inside."

"I think it's going to be difficult for her to trust if we don't find some way of verifying that there was an intruder in her house, who took her son. Then if something has happened to her son, she'll have to deal with the grief and anger and guilt of his loss. She is in a tough situation, but she needs the truth, which will complicate her recovery as well. No matter what the case, you'll have a challenge on your hands with this one."

"No worse than you were," Doc said with a smile and a quick wink.

"That's true. If you could get through to me, you can get through to anyone," Lucy said, as she grabbed his arm and continued down the hall.

"I don't know about that, but I'm glad you and others like you come back to remind us that we are successful sometimes. Now go and do your job and let us do ours." She was dismissed. Lucy was dismissed for a third time that day.

Chapter 5

Ray

Lucy was beginning to think she knew what snow blindness was like, as she turned her snowmobile up another trail. Everywhere she looked, she saw white. With all the new snow, there was no evidence of anything. There were no footprints, no bloodstains, and—luckily—no tiny bodies anywhere in the snow. As darkness closed in, she gathered with the other searchers, and they each reported the same. They saw nothing.

The next day, they tried snowshoes so they could get off the trails, but disappointingly, still found nothing. Lucy did come across a hiking trail that she didn't know existed, and it appeared that someone had been on it at some point either before or during the storm. However, she found nothing on it that would indicate the kidnapper might have used it. It was narrow and cut in such a way that would strongly discourage snowmobilers from traveling on it. Not only that, occasionally a large tree stood in the middle of the trail, and the tracks went to one side or the other. Lucy stopped and looked around frequently for anything that was remotely helpful.

She saw nothing, but on occasion, she did appreciate that seeing nothing meant there was no evidence of foul play and she could instead savored the beauty. The woods were completely quiet. She saw evidence of deer tracks in the snow. The small thin saplings, which had to grow up rapidly to fight with the taller trees for the sun, would bend over under the weight of the snow and touch the ground. They created arches of white that reminded her of the ones that brides would walk through in the magazine ads she saw. Her mind drifted to her own life, and she wondered if there would ever be a man in her life again. In her first marriage, she and her husband had been much more married to drugs than to each other. They finally killed him and would have probably killed her, if Karen hadn't intervened.

Her life since was filled with recovery, her children, her job, and recently some courses at the College of Menominee Nation. It was a full life, but as she learned about real closeness with others, she began to think it might be interesting to be in a relationship again that could be a barometer of how far she had come.

Coincidentally, she heard Ray's voice softly behind her. "We better start heading back. It will be dark soon, and we move a lot slower on these snowshoes."

"You startled me," she said. "How long have you been following me?" Lucy knew her reaction was more than just surprise. She felt her face flush. Butterflies were fluttering in her stomach, and she had to stop herself from giggling.

"I've been about a hundred yards to your right and slightly behind you for a while now. You know I walk in these woods a lot. I drive a four-wheeler during the summer and hunting season, and I never came across this trail before. It must be new. I wonder who built it and where it leads." He gently put his arm around her shoulder in a safe brotherly way. Lucy leaned into him briefly.

"I don't know, but is there any reason to believe it has anything to do with Michael's disappearance? We've been searching these woods for two days now, and for all we know, the person might have left in a car. Come to think of it, we don't even know if there was such a person." Ray and Lucy were heading back to Dawn's house, where they would meet up with the rest of the search party.

"Well, we do know that there is a child and that he is missing. He has to be somewhere. We know that there is probably not going to be a ransom demand, since Dawn has no money. It could be someone to whom she owned money, but still, how do you get blood from a turnip? We have to hope that this person wanted to keep the child alive, but why this child? I'm sorry, but the most logical explanation is the mother or her boyfriend lost their temper and that they disposed of the child somewhere." Both of them felt a tightness in their stomachs.

"Why don't you let me talk to the boyfriend tomorrow to see what his story is?"

"I'd appreciate that, but this is three days you're spending on this case. You sure you're not going soft on me?" Lucy tilted her head and smiled with her eyes.

Ray smiled. "You need a lot of help. Since I know you're not going to leave this alone, I might as well do what I can. What is your next move?"

"I don't have one. I thought after the kids get out of school tomorrow, I'd take them up to see the Brandts. It would give my mother a break that I think she'd appreciate. Maybe she could even go to the casino and play some bingo with her buddies. I'd like to see how the Brandts are doing. I'm hoping that getting away from this for a while will give me some new ideas."

Lucy didn't know how true that might be. She didn't know what was coming her way.

Chapter 6

Hank?

When the kids came home from school, she took the three of them on the hour-long drive to the Brandt's house. Her two would normally have fought most of the way, but with Lisa between them, they took turns entertaining her and listening to music. When they arrived, she thought she had maybe taken the trip for nothing, since there was nobody home. The children were getting tired of being in the car. Just as she was getting ready for the ride back, Hank Brandt slid across his lawn on cross-country skis. Lucy thought his face looked more relaxed, and when he saw her, his face brightened considerably.

Using his poles, he loosened the bindings on his skis and quickly opened the front door. She introduced her children to him, and Hank quickly made them feel welcome with cups of steaming hot chocolate. Lisa was very quiet and even seemed Witch of Winter to hide behind her for the time they were there. Lucy thought it might help to tell her that this was Scott's father, but it had little impact. She had never met Hank, because she never had to testify at Mr. Riely's trial. Because he had abducted Lucy and threatened to kill her, he was tried on that, and his confession in Scott's murder. Hank had attended the whole trial, and the other family members when they could. They did it as much to support Lucy as looking for justice. Unlike others, they didn't believe that bringing the killers to justice would do much for their healing, only that it would serve to keep them from hurting others.

One by one, the rest of the family trickled in. Lisa seemed to warm to Molly, Bobbie, Paul, and Sally, but not to Hank, hard as he tried. Lucy began to wonder what kind of relationship Lisa might have with Dawn's boyfriend. Why was this little girl afraid of this gentle man?

The Brandt's home seemed much less somber than her last visit, and the kidding and laughter were pleasant for Lucy to see.

When they left, Lisa was quiet for the beginning of the ride, but Jerrod and Tara made plenty of noise to make up for it. Lisa spoke softly, and Lucy almost missed it.

"He had witch's feet," was all she said.

Lucy slowed the car and made a U-turn. Her heart was pounding, and she was more excited than she had been in a long time. Within minutes, they were back in the Brandt's driveway. When he answered the door, Hank had changed from his cross-country gear to jeans and a flannel shirt. Lucy apologized for the interruption and told Hank what Lisa had said. Hank was confused at first, until Lucy told him about the description that Lisa had given her about the intruder. Hank immediately excused himself and returned with his ski boots. They were an old pair, the kind with a solid rubber square front with three holes in the bottom that fit on three pins that stuck up from the ski.

Lucy assured Lisa that Hank was not a witch. When Lisa saw that the shoes came off, she was less afraid. Lucy began to think of the trail that she and Ray were on earlier. Maybe it was important. Still, there were all the other weird things that Lisa had described. Now Hank was excited; part of his recovery had come from nature. He loved it and participated in something every season. Molly and the kids were constantly teasing him about his gear.

They never ran out of Christmas and birthday gifts to get him, because he always wanted more gear. He kayaked and canoed in the summer, as well as biked. He and Molly had gotten a tandem that they road on trails throughout Wisconsin. In the winter, he loved cross-country skiing and even did downhill, because the kids liked that better. Lucy could see the wheels turning in his head as he kept repeating the description. He soon returned with his arms full of gear.

"You said it was most likely dark when the abduction took place, and that it was snowing?"

"Yes," Lucy answered.

They asked Lisa if she was aware of the time, but all she could say was that it was dark, and she had been sleeping.

Hank pulled out a small flashlight attached to straps and placed the straps over his head. He positioned it so the small flashlight was facing out from the middle of his forehead. Lisa jumped back.

Witch of Winter

"Is that how the man looked?" Lucy asked her.

"Sort of," Lisa said. "But the Eye was in his forehead.

Hank took a stocking cap from his pile, went to the kitchen, and got a scissors. He cut a slit in the cap and pulled it over his head. The lens of the light came through the slit. Lisa grabbed Lucy's arm. "But it had an eye." Lisa looked very confused and was moving behind Lucy.

Hank called his daughter Sally. Sally was becoming quite the artist and had paint supplies in the house. She painted an eye on the lens of the flashlight. Hank then reached up and twisted the light. It not only looked like an eye; it cast a strange shadow around the room.

"Creepy," Tara said, making a noise for the first time. She and Jerrod had been totally dumbfounded prior to this. They thought it was funny that adults were playing such a game.

"If he were skiing through the woods, he would have needed his hands free for the poles. Also, if the house was dark, this would have been great for seeing where he was going, without turning on any lights," Lucy whispered, not wanting to startle Lisa. "He must have known your mother would be taking her medicine, and you'd be the only one that could tell. If you described something strange, no one would believe you. This get-up is strange enough by itself, but he made it more in order to scare you and make him look like a witch." Lucy turned to Hank. "But what about swallowing the baby through a hole in the back of his neck?

"Yeah, what about that, Dad?" Paul, Bobby, and Sally asked. Everyone seemed to be getting involved.

"Yeah, what about that, Hank?" Molly asked. They now had everyone's interest.

Hank again reached into his pile. He pulled out a frame backpack. He told Sally to get one of her old dolls she kept in her bedroom. He stuck his hands and arms through the straps. The bag stood open on his back like a large box on its side, so that the opening was by his shoulders and facing up. He then put on a large coat several sizes too big for his normal frame to accommodate the backpack.

"I sometimes go to the grocery store on my skis. If it's cold and I don't want something to freeze, I do this. He wouldn't have wanted to take the time to dress the baby." Sally came with a doll. He took the doll, moved the collar backward, and put the baby inside the backpack.

"Swallowed the baby through a mouth in the back of his neck," they all said in unison.

"This is crude, of course, but if I had time to fix it up, I could make a comfortable compartment for a baby. I could also put diapers and bottles in the side compartments. I could even put a little hand warmer in there to keep the baby warm, and a breathing tube to bring in plenty of oxygen."

All eyes turned toward Lisa. She stood shaking behind Lucy with tears in her eyes. "That's what I saw. I thought it was a witch that came to steal my baby brother."

Hank, realizing she was scared all over again, took off the outfit as quickly as he could.

Lucy asked, "Lisa, is it O.K. to hug you?"

Lisa just nodded her head.

Lucy knelt down slowly and gave her a long hug. "I know that was scary for you, but now we understand what you were describing. We also know it wasn't a witch. Just like Mr. Brandt, it was someone pretending to be a witch. This will really help us to find your brother. You are a good helper, Lisa."

What Lucy didn't say was, for the first time, she had hope that he'd be alive and that neither Lisa's mother nor her boyfriend was guilty of murder. Anyone who went to this much trouble, wasn't about to kill the child, at least not right away. She wondered how much time they had. With such a big lead, could they ever catch him?

"So when do we start going after this guy?" Hank asked, as he stood up quickly.

"We?" Lucy asked sarcastically.

"I can start in the morning. It's winter. The construction company is closed for a couple of months, and you need lessons in skiing. Besides, I've lost a child. Nothing would give me more joy than helping to find one. I know what it's like to desperately want to fill the void of a missing child."

"Just because we now know this guy isn't a witch, doesn't mean he isn't dangerous. I can't ask you to risk your life for this."

"You're not asking. I'm volunteering," Hank stated firmly.

"Hank, don't you think you and I should talk about this? Don't you think this family has suffered enough? What if something happens to you? How do you think we're going to feel?" Molly was only starting with her questions. She spoke quickly and quietly.

Hank turned toward all of them. "You guys have to let me do this. You are all busy now with school, work, and friends. All I have is time to think, and I don't need that. I feel like I have a sense of this guy, and I don't think he's dangerous. He went to too much trouble to protect everyone."

"That doesn't say what he'd do if we got him cornered," Lucy replied.

"I don't want to apprehend him. That's your job. I just want to help you find him and the baby," Hank said with pleading eyes.

"I'd like to help, too. I'm not in school at the moment." All of a sudden, Bobbie realized what she had said. She looked at all of them with guilt in her eyes and shame in her voice. I dropped my classes." She paused. "It was either that or fail them. I just couldn't get motivated or concentrate. This would do me good, too. I need to do something to make me feel better."

"Oh great, let me lose two more family members." Molly threw up her hands and sounded sarcastic, but she had tears in her eyes.

Hank put his arms around Bobbie and his wife. "We'll be back, and we'll have something to celebrate, too." Molly rolled her eyes. She appeared deflated.

Lucy was in a dilemma. She wasn't as optimistic as Hank. Nor was she as certain that there wouldn't be trouble. But she also knew snowmobiles wouldn't work on the trail she was on yesterday. Hank was the only person she knew who cross-country skied. Snowshoes were too slow. "O.K., if you guys decide as a family that you want to help, I'll clear it with my boss, and we can head out day after tomorrow."

When Hank crawled into bed that night, he could hear Molly sniffling.

He lay there quietly for a while, not knowing what to say. Finally, he spoke. "Molly, I know this is hard for you to understand, but all my life I've wondered about whether or not I have courage. I've never been in a war or in a situation where I had to put my life on the line for the good of another. I see an opportunity here to prove something to myself, and maybe Bobbie needs to do the same. If I walk away from this, I feel I will have failed, and I just can't take another failure right now."

"Hank, you show courage every day. Don't you think I know how hard it is for you to get up every day and go to work, to fight your addiction, to be a good father, to live with me, Especially to live with me? You are all about courage. Perhaps it would take more courage to not do this thing, and stay home with your wife and family who need you."

"I understand what you're saying and appreciate your love and concern for me, but let's all sacrifice for the good of this child. I promise I will not try to be a hero and get myself killed. I know my limitations. I just want to help."

"You already have, Hank. Lucy didn't have a clue in this case until she came here today."

"Can I ask for your support in this? Will you make this your sacrifice?" Molly sighed. She rolled over and kissed him. "Come home to me," she said.

"I'm just beginning to feel connected to you and to life again. I don't want to lose that."

Hank reached out for his wife. They made love with a greater intensity, knowing it could be the last time. They were both praying silently that it wouldn't be.

Chapter 7

Lucy?

The next day Lucy needed to talk to several people. She started with Ray. She called the station and asked to be patched through to his radio. First, she asked Ray what he had learned from the boyfriend. She was hoping he had valuable information.

"Not much. He skipped town. I issued a warrant for his arrest and notified the police in other reservations. I think we may have our man."

"I don't think so," Lucy said, and she related the events at the Brandts.

"Damn. That guy's good. Maybe we should offer him a job," Ray said.

"Well, we kind of have." Confused silence was all Lucy heard on the other end.

"He offered to take me down that path we were on yesterday on Cross Country skis. You interested?"

"You know I've always wanted to try that," he said. "How are we going to get equipment? And how do we dress?"

"Hank says to dress in layers. Wear a wool sweater if you have one. It insulates even when it's wet, and if you have any kind of underwear that wicks the perspiration away from your body, wear that. Wear a windbreaker on the outside. If it's waterproof and breathable, all the better. He said he'd bring food and gear for overnight, if we need it.

The reservation totaled 240 thousand acres. Trees covered 95% of it, and it butted up to the Nicolet National Forest, which was several hundred thousand acres more. Their kidnapper could be anywhere in those woods. He could have a car on any of the highways that travel through it. If they got too far from a highway and a patrol car, their radios wouldn't work. Lucy wondered what she was getting herself and her friends into.

Next, she talked to her supervisor. When she went into his office, she knew she was in more trouble than usual. Standing next to the Lieutenant's desk was a tall, slender man with glasses that shouted FBI. The look on his face was well past confident and heading straight to cocky. He smirked as she entered the room. So not only did she have to try to convince the Lieutenant that Lisa's story was beginning to make sense while he frequently looked over his glasses at her, she had to try to ignore FBI agent Scruggs who was beside himself with amusement. He didn't even bother to address her as he spoke directly to the Lieutenant. "Why don't you let the little officer here go on her witch hunt while I and my men engage in serious police work?"

Then she asked for time to cross-country ski through the woods and to take another officer, Ray Waupuse, and two civilian non-natives with her. This gave Agent Scruggs a good chuckle. The Lieutenant was at least happy not to have to assign additional officers to find Dawn's boyfriend. That would be the FBI's job. They might have better luck, since there was a good chance he would have left for another reservation anyway.

The next and biggest challenge was her mother. Luckily, the kids were on her side with this, but she had to convince them that they couldn't go with her.

"I put up with your playing Injun with short runs and smudging, but this is ridiculous. It's cold out there and dangerous. You know nothing about surviving in the woods in the summertime much less the winter. You're crazy. And then you're going to trust some white man to lead you around who probably knows less than you do about survival. You're crazy."

"Mom, I promise the kids will be good and that Jerrod and Tara will help." Lucy turned to them with a threatening tone. "Won't you?"

"You haven't heard a word I said, have you?"

Lucy just looked at her, confused. She was searching for the right words to convince her mom.

"I don't have a problem with these kids. It's you I'm worried about, you dope," said Lucy's mom.

Lucy wasn't sure how to deal with this. "Hank knows what he's doing as far as skiing and camping are concerned, and I have Ray to help me with the police part of it. I don't think this guy is a killer."

"Just because you got some explanations of some things he does, don't you convince yourself he's not a witch and has powers you don't understand, young lady."

"I promise I won't take him lightly," Lucy assured her as she moved closer to her mom.

"You already are." Her mother replied with fear in her eyes. "You were easier to deal with on drugs." Her words were not intended to be hurtful, but they stung Lucy all the same. She stepped back and recoiled at the pain.

Her final stop was at the treatment center. She told Dawn about the recent developments and what she was planning to do. Lucy was hopeful as she spoke to the lost boy's mother.

If Dawn heard any of it, she didn't speak to it. "You need to find my boyfriend, and he needs to bring me a little something just to take the edge off. Then maybe I can survive in here." Dawn was rude and very angry.

Lucy tried to understand and place herself back to when she was just like Dawn, but it was hard. Here, while Dawn remained warm and dry, Lucy would be cold and wet and working her ass off trying to find Dawn's kid. The thing that helped was that no matter how uncomfortable the elements were she knew she'd be in less pain than Dawn was, because Dawn's was physical, emotional, and spiritual.

"We'll do our best," was all Lucy said before leaving the room. This time she dismissed Dawn.

Chapter 8

The Trail

The next day, Ray and Lucy met Hank and Bobbie at the Pine Hills Golf Course for breakfast. Pine Hills had been bought by the Mohecan nation a number of years ago. They had added an extra 9 holes and built a beautiful resturaunt several years ago. Hank encouraged all of them to eat a heavy breakfast. Each of them had eggs and meat, and whole-wheat pancakes or toast. Hank said, "Meals from here on out will be fast and not that exciting." He spoke as an authority.

As they were eating, Hank went over with them what they had brought for clothes. He was concerned that Lucy had jeans and cotton long underwear. She did have a lightweight nylon jacket, but it wasn't breathable. Both Lucy and Ray had layers of clothing, but they found it hard to believe they'd be warm enough. When he heard about the layers that Ray had planned to wear, Hank convinced him to take a few off and put them in his backpack.

"It's better to start off cold," he told them. "You can always add layers if you continue to be cold, but if you start to perspire, and your skin gets wet, it will be Witch of Winter hard to warm up again. If your core temperature begins to drop, that's hypothermia and can be fatal if we can't get it up again. I'm going to let you guys worry about the enemy we're chasing; my main enemy is winter. Winter can be just as deadly as anyone with a gun." He had brought a pair of Gortex pants and a Gortex Jacket of Molly's for Lucy and a pair of Ryan's for Ray.

When they had finished, they drove in two cars to Lisa's house. Hank took out skis, poles, and boots for everyone. He had a backpack filled with some of the food, her clothes and a sleeping bag, and for Bobbie and for himself he had a sled he would pull behind him on the trail with a four-person tent, and the remainder of the food since they were the experienced skiers. He gave smaller and lighter packs to Lucy and Ray for their clothes, personal items, and sleeping bags. After putting on their boots, Ray and Lucy got their first skiing lesson. Hank taught them how to put on the skis first, then he had them practice gliding without their poles.

"You want to press down and backwards when the ski is directly beneath you," Hank instructed them. Lucy was excited and relieved when both she and Ray picked this up quickly.

Next, Hank handed them poles. They put their hands through the straps first and then grabbed the poles on the grip with their thumbs over the straps. "Many people use the poles just to help them with balance, but you need to use them to push you forward down the trail. Pretend you're holding a glass of water and you want to shoot it out in front of you, then place the pole in the snow and push yourself forward. You ski like you walk, with your feet and hands opposite one another. As your right foot is going forward, your left hand is going forward." Hank waited for them to try.

Lucy and Ray tried with the poles. This was a little more complicated, and Lucy soon fell.

"That's good," Hank laughed. "Now I can teach you how to get up."

Lucy was glad there was a trick to it, because otherwise she might be lying there until spring. The more she struggled, the deeper she got in the snow.

"First get your skis parallel. Then take your poles off from the straps and put them together. Hold them in about the middle of the pole and push while you raise yourself to your feet. When you're wearing your pack, take it off before you try to get up." It worked, and soon Lucy and Ray were doing pretty well.

"There are some other skills you'll need for going up and down hills, but I'll teach you that when we get to them. We'll go in the following order: I'll go first to make a trail, then Lucy and Ray, and Bobbie will bring up the rear. Try to stay in the tracks I set. That way, we should have it easy coming back out, unless it snows some more."

Hank gave them each two large water bottles that were held in insulated pouches on the hips of a belt. He encouraged them to drink often and to fill them with snow as the bottles emptied. In spite of the twenty-degree temperatures, they'd be perspiring and would need to stay hydrated to avoid fatigue.

"I don't like the idea of you being first. What if we run into the kidnapper? You're not even armed," Lucy said.

"Well, we know we're pretty safe for a while. We can talk about switching as you get the hang of skiing some more."

Before they left, Ray went to his truck. Lucy followed. He opened a box in the back. Lucy's forehead raised an inch, and her eyes grew wide. In the box was an arsenal of weapons and ammunition. He took out a collapsible rifle that was similar to the one the Olympians use when they ski, then stop and shoot at targets, but this one looked more powerful. He also took a Smith and Wesson handgun with a holster, and gave another one to Lucy, with an extra clip of bullets.

Lucy said nothing, and Ray just smiled at her expression. She felt the deep respect and affection he held for her.

They all took off on their skis and walked across 55 and into the woods. They started on the snowmobile trail. The snowmobiles had packed down the snow, and the skiing was easy, but Lucy found it hard to ski with no snow to keep her feet in line. Her skis crossed over one another, and she fell twice in the first mile. She didn't feel too bad though, because Ray fell three times, and even Bobbie fell once. Bobbie was a good skier, but she wasn't used to carrying as much weight as she had on her back.

When they made it to their first hill in the woods, Hank taught them how to snowplow. He pointed the tips of his skis in and the rears out. He proceeded slowly down the hill, and his skis looked like the big plows that clean the highways of deep snow.

Teaching these skills, Hank was feeling needed and valuable, and the hardness and anger that had become part of his daily life since Scott's death began to ease and the tension leave his body.

Bobbie went next to give them another model. "On the smaller hills, if you feel comfortable just bend your knees and lean slightly forward at the waist and separate your skis a little more but keep them parallel. You can even double pole if you want more speed, but don't be afraid to take off your skis and walk down if it looks too steep."

Bobbie went down the hill much faster, and by the time she stopped she was halfway up the hill on the other side. Both Ray and Lucy chose the more cautious snowplow, and each fell once going down. Once they reached the bottom, Hank taught them how to herringbone up the other side. This time he pointed the tips of his skis out and the backs in, and he stepped up the hill, slapping his skis as he landed. He placed the poles behind the skis for an extra push. It looked easy enough when Hank did it, but Lucy and Ray struggled up the hill, and Lucy was breathing hard by the time she reached the top.

Soon they reached the trail that Ray and Lucy had found the day before. Now Hank went forward and began making a trail in front of them in the unbroken snow. The going was slower now, but Lucy and Ray had a path to follow which made skiing easier. Little by little, they began to improve their form. In the slower powder snow, they began to use the parallel technique down the hills, and soon they were past the point they had reached on snowshoes.

Lucy was so intent on watching the tips of her skis that Bobbie had to remind her to take some time to look around the woods and listen to the quiet. They were far away from any roads now, and everything was white. Lucy had never seen the woods so beautiful. She could see so much farther because the leaves and underbrush were gone.

They were at the top of a ravine, and a herd of deer had gathered at the bottom three or four hundred yards away. Something seemed to have spooked them, and soon they ran out of sight. At that moment, Lucy remembered that they were after a kidnapper and possible murderer who probably knew these woods a lot better than they did. She spent less time looking at her skis after that. She did not have to remind herself again. She became more alert and focused her attention on any clues that might be evident.

By lunchtime, they had reached a point in the woods that Lucy and even Ray had never seen before. Lunch was simple: trail mix, crackers, cheese, and salami, washed down with water.

They weren't sure where they were. Lucy could tell that everyone was getting tired. Hank was the oldest of the group and was carrying the most weight, but the sled may have made it easier. He had the hardest job, making the track in the front of the group. She knew her own body, and it was screaming at her. Her inner thighs especially ached. She looked at Ray and Bobbie and saw fatigue in their faces.

"You need to teach Ray and me how to make a track," she said to Hank. "You have the heaviest load, and it's not fair that you have to bust the trail, too. Besides, we could be skiing right into the sights of a rifle for all we know." Lucy was hoping that was not the case, as a shiver went up her spine. Hank didn't argue.

"I don't mind keeping it up, but I'll do what you think is best."

"I think we need to start looking for a place to make camp soon," Ray added. "It'll be dark shortly after four, and it's one-thirty now. We'll need light to put up the tent, and we need to stay rested in case we catch up to this guy. If there is shooting, we need to be alert, not exhausted." Lucy felt the shiver return; it was not from the cold.

They rested a while after lunch, and when they started again, Lucy wished they hadn't. The rest had given her time to get stiff, and it was an effort just to move again. The groans of the rest of the group told her they felt the same. Ray took the lead, and they moved more slowly while he got the hang of making the trail. By three o'clock, the sun was getting low in the sky. Every muscle in Lucy's body hurt, and she could tell that her long underwear was soaked. She had only cotton long underwear, and it held the moisture. Spending the entire day in twenty-degree weather was beginning to take its toll. She felt chilled all the way to her bones.

All day they had been following the tracks the kidnapper had made that had been covered by several inches of snow. The only way they could discern the tracks was by a tiny dip in the snow out in front of them. Looking over Ray's shoulder, Lucy could see a spot where the tiny dip veered off. She called to Ray, who was so busy making track that he hadn't noticed what she saw.

Ray calmly pulled his handgun and took off his skis. He went underneath the bushes and disappeared. Lucy pulled her weapon as well. It only took a minute or two, but to Lucy it seemed like ages. Ray returned to the group with a smile.

I

"We won't have to put up that tent, and I'm pretty sure we're on the right track. Come see this," he said with excitement.

As they took off their skis and scurried under the bushes, they saw a small field. In the middle of it was a mound of snow, and on the opposite side, they saw an entrance to a snow fort similar to an igloo.

When they crawled inside they first went down and then up this kept more of the cold out of the enclosure, they could see the remains of a fire that was vented through the roof. There was a small table with a plate and silverware, as well as diapers and some bottles. They each smiled at one another. It was a hard day's work, but right now it seemed worth it.

They soon collected wood for a fire, and Hank pulled a pot out of his backpack and boiled some snow. When the water began to boil, he opened a bag of freeze-dried chicken and noodle casserole and added it to the water. Everything was in one bag. Within a half hour, it was ready. He took four tin cups about twice the size of a coffee mug with a long metal handle out of what seemed like his bottomless bag and gave each a full portion.

Lucy could have spent hours cooking, and it wouldn't have tasted any better than at that moment. Since she didn't sleep well, Lucy was often tired, but she wondered whether she had ever felt this exhausted before today. She felt bruised and battered, but she knew she had to go on.

Silently, they all helped clean up, and then they sat around the fire. It had the look of a seance as each of them stared silently into the fire, but their eyes were out of focus, and no one moved. Ray finally broke the spell and pulled Lucy aside.

"I think you and I should take turns keeping watch outside. We don't know if he will return. How about if you take the first watch? It's about eight o'clock now. I'll bring you some coffee when it's ready, then I'll start about ten. We can switch every three or four hours till morning."

Thank God for Ray. Lucy had never thought of posting a watch.

"That sounds good. Come and get me about two, and I'll take the rest of the night. I haven't slept for more than four hours in years. At least my staying awake could serve a purpose for a change." Lucy sounded sarcastic, but her smile was gentle and welcoming.

Hank and Bobbie had volunteered to take a turn at guard duty, but Lucy would have none of it. It was a clear night, and Lucy had never seen so many stars. At eight thirty, Ray came out with coffee and they both watched the Northern lights put on a show for more than an hour. They called to Hank and Bobbie, and the four of them watched for a while until Hank and Bobbie turned in about nine thirty.

Lucy stayed out until ten, but the night was getting cold with plenty of snow, no wind, and clear skies. It would soon be below zero outside the snow cave. Lucy was shivering as she stripped down to her long underwear and crawled into the sleeping bag. She could tell by their slow rhythmic breathing that Hank and Bobbie were already asleep. She was prepared to keep her regular vigil, staring at new surroundings, and sleeping with other people in the room, but eight hours of skiing caught her and pulled her into a deep sleep.

Just before Ray was supposed to wake her for her watch, she saw a baby's face smiling at her in a dream, and then she felt a cold hand by her face. She woke with a start. Ray put a finger to her mouth and gently shushed her.

"I wish I could let you sleep, but I'm shivering and falling asleep at the same time, and it's bitter cold out there. It's two-thirty and below zero. Maybe we can figure our guy is somewhere warm and sleeping now."

"No, I've already set a post treatment sleep record. I'll keep watch." Lucy's long underwear, which was damp when she got into the sleeping bag, was still wet. When she got out of the bag and hit the air, she began to shiver. As she grabbed her jeans and pulled them on, her hands were now shaking so badly she couldn't button them.

She felt a hand slide over hers. Ray said to her, "Right now, hypothermia is a bigger threat to you than anyone or anything that might be out there. You need to take this underwear off and hang it by the fire so it's dry by the time you put it on in the morning. Then you need to crawl into the bag with me so I can warm you up." Ray pulled his underwear top off so he was bare-chested. He was firm, and she welcomed his strong arms surrounding and holding her.

Lucy had men use a number of lines to get her to bed, but this was a first. "Why are you taking yours off?" It had been a very long time since she had been with a man. She was surprised at the strong stirrings she was feeling.

"Only so my body heat can warm you."

Lucy just smiled an "I'm not buying this" smile.

"Do it. We'll be lying back to front. This is not the time or the place for anything more than that." The thought of something more happening was playing in her mind. She was hopeful that there might be an opportunity in the future.

For the first time, Lucy heard the concern and urgency in his voice. She took off her top leaving only a bra, and then the bottoms leaving her panties. She crawled into Ray's sleeping bag. Just as Ray said, they laid back to front. The only sign he wasn't being totally honest was the swelling that she felt on her lower back, but no other part of him moved. Lucy was curious, but soon she stopped shivering and fell asleep. Ray soon followed.

There were only two people awake in the area. One was Hank, who had been fighting with his bladder for the last half hour. He'd heard the conversation and was ready to add his two cents worth if Lucy didn't listen. He was glad he didn't need to, and he smiled when he heard their breathing indicating they were asleep.

There were newer methods of dealing with early stage hyperthermia. Usually you would brew the person some hot tea or soup and have them do Jumping Jacks to warm up, but Hank thought the interpersonal value of Rays methods were superior.

He liked both Ray and Lucy and thought they would make a great couple. Shortly after, the warmth of his sleeping bag won out, and he fell back asleep.

The other person awake was in the trees just past the clearing. He wore a headlamp now turned off. He waited for another guard to appear, and when none did, he made his move silently and quickly.

Witch of Winter

Chapter 9

Blood on the Snow

It was light when Hank's bladder could be ignored no longer, even though the fire had gone out, and it was cold inside the cave. He slipped into his pants and shirt and headed outside. The sun was rising over the trees, but it was too ineffective to do much to the frigid air at that time. The cold didn't matter to Hank though; as a matter fact, even his bladder had lost his attention. He wondered if his legs could move.

The blood, lots of blood, in the snow just outside the snow cave was the only thing he could see.

He immediately thought of the people inside. He ran first to Bobbie's bag and breathed a sigh of relief as he saw her sleeping. Or was she? He shook her, and her eyes opened. She smiled until she saw the fear in his eyes.

"What's the matter?" She was quickly wide awake and alert as she sat straight up.

"Stay there for a minute," was all he said. He turned next to Ray and Lucy. They also were still in their bags. As he approached them, they both opened their eyes.

"You need to check the outside of the entrance. Something happened out there, and I don't want to screw up any evidence."

"What makes you think so?" Lucy asked, already kicking herself for not being out there. "I would have to pick this night to get my first good nights sleep in four years," she thought to herself.

"I just saw what looks like lots of blood in the snow, and I came right back to check on you guys." Hank was rocking back and forth holding his stomach. Lucy was sure his stomach was tied in knots. He looked very pale.

Ray was quickly out of his bag and into his clothes. Lucy realized she had little on and hesitated getting out of the bag in front of Hank. It took a while for Hank to realize that, turn around with his back to her, and check on Bobbie.

Ray stopped abruptly outside the door. Hank was right; there was lots of blood. Ray's own blood ran cold at what he saw next. A baby's head was stuck to a stake and planted in the snow. He turned away quickly. Then his brain registered that something was wrong with the gruesome image that seared its way so rapidly into his memory. He looked again. At the same time, he realized Lucy was now standing next to him, experiencing her first reaction, and turning away. She was fighting not to vomit.

Lucy repeated to herself, "Control your breathing, control your breath." The baby's face was covered in blood, and blood had dripped onto, and then frozen to the stake. The neck of the baby was what bothered Ray, and then caused him to breathe in relief. The neck was smooth, with a lip at the bottom of it

"It's a dolls head," he told Lucy, letting out a deep sigh.

Lucy opened one eye and looked again. Then she opened both eyes to be sure. She stood frozen with many different emotions churning through her body: dread mixed with fear, mixed with relief. Surprisingly, she was not angry yet.

Ray retreated into the snow cave. He came out with his rifle. He walked to the point where they had left the trail and looked at the tracks. He walked around the whole perimeter of the field where the snow cave was located. He found no other tracks.

"Is it o.k. to come out?" Hank asked from the doorway.

"Do you still have the bag that dinner came in last night?" Lucy asked, trying to sound calm.

"Yes. It's in a side compartment of my backpack."

"Great. Bring it out, but let me warn you, you're going to be horrified by what you see. It may not be as bad as it seems though."

Hank got the bag and walked out. Like Ray and Lucy, he looked and then looked away.

Witch of Winter

"It's a doll's head," Ray and Lucy said in unison.

Horrified, Hank looked again. "What's all the blood from?"

"I don't know." Ray said, shaking his head. "What I find even more disturbing is how it all got here." Hank and Lucy both looked at him curiously.

"There are no new tracks in the snow other than ours."

Lucy's face turned white. Her mother's words came back to her and softly left her mouth. "You're dealing with powers you don't understand."

Ray took the bag from Hank, stretched over the frozen pool of blood, wrapped the bag around the head and stake, and pulled them from the ground.

Bobbie appeared outside the snow cave for the first time. Her face blanched, and she looked very afraid.

"We have to go back," Lucy said.

"That's just what he wants us to do. That's what this whole thing is about," Hank said.

"If he wanted us dead, he could have killed us all in our sleep."

"We don't know what we're dealing with, and we've gone from the hunters to the hunted."

Ray went over and peered more closely at the footprints. "Hank, let me see the bottom of your boots."

Hank looked confused, but obliged.

"I agree. We need to go back."

"What does that have with the bottom of my shoes?" Hank asked.

"Because he's using our tracks to cover up his own. I bet he used our ski tracks, too," Ray said.

Hank and Ray looked at Lucy and Bobbie. Bobbie was still staring at the pool of blood. Hank was thankful that she had missed the doll's head on the stick.

"We're lucky to be alive, and I don't think we should push it. Even if it was a doll's head, he may be saying, "I'll kill the baby or you, if you get any closer," Lucy said.

"I still don't believe he wants to harm that baby," Hank said. "Do you think he's wandering around in below zero weather with that baby in a backpack?"

"I don't know," Lucy said.

"We have no guarantee that the baby will be safe if we stop looking either," Bobbie said. "He may have used the doll's head because the baby's already dead and buried. Let's find this guy." Hank turned toward Bobbie as they all did, marveling with what she had said. He knew how afraid she was, and yet she voted to continue.

He remembered reading once that the person with the greatest amount of courage is the one who has the greatest amount of fear to overcome. His children continued to amaze and impress him. A strong wave of grief passed quickly over him as his son, Scott's, face crossed his mind.

"Well, let's do first things first. We need some coffee and some breakfast; though probably none of us is hungry, we'll need the energy. Then we have to break camp and head back because that's the direction he's going anyway. Let's see what we find. Maybe we'll end up back at Lisa's house," Hank suggested.

Lucy shook her head—first things first. It is a simple AA philosophy, but if she followed it, it usually worked. "Sounds good," she said.

Hank started a fire and made coffee and hot water. They each had coffee, and then he pulled out several packets of oatmeal. They used their Sierra cups to eat their fill, and then they put everything back into their backpacks and started back the way they come the day before. The skiing was much easier with the trail already established, but the effort was greater. Each of them was now aware that the kidnapper knew they were out there and that they were after him. Their eyes constantly scanned the woods, but unlike the day before, they weren't able to appreciate the beauty. They were all ever vigilant and very determined to find this lunatic.

After a few miles of skiing, they reached a grove of pine trees. Ray, who was in the lead with his rifle in the ready, noticed a spot where the snow had been altered. It could have been a mound of snow that had fallen from the pine tree boughs, but it could have been where the kidnapper left the trail and attempted to cover his tracks. Ray asked the rest of them to stay back while he proceeded forward alone. He disappeared into the pine trees and was gone for what seemed to the rest of them to be a long while. When he reemerged, they all breathed a sigh of relief.

"On the other side of the pine trees, it looks like he circled back on a different path."

They all looked at Lucy. "Let's vote," she said.

Soon they were skiing under the pine tree. Now they were following him again, or so they hoped.

Chapter 10

Ezra Marsh

Now they could see his tracks in front of them and follow them. After two days of skiing, Lucy and Ray's skills were much improved. They still fell occasionally on some of the steep hills, but the snow was soft and broke their falls. Hank and Bobbie never fell, and that helped save energy for them because, even with the techniques Hank taught them, getting back up in the deep snow was hard work.

They had skied for several hours when the tracks led them to a cabin. They all stopped and ducked back under the cover of some pines. They were discussing what to do next when a man appeared outside. He was staggering and had a bottle in one hand and a rifle in the other.

"What do you people want?" The man was tall and slender and older, with a dark wrinkled face.

"We're police officers. We'd like to ask you a few questions. Is it o.k. if we come up?" Lucy hollered.

"If you're looking for that guy who came through here earlier, he continued down that way." He pointed to some fresh tracks that headed in the same direction they had been traveling.

"We're cold and hungry. Do you mind if we come in and warm up? We'll pay you for your time," Lucy asked.

There was a pause. "Come on in," the man shouted. Lucy and Ray went first, screening Bobbie and Hank. The man's rifle hung from the crook in his arm, and he never moved it. The man's name, they found out, was Ezra Marsh.

In the cabin, he set his gun down on a gun rack by the door. The inside of the cabin was just one big room, with a Franklin stove for heat. The floor was plywood. It had a sink with an old-fashioned pump for water, and the drain just ran out of the house. There was no bathroom, and Bobbie asked permission to use the outhouse, which was about fifty feet from the cabin. There was only one chair at the kitchen table and a single bed in the corner. A rocking chair stood by one of the few windows, and there were cans of beans, soup, chili, vegetables, and canned fruit lined on shelves in the kitchen.

A deer was hanging from its hind legs from the porch rafters. It looked like a fresh kill. Hank used the kitchen table to spread out gorp, salami, and crackers. He Witch of Winter invited the man to join them for lunch. Ezra simply held up his bottle and said he'd be drinking his lunch.

"I'm chilled to the bone," Lucy said. "How about a hit of that?" She pointed to the bottle.

"Sorry," the man said. "This is my last one, and I have to go all the way to town to get another. Why are you looking for that man?"

"It's not so much the man we're looking for. It's a baby we think he might have. There was a nine-month old baby taken from town the other night during that big snowstorm. We think he's got the baby."

"How do you get to town when you go there?" Lucy asked.

"I've got a snowmobile and a truck in a garage at the fire lane, where I'm sure that skier was headed. This time of year, I usually take the snowmobile."

"What does a man want with a baby?"

"We don't know. How far is that garage from here?" Ray asked.

"About five miles."

"How do you get to the garage?" Lucy asked.

"I walk or snowshoe," the man said.

"How far do you think the man on the skis is ahead of us?"

"I would guess three or four hours."

"Did he stop here?"

"No, I just saw him go by. Seemed he was in quite a hurry."

"How was he dressed? Lucy asked.

"Lot like you guys. He had a light jacket, but he seemed to have his over his backpack. Now that you mention a baby, he might have been keeping it warm that way."

"How was he built?" Ray asked.

"He seemed tall and thin."

"Where does the fire lane come out? Lucy asked.

"On W. Near Berry Lake."

"How many miles is it on the fire lane to W?" Hank asked.

"'Bout eight miles."

"If we start now, we might be able to make it to the fire lane by dark. Your radios should work from there. Maybe you could have someone pick us up."

They gathered the leftover food, said goodbye to Ezra, and left.

Chapter 11

Ezra Marsh

They started down the path away from Ezra's cabin. Ray continued to lead with his rifle slung across his arm, and Bobbie went next, still carrying a larger pack. Hank followed her, and Lucy was in the rear. Hank had been fairly chatty on the trail unless they had been concerned about an ambush, but now he was quiet. Lucy finally asked him why he was so quiet.

"Aren't we worried about the guy ahead of us?" Hank replied. "I'm not, but I don't think that's why you're quiet," Lucy answered. "OK," Hank answered, as if a cork had been let out of a bottle. He was building pressure inside for a long time.

"Why did you ask that guy for a drink? You know you can't drink alcohol." "I'm surprised you of all people would ask me that question," Lucy said, genuinely confused.

Hank actually stopped and turned around. "Me of all people. What am I supposed to do, just let you relapse?"

Locking eyes, she said, "Hank, when you walked into that place where he had been drinking all day, what did you smell?"

Hank was the one confused now. "What did I smell? What does that have to do with you not only relapsing but also putting all our lives in jeopardy because you lose focus and make the wrong decision out here? You're worried about what I smelled? I didn't smell anything."

Hank paused, suddenly aware of where Lucy was going with this.

They say a shark can smell a drop of blood in ten million gallons of water. A recovering alcoholic is at least as adept at smelling alcohol. Often, it is very aversive to them and makes them sick. If Ezra had had a bottle of whiskey open in his cabin for quite awhile, not only would there be the smell from the open bottle, but also on his breath; his body would even be secreting it. But Hank had smelled nothing.

"You knew it wasn't alcohol. How dumb am I, not only for not picking up on that, but also for doubting you. I'm sorry. Can you be sure, besides the smell, that it wasn't booze in there?"

"Well, for one thing, I've never known a self respecting drunk who was unwilling to share."

Hank thought about this, smiled, and nodded.

"Besides, the bottle he was drinking out of had an old label on it, like the one it had when my father used to drink it. I used to drink the same stuff, and by then the label was different. How long did you keep liquor?"

"I remember once when I had the flu, a case of beer lasted me an entire week. But why would he pretend to be a drunk? I could tell him that it's just not all that glamorous."

"He had to make us think he wasn't out all night stalking us and pouring blood next to were we slept," Lucy answered. "I'll bet that deer on his porch donated the blood you found this morning. He's our kidnapper."

Hank had started skiing again, but this made him stop and turn around.

"That's the guy? What makes you so sure?"

"Well, for one thing, why else would he pretend to be drunk? Two, he matches the description that Lisa gave. I bet if we searched underneath that cabin of his we'd find cross country skis, and maybe even a doll without a head."

Bobbie no longer pretended not to listen. "Why don't you arrest him then?" she asked anxiously.

"He obviously doesn't have the baby now. I think if we arrested him, he wouldn't tell us where it is. I'd rather have him think we bought his story, and maybe he'll lead us to where the baby is. What do you think, Ray?"

"I think you are one smart cop, Lucy. I also think I should quit busting my ass trying to catch up with some mythical character ahead of us." Ray slowed to a stop and took a long slug from his water bottle.

Lucy suddenly felt warm all over. She had been so busy since her eyes opened this morning, she never even thought of the night before. It had been so long since she had slept next to a man. She remembered how good Ray's body felt next to hers.

What she liked even more than that was that she trusted him. He kept his word, even though she wasn't sure she'd have resisted if he hadn't. She felt secure with him as evidenced by the fact that she slept like a baby, safe and secure in his arms.

And finally, he respected her and wasn't afraid to let other people know that he did. How many other men would have pretended to know what Lucy had figured out? Ray gave her all the credit. Now she was beginning to understand some of the feelings she had when she was around him. First was confusion. She had never known a man like Ray Waupuse. Second was also confusion: she had never felt what she felt toward him, not even toward her husband, God rest his soul.

They each rested awhile on the trail and drank some water. Hank pulled out some trail mix, and they snacked on it. Then they heard a snowmobile in the distance.

They realized they were close now to where Ezra said he kept a snowmobile, and they wondered if he had slipped out ahead of them on another trail. They quickly stowed their gear and continued down the trail. When they arrived at the fire lane, they looked for the shed where Ezra stored his snowmobile and truck found it quickly. Inside, they found both were still there. Ray felt the motors, and they were cold.

Lucy pulled out her radio and tried to reach someone, but all she heard was silence. It was getting dark, and now the question was what to do next.

"Should we pitch a tent and stay out here another night, or use our headlamps and go the eight more miles to W?" Hank asked.

It was about 5:30pm and already getting dark.

"Eight miles seems like a lot of skiing, especially in the dark," Ray said.

"I agree. I'm pretty tired, but I don't relish the idea of pitching a tent and being a sitting duck for some wacko either," Bobbie added.

"We can keep going and keep trying the radio. As we get closer, we're bound to be able to reach the station or a squad going by on W," Lucy said.

"We might hook up with a snowmobiler on this fire lane also. I know I've been on this stretch myself. There are some bars on W that they like to stop at," Ray added.

"That's another thing that scares me, speaking of being sitting ducks," said Hank. "We've got to be careful of some drunken snowmobiler heading down the lane at one hundred miles an hour."

They turned on their headlamps and started cautiously down the lane. They had skied about an hour and had gone a few miles when they heard a snowmobile behind them. Lucy immediately thought of Ezra. He could easily hit them and say he hadn't seen them in the dark.

"Let's move off the lane," she yelled to those ahead. They moved, but the snowmobile quickly closed the gap between them. When the rider caught them, he stopped.

"Teller, is that you?" The man on the sled was wearing a helmet with a face shield, but Lucy had no difficulty identifying Lieutenant Moon's voice.

"Yes, Sir," she answered.

"We've been looking for you for hours now and trying to contact you on your radio. Do you have it on?"

"No, Sir. I was trying to save the battery." She wondered if he had his glasses on under his helmet and if he was looking over them right now.

"Speaking of the battery, when the last time you changed it?" Lieutenant Moon asked firmly.

"It might have been a while, Sir." She felt herself flushing, but it didn't matter. It was too dark for him to see, and no matter what, she was never happier to see anyone.

The lieutenant used his radio, and soon there were enough snowmobiles to get them to W, into squad cars, and back to their cars at Dawn's house. Hank used Bobbie's cell phone to call Molly and let her know they were both all right. Neither he nor Bobby felt capable of driving the hour home without risking falling asleep, and Lucy had asked if they could help her with her report in the morning.

Hank promised to fill Molly in as soon as he arrived home. He told his wife he loved her and said goodbye. Ray lived alone and had room at his place for them to stay the night. While Hank and Bobbie took turns using the shower, Ray cooked some food, and it smelled delicious. Their mouths were watering as the three of them sat down to eat. Bobbie and Hank cleaned the dishes while Ray took his turn in the shower. They watched TV for a while afterwards, but none of them was able to make it through the first show.

One by one, as their various dreams awoke them, they made their way to bed. It was well past dawn before they touched their feet to the floor.

Lucy had gone home and spent the better part of an hour soaking in the tub, occasionally adding more hot water.

When she got out, there were four people who were anxious to hear what she had found. She left out all that they had discovered after their first night in the woods, but for Lisa, she gave enough information to help her believe there was still hope of finding her brother alive.

For her children, she talked about skiing and the spot where they had spent the night in the icehouse. She told them all about the things she had learned about winter camping and surviving in the woods. She kept to herself what she had discovered about her feelings toward Ray. She led them to believe that they spent the night in their own sleeping bags.

When she finally crawled into her own bed, she wondered what would await her. She had so much to review and so many decisions to make about what to do next, but she knew also that she was exhausted and needed rest. What would win: her tired-to-the-bone body, her head full of thoughts and ideas clamoring for her attention, or her newly awakened feelings waiting to be explored? A wave of sleep washed over all of it, giving her body the rest it needed, and leaving her unconscious mind to sort out everything else. The result was a series of bizarre dreams, most of which she couldn't remember. Unfortunately, just before dawn, she awoke abruptly after a smiling, contented baby was stuck to a stake.

She got up, made some coffee, and started her report.

Chapter 12

Bobbie and Kathy

The next day, Bobbie decided to take the car and drive in to see Kathy, who was now working in the same classroom where Scott had worked before he died. Kathy felt a connection to Scott there, so she had called Lucy and volunteered to take Lisa to school.

Kathy was disappointed she couldn't have joined them in the search for Lisa's brother when she heard about it. She and Brad had begun to date regularly now, but she hadn't told Bobbie yet. Brad had for the first time spent the previous weekend with her in Shawano. Kathy didn't feel this was the time or place to confide that to Bobbie, however, so they talked about their time in the woods.

Bobbie also withheld much, since she wasn't sure what Lucy would want her to reveal about an ongoing investigation. Kathy talked about her experiences with the children, and Bobbie was quite interested in that, since she had been an education major herself and had thought she'd go back to it when she returned to school. She was also toying with the idea of a criminal justice career after her experience over the last couple of days.

She told Kathy she had never been so frightened in all her life, but she felt that she had never been involved in anything more meaningful or exciting.

Hank sat down with Lucy and read what she had written in her report. There wasn't much he could add or alter since he agreed with what she had written.

"I don't see anything in here about Officer Teller faking hypothermia so she could crawl in the sack with Officer Waupuse." Hank laughed and Lucy turned red.

"You know I was awake then, and I was just going to give you the same advice if you hadn't agreed with Ray. As a matter of fact, had your shaking not subsided I was prepared to wake Bobbie and have her strip to her bra and panties and lay in front of you in the bag. Hypothermia is nothing to take lightly. If you had finished dressing and gone outside, I'm convinced you'd be dead right now. Ray saved your life.

"I like him a lot, Lucy, and I like the two of you together. Not that it's any of my business, or that you care about my opinion."

Lucy smiled, trying not to reveal too much about what was happening to her at the thought of that night or how good it felt to hear that someone she respected, liked how she looked with Ray and seemed to be telling her to pursue the relationship.

"I do care what you think, but I have to simplify my life a little before I can think about adding anything more to it," she said. Partly to change the subject, she asked, "Had any more dreams about Scott lately?"

"No. I wake up every morning feeling disappointed that he hasn't visited me again. I can't tell you what it meant to me to have the opportunity to do this with you over the last couple of days. Not only did I get a chance to prove something to myself, but also I was able to get out of myself for a while and my own grief and guilt. How about you?"

"No. I guess like you I've focused on finding Michael and haven't focused on Scott as much. But I have the feeling that we're doing what Scot wants us to do, and eventually this is going to lead us back to him."

"The next right thing: that's what both of us have to remember, I guess," Hank said.

Bobbie walked in on the last of the conversation. "I've come to know AA talk when I hear it. What is this about?" she asked.

Lucy gave Hank an "I defer to you" look.

"We were talking about Scott," Hank said.

"Oh," was all Bobbie said, and she looked down.

An awkward silence filled the room. At least, awkward for Hank and Bobbie who were used to the room being filled with words when three people were present. Bobbie broke it. "So should I look at your report?" she asked Lucy.

Lucy handed it to her, and she began to read. Ray came in a few minutes later and offered to show Hank around. Hank accepted.

After they left, Bobbie handed Lucy the report. "It looks pretty thorough."

On the ride home, Hank and Bobbie talked openly about what they had shared together. There was a closeness between them that had been interrupted with Scott's death. When they reached home, the whole family was there to greet them.

Even Ryan had come home, supposedly because he was running low on laundry.

Chapter 13

Doc Wolf

At the treatment center, Lucy's first stop was at Dr. Wolf's office. He was there, riding an exercise bike in the corner. He had run cross-country in high school and was pretty good at it. Then, with medical school and his drug involvement, he had gotten very out of shape. Now, partly to relieve the stress of working with addicts all day, he had started running again. As he began to regain his former condition, he had gotten into cross training. He not only ran, but also started bike riding, rollerblading, canoeing, and swimming. He had won a few of the 5K races the tribe sponsored during the pow wow. He had also won the first triathlon that took place on the reservation the previous summer.

He had gotten a group together to put on an "experience the rez" event for the following summer. Similar to one put on in Duluth, Minnesota, it would involve not only the swimming, biking, and running of a triathlon, but also canoeing, kayaking, rollerblading, and mountain biking.

"How's my favorite patient?" he asked, not slowing down his pedaling in the least, keeping up a cadence of 90 repetitions per minute.

"Oh, you say that to all the girls, Dr. Meany," Lucy said, with a mock tone of dejection. "How is our new favorite patient doing?"

"I think you'll be pleasantly surprised. She's been going to group, and they've been calling her on her lack of responsibility, and getting her to deal with her feelings honestly. She's sure not out of the woods yet, and you know the recovery rate of heroin addicts, but I'd say she has a fighting chance. Any news on her son?"

"Nothing concrete." Lucy didn't want to burden Dr. Wolf with details that he would then have to keep from everyone else. "I do believe that the baby is still alive. By the way, I've got a great new aerobic exercise for you to try. We've been searching the woods on cross-country skis, and I now have to use my arms to lift my legs to operate the clutch and brake on my truck; that's how sore my legs are."

"I've tried the machines a few times, but never the real thing. I understand it's the best aerobic exercise you can get. I'm surprised you're that sore. Aren't you in pretty good shape? You've been telling me you run twenty miles a week."

"I thought I was. I guess it's different muscles, but I sure feel it."

"Well, do you think you're good enough to give me a lesson?"

"I don't know if I am, but I'm sure my friend Hank is. Maybe we could arrange an outing for the Alumni group. I know a great trail we could try near here, or we could head up to Hank's. There are a bunch of them up his way, he tells me."

"That sounds like a plan."

"I might even get my kids to try it. We could make it a family outing. I have to get some time though. Do you know if Dawn is free now?"

Dr. Wolf looked at his watch. "She should be just getting out of group. You know where they meet. I have five more minutes left on this. Stop by on your way out."

Lucy walked down the familiar hall and thought about how her life had changed over the last four years. She had spent the first two getting sober and taking care of her children. After that, she had started working for the tribal police. She had spent one year as a dispatcher and the last as a patrol officer.

At her AA meetings, the question sometimes came up: if scientists invented a pill that allowed you to use socially, would you go back to drinking and using? Lucy was convinced even if she was guaranteed that it would work, she wouldn't try it. She liked what she had too much. First of all, as a native, she didn't know what social drinking even was.

She smiled to herself. Every drinker she had ever known drank to get drunk. And then she didn't know anyone from any culture who took other drugs socially, certainly not heroin.

As she approached the group room, she could see Dawn exiting with a group of patients with whom she seemed to have made friends. Even at a distance, Lucy could see the change. She was arm in arm with another woman, and they were laughing together. She looked like a different person. What a change a smile can make, Lucy thought.

When she saw Lucy, she let go of the woman, and the smile left her face.

"Do you have news about my children?" she asked Lucy, rushing toward her.

"Well, I can tell you that Lisa's doing o.k. at home with my family. I talked with her teacher just before I came here, and she's doing well at school also. I wish I had good news about Michael, but I don't have any bad news either. I can't give you details, but I'm more optimistic about Michael than I was the last time I was here."

Dawn looked relieved. Lucy braced herself for a barrage of criticism and questions that never came.

"I appreciate what you're doing for all of us," was all Dawn said.

"You seem much better than you were the last time I was here. How has treatment been going?"

"I've got a lot to deal with. As I get the drugs out of my system, I realize more and more why I took them. I have issues with my own growing up that I never addressed, and I used drugs to dull the pain. I looked for a relationship that would keep me safe, and instead I found someone who used me like my father did.

The counselors are suggesting a halfway house after this so I can continue to deal with all this. They say if I don't take that extra time to heal, the pain of it will lead me right back to using. But how can I abandon my children any longer? I feel like I have so much to make up to them. I don't understand why I never saw this clearly until now."

"Lisa is fine staying with us, and as of now we don't know where Michael is. So you go ahead and concentrate on living one day at a time and keep healing. Each day without drugs, your mind will get clearer, and you'll see the path you need to take."

Dawn smiled. "You sound like Dr. Meany."

"You know, I'm the one who gave him that name," Lucy said, feeling proud on both counts. Lucy gave her a goodbye hug and walked back down the hall.

Lucy stuck her head in his office. Dr. Wolf was toweling himself off.

"You're doing a wonderful job, and she says I sound just like you," Lucy said.

Doc. gave her the thumbs up, and she continued from the building.

Chapter 14

Bobbie

Bobbie sat on a snowmobile in a clump of pine trees right near the shed where Ezra kept his snowmobile. Neither Lucy nor Lieutenant Moon was very thrilled with the idea of a civilian doing surveillance, but they didn't have enough officers to watch the shed twenty-four/seven so when Hank and Bobbie offered to help, they had finally relented. Hank had told Lucy that she'd be doing him a favor not only because he wanted to continue to help, but as he put it, he needed help with his daughter as well.

"The good news is she's now anxious to return to school. The bad news is that since our adventure she's considering switching her major to law enforcement. I figure if you can put her on a boring stakeout, maybe she'll find out that a lot of police work isn't so glamorous. Besides, it's not like you want us to confront Ezra, just find out where he's going."

Hank and Bobbie were both given strict orders to give Ezra plenty of room and make sure they weren't discovered. Lucy gave them fully-charged radios that were powerful enough to reach the dispatcher. They each took four-hour shifts in the daytime.

Bobbie had been sitting behind the trees for about an hour, and though she was dressed for the worst, the bitter cold of the day was already beginning to seep through her snowmobile suit and the layers she had under it. Her mind wandered to her boyfriend, Tom. She had gotten used to seeing him every day, and she missed him since she wasn't at school. They talked every day on the phone, but it wasn't the same. She smiled as she thought of him telling her he was going to parties every night. First, she knew he was teasing, and she had enough spies to let her know he hung around mostly with his friends and was studying hard. Second, she trusted him completely. Tom was not a partier.

She didn't even see Ezra enter his shed and was startled to hear his snowmobile fire up. After warming it up for a while, he exited. He sped quickly by the trees she was hiding in and seemed to pay little attention to anything around him. She could tell by his speed as he passed that she'd have no trouble giving him plenty of room, because there was no way she was going to be going that fast. She just hoped that she'd have the nerve to go fast enough to be able to tell where he might be going. It had snowed an inch or two the night before, and he was the first to use the logging road, so she didn't have to stay that close.

She radioed that Ezra was on the move and that she was following cautiously behind him. Bobbie was careful to use the word 'cautiously' because she knew Ray, Lucy, and her dad would all be listening. Lucy, waiting in her squad car, turned on her dome lights and headed up W toward Berry Lake, hoping to reach the spot where Ezra would get on the highway. As she got close to the spot where he would exit, she turned off her lights and slowed down.

Soon she saw a flash cross the highway and quickly disappear in the woods on the other side. A few minutes later, Bobbie appeared in the same spot and stopped on the highway. Lucy pulled up in front of her.

"Where did he go?" Bobbie asked.

"He headed straight across the highway. Do you want me to take it from here?"

"No, you're not dressed for it," Bobbie answered. "I'll follow,"

Before Lucy could argue with her, Bobbie was around her car and across the highway.

She had been following Ezra's tracks for nearly an hour. She occasionally stopped her sled and turned off her engine to listen for other sleds in the area. She could hear one or more, but usually at a distance from her. The sun was dropping low in the sky, and Bobbie wondered if she should turn on her headlight or not. She picked up speed to try to gain on Ezra. Just past a clump of pines, another sledder cut in front of her, and she turned sharply to avoid him. In the next instant, she was heading for a large tree.

She turned sharply again and the sled turned, but it was sliding sideways toward the tree now.

Bobbie felt things moving in slow motion even though the sled was moving at a dangerously fast speed. She leaned on it, trying to avoid hitting the tree and turned the sled on its side. She hit the tree with her runners, and the impact knocked her radio into the snow and the breath out of her lungs.

Bobbie lay in the snow motionless, as darkness fell around her. Even if she could yell, no one would hear her. Bobbie lost consciousness. The snowmobiler who had cut her off continued down the trail, either oblivious of what had happened or intentionally leaving her to freeze in the cold night air.

Chapter 15

Bobbie and Ezra

The radio had been silent too long. Hank had started his shift shortly after he had heard that Ezra had crossed W. He drove his SUV to a parking lot near where Bobby had crossed W and pulled his sled off the trailer. Bobbie had radioed a couple of times since crossing W when she'd stopped her sled to listen, but he had heard nothing for an hour. It was dark now, and his headlight lit the trail in front of him, but the woods on either side of him were dark.

Lucy and Ray, also concerned, were out on the trail, searching less now for Ezra than for Bobbie. The three of them radioed back and forth, each with nothing to report and hoping their fears would not become reality.

Bobbie came to slowly, first aware of the cold on her face. Her foot was wedged under an exposed root, and the sled was on top of her leg. Surprisingly, she felt no pain. She could see the radio half-buried in the snow and reached for it, but it was inches beyond her fingertips. Willing herself, she stretched with all her might, but she could not reach it. She could hear Ray, Lucy, and Hank talking among themselves.

They came up the path she had followed. Bobbie felt such relief. When they got near where she was, she began to yell, but the noise from their sleds drowned out her call for help, and the branches of the tree blocked their view of her from their direction. The tears ran down her face as they turned the way that the snowmobile that cut her off had gone, away from where she was.

She felt the cold seeping into her, and she fought the urge to fall asleep. She knew she had to stay awake to survive. After what seemed like eternity to her, laying in the dark and giving up hope, a snowmobile pulled up next to her. A tall, thin man got off the sled and walked toward her.

"I know you guys want to find that baby, but do you really think you're going to find it under that tree in the dark?"

Bobbie panicked when she heard Ezra's voice and lunged as hard as she could for the radio. She touched it with her fingertips just as Hank's voice rang from the speaker. She could hear the panic in her fathers' voice.

"Bobbie, if you can hear this please respond."

Ezra picked up the radio. He stared at it for a long time. Bobbie was sure he was contemplating throwing it into the woods. Finally, he turned to her.

"How do you work this thing?"

Bobbie started crying. She started to pray silently. "Push the red button to talk," she said through her tears. "Then let it up to listen."

Ezra did as he was told. "This is Ezra. I've got your daughter. She seems scared and might have a broken leg, but otherwise she's OK."

There was silence on the phone. Ezra turned to Bobbie. "I don't think it worked." He set the radio on his sled.

"Press the button again. Tell them you found me under a tree and that my snowmobile had fallen on top of me."

This time Ezra ignored her. Bobbie heard him say, "I think we need to check you out first. This might hurt." Again without waiting for an answer, he dislodged Bobbie's leg. Probably because it was numb, the pain was bearable. Ezra immediately noticed the leg was bleeding. "The pressure of the sled and the cold kept you from bleeding to death. I need to fix this cut right away." He went right to his sled and pulled out a first aid kit. He took his head lamp and a needle and thread and began to sew the skin of her ankle. He worked patiently but quickly. When he finished he took guaze and wrapped the leg tightly.

"Now pull yourself out from there, and I'll straighten out your sled and see if I can't get it started," he barked at her. Bobbie pulled herself out from what would have been her grave, but remained on the ground afraid to test the leg. Then Ezra quickly picked up the sled, with what appeared to Bobbie to be incredible strength. He started it and pulled it back out to the path. "Can you stand on that leg?"

Then he tried the Radio again.

"This is Ezra again. I found your daughter under a tree. She had an accident. Her leg was stuck under her sled."

This time, the response was immediate. "Where are you, and how can we find you?" Bobbie gratefully heard her father's voice.

"I'll fire my rifle in the air. Let me know if you hear it."

It was then that Bobbie noticed Ezra had his rifle strapped over his shoulder again. He removed it with one hand. Bobbie watched as he raised the barrel to her face. She closed her eyes and flinched as she heard the shot. When she opened her eyes, he held the rifle straight up in the air. "Did you hear that?"

"Yes. Fire it again in about a minute," Lucy answered back.

Bobbie stood up slowly, keeping the weight on her good leg, and then slowly placing weight on the other leg. It felt sore, particularly by the ankle, but it supported her body. She walked to her sled, and Ezra vacated it as she approached. He went to his rifle and fired it in the air again.

"We saw the discharge that time," Lucy said. "We'll be there in a minute."

"Why don't you let go of this hunt before someone gets hurt? Maybe the baby's in a better place." After saying that, Ezra threw the radio to Bobbie. "Get inside right away," he told her.

"Thanks," she said.

Then Ezra got on his sled and left.

Chapter 16

Bobbie

Hank, Lucy, and Ray arrived moments after Ezra left. Bobbie hugged her father the moment he pulled up.

"Am I glad to see you," she said as her voice cracked.

"And I you. What happened?" Hank replied.

"Let's get her to my place by the fire, and then we can ask her questions," Ray said with concern in his voice.

All of a sudden, Bobbie realized how cold she was, for the first time since Ezra had arrived, as she got on her sled. She started to shiver as the speed of her sled created a wind on her body, but the heat from the motor soon began to warm her. Ray went ahead to start his car and began to warm it up. As soon as Bobbie arrived in the parking lot, Ray took her in his car, and she sat there with the heater running high while the rest of them loaded up the snowmobiles.

"Ezra said something about a broken leg?" Lucy said with a question in her voice.

"I wedged my foot in an exposed root, and the sled fell on top of my leg. My ankle is sore, but I know nothing is broken. He talked to you after he had gotten me loose, but before I stood up. I had a cut on my leg and he stitched it up. He said if it wasn't for the cold and the pressure my leg was under I probably would have bled to death." Bobbie answered.

They made a quick stop at the tribal clinic just to make sure the leg wasn't broken, and to have the doctor look at the stitches.

"I couldn't have done better myself. Who did this?" The doctor asked.

"Ezra Marsh" Lucy answered.

"That explains it." The Doctor said. "He was a medic in Viet Nam. He has a number of awards."

Lucy thought back to his cabin and they were definitely not displayed. She asked the Doctor what else he knew about Ezra. He told her he had never even met him just that he had heard he was an Army hero and a medic. The x-rays were negative.

Once at Ray's, she wrapped up in a blanket.

"How did you tip?" Hank asked.

"I reached a point where two trails merged. I didn't have my lights on even though it was getting dark, because I didn't want Ezra to know where I was. Another sled came from the other direction, and I swerved to avoid him, I was heading toward a tree and had to swerve again to avoid it. That's when the sled and I tipped."

"The person whom you avoided didn't stop?" Lucy asked.

"I'm not even sure he knew I was there. I came from behind some pine trees. I was slightly behind him, and I didn't have my light on."

"How could anyone not know?" Hank asked in disgust.

"There are several bars on W. These guys go from one to the next and have several drinks at each one. He could have hit his mother head on and not known it," Ray said.

"But it could have been Ezra, too," Lucy said. "Do you know for sure it wasn't him?"

"No. As I said, it was getting dark. All I saw was a shadow. But why would he wait over an hour to come back?"

"Maybe his conscience began to get to him, or maybe he just waited around to see if we'd find you first. It could have been another one of his little messages, like the blood and the doll's head."

Bobbie shivered. This time it wasn't from the cold. "I don't know what to think. I have to feel grateful to him for helping me, but I got the strong feeling he was trying to intimidate me also. I know the man gives me the creeps. I do not trust him at all."

"Well, there's no sense in keeping tabs on him now. He knows we're watching him," Lucy said.

"I'm sorry I blew it," Bobbie said, sounding dejected.

"You didn't do anything wrong. I'm sure he was suspicious of us being on to him, since we went to his cabin. Maybe we need to let him think we've heeded his warning and are staying away. I have some other leads I can follow. He's been in this area for a while. He must come into town for supplies. This is a small area. Someone must recognize him."

However, Lucy was surprised at just who that might be.

Chapter 17

Karen

The next day, Lucy decided to see Karen. Karen knew more people in the area than anyone and always had her ear to the ground. The best she hoped for was that Karen knew someone who knew someone, but as soon as she mentioned Ezra and where he lived, Karen was on a roll. Lucy didn't even tell her why she was interested in Ezra.

"I know that man. There was a time he could drink you and half the village under the table. He was abusive to his wife and his daughter. He learned to be mean from his own parents. I've heard he was beaten as a child and came close to death on two violent occasions. Finally, his wife got the nerve to take the daughter and go to a shelter. Ezra, like all abusive men, promised to change. Said he'd quit drinking, brought her presents.

Finally, against all her DV counselors' advice, she agreed to give him one more chance. Her counselors were sick about it because the large majority of abusers never change. They had all too often seen women go back with their heads filled with promises, only to be abused again or worse. But to their surprise, Ezra straightened out. He gave up drinking and became a devoted husband and father. What made it even more amazing is he did it without help. He never attended AA or group counseling for his abuse.

I stayed involved with the family for years afterward because I always believed he wouldn't last. I kept encouraging him to get help, but he never did. There wasn't a whole lot I could say about it, because not only was there no evidence of problems, but also I believe they were a loving couple and family.

When their daughter went off to nursing school, they left the reservation to be close to her. They moved back a couple of years ago, when their daughter got a job in Shawano. They were doing great. I'd see him and his wife out cross-country skiing in the wintertime. They had picked it up while their daughter was in college.

Then Ezra's wife got breast cancer and died quickly. I went to the funeral. Ezra didn't say a word to anyone. He just stared. After the funeral, he moved to his hunting shack in the woods, and I haven't seen him since. I think all that untreated alcoholism finally got the best of him. He never completely escaped the emotional wounds inflicted by his parents and himself."

"What about the daughter? What happened to her?" Lucy asked.

She met a man in college of whom the parents were quite fond. They settled in Shawano, and she still works at a hospital in Shawano."

"What unit does she work in?" Lucy was curious.

Karen hung her head. In a soft, sad voice, she answered, "She works in maternity. She's so good with those babies. She and her husband have been trying for so long to have a child. They've even tried a fertility clinic, but they have now given up. It's so sad. She'd be such a good mom."

Light bulbs were flashing in Lucy's head. "When did you find out they had given up?"

"Just last week. She even said she might give up maternity nursing because it's just too painful for her. She told me her husband was getting promoted, and it might require a move. She said she might take the opportunity to train in a new area of nursing. Might even go back to school for her master's degree and take some time off."

"Where does she live in Shawano?" Lucy asked.

"I've never been to her house, but she told me once she lives on Loon Lake. It's north and east of there. You know how nice it is around that lake," Karen answered, beginning to look a little confused at Lucy's interest in the daughter.

"Do you suppose you could introduce me to her?" Lucy asked, standing up quickly.

"Sure. I talked with her this morning about a cocaine baby that was born there. I'm on my way over now, but what's the big deal with her?"

"One more question. Was Michael Lake born in Shawano Hospital, and was Ezra's daughter his nurse?"

Karen's face turned white. She had been in the business too long not to be able to sort what little she knew about this case into a puzzle inside her head that was beginning to look like a scene she didn't care for.

"Her name is Gabby. She thought he was the cutest thing. He stayed in the hospital longer because of low birth weight. She got real attached to him and often asked me about him. She always looked sad and angry when I'd tell her about him. Once she even blurted out, 'it's not fair.'

"I never thought much about it, because I felt the same way. She seemed concerned when I first told her Michael was missing, but the next time I talked with her about it, she said, 'I'm sure the mother or the boyfriend killed him,' and she didn't seem to want to talk about it any more. I thought at the time it was just too painful for her, but now I see where you're going with this."

"I think Ezra is still trying to make up for what he's done to his wife and daughter, and now she's in a bind," Lucy said. "Let's go see Gabby at the hospital and hint to her that we know what happened. Do you think there's any chance she would hurt the baby to save her father?"

"No, and I'd stake my life on that," Karen said. Then she continued to look thoughtfully at Lucy.

"What?" Lucy asked, because she knew the look.

"Will you have to charge Gabby with aiding and abetting or something like that?"

"That's not up to me."

"But right now, you and I are the only ones who've figure this out, right?"

"We don't even know for sure that we're right. Where are you going with this?"

"If the baby is in her home, and my gut tells me you're right and he is, and she's charged with a crime, then I'm going to have to remove the baby and take him somewhere else. I'm removing that child from the best possible environment to someplace less suitable. She's a caring and loving person, and this baby has been through enough. Let's think about him for a while.

"Can't we at least slow things down? Let me talk with her myself. Let her know I'm on her side and that I think you might be onto what's going on with the baby. You go talk with the mother, tell her the situation, find out what she wants. If she's still in treatment, the baby needs to stay somewhere. Why not where he is?"

Lucy's mind was whirling. "But is it helpful to Gabby to allow her to become even more attached if eventually she going to have to give him up? Wouldn't it be better to remove him right away?"

"I don't know. My first thought is for the child. Failure to thrive children can sometimes turn around in the right environment. Let's give him a chance at a healthy life," she pleaded.

"I'll go talk with my sponsor and Dr. Wolf and see what they suggest about talking with Dawn. Make sure you stress to Gabby that if she and her husband do something stupid like take the baby across state lines, it will be out of my hands, and I'll have to report it to the FBI.

"By the way, they call it Reactive Attachment Disorder now."

Karen waved her hand in disgust. "I gave up trying to keep up with unimportant changes years ago. I think Gabby will be relieved if there is a way out of this for all concerned. Besides, I'm not powerless in this either. If Gabby is the best environment for that child, and we're not tied by criminal charges, Michael just may stay there. The judges around here will listen to me."

"You're getting way ahead of me. I think you are still kicking yourself for not acting fast enough, and now you're trying to act too fast. Breathe, Karen, breathe."

"I hate it when my client becomes my counselor. You're right. I promise not to get ahead of you in this. I appreciate your giving me some time."

They talked about what Karen would say exactly to Gabby. Once they were clear, Karen gave Lucy a hug. "You have been a gift in my life, Lucy Teller."

Lucy smiled with pride. "Funny, I always thought it was the other way around."

Each went her way with a task neither wanted.

Chapter 18

The Plan

Lucy decided to include Ray in on the plan as well, since he could advise her in police matters. She called him and asked him to meet her at Maehnowesekiyah Treatment Center. On her way there, she stopped by her sponsor Sophie's house and found her at home.

"Hey girl, I need you to take a ride with me. Are you up for it?"

"I don't know. I usually don't make a habit of riding with strangers," Sophie snapped.

"Oh, cut it out. It hasn't been that long."

"Sure, I'll go. Where to?"

"I need to talk with Dr. Wolf out at the treatment center. I'll fill you in on the way."

"Told you you'd relapse if you weren't careful." She stuck out her tongue at Lucy.

"It's not about me. I'm fine."

On the way to the treatment center, Lucy filled Sophie in on what had happened to Lisa, Michael, and Dawn. As they pulled up, they spotted Ray waiting for them out front. When they had gathered in Dr. Wolf's office, Lucy explained what she had talked about with Karen.

"I think the baby is in the right place for now, but I don't know what will happen if I tell Dawn I found the baby and then suggest he stay where he is for now."

"What is the purpose for all of us being here?" Ray asked.

"Dr. Wolf is here to help decide what is best for Dawn; besides it's his office. He'd be here anyway. Sophie is here to help me decide what's best for me and my recovery. You're here to advise me what's best from a police standpoint."

"Well," Sophie said. "I bet Ray and I agree. It sounds like you're taking the law into your own hands, and I say it's dangerous for you personally and professionally."

"Dawn has come a long way even since you saw her last, but I don't know if she could handle hearing that you want to leave her son with a person who was an accomplice in a kidnapping."

"What if we tell her that we found the baby and put him in foster care for now? It's partly true, and I could be the one to tell her so the treatment staff doesn't have to be a part of a half-truth."

"You still haven't answered my question about taking the law into your own hands. Now you're adding dishonesty to my concerns about you," Sophie said, rolling her eyes and stepping away from Lucy.

"I think at the very least, you need to include Lt. Moon in on this," Ray added, taking a large step closer to Lucy.

"O.k., help me decide on priorities. We have to tell Dawn something. We have to tell Lt. Moon something. I'd like to tell Lisa about her brother as well, and at this point we're not even sure that Michael is where I think he is." Lucy's head was beginning to hurt. She was wishing for a simpler life at the moment.

For a long time the room grew silent. This would be strange in the white culture, but Lucy and the others let the silence settle over them like a warm blanket on a cold night and waited for it to provide the answers. When they spoke again, the room was calmer, and they were working with one voice. Between the voices and the silence, a plan emerged, and the values of honesty and respect took charge. They decided to wait a while longer to tell Dawn until they were sure Lucy was correct. Ray would fill in Lt. Moon. They would let Karen talk with Ezra's daughter, and then Lucy would bring Lisa to visit her brother if indeed he was where Lucy thought he was. She could then bring Lisa to visit Dawn, and together they could tell her that her son was safe. Lucy was satisfied with the plan, but that might have Witch of Winter been because at the moment, she wasn't thinking of the expression that life is what happens when you're planning something else.

Before they could leave the parking lot, the dispatcher called and told Ray he and Lucy should report immediately to Lt. Moon's office, and she warned Ray that the Lieutenant was not happy. Lucy dropped off Sophie and met Ray outside the Lieutenant's office.

Chapter 19

Ezra

Lucy felt better walking into the Lieutenant's office with Ray, but her good feeling was short-lived when she saw Agent Scruggs of the FBI standing next to the large desk, looking even more smug than usual. Before Lieutenant Moon had a chance to say anything, Agent Scruggs started in.

"While you were busy with your little witch hunt, Officer Teller, I and my fellow agents were busy doing real police work, and as usual, it paid off with real results. We have located the boyfriend, apprehended him, and gotten him to confess to the murder of Michael Lake. You can therefore go back to patrolling the highways for which at least you have some training," he said sarcastically.

Ray, who was standing behind Lucy and whose mouth was right by her ear, growled just loud enough so only she could hear, "Witch hunt?" Just as Lucy was going to congratulate Agent Scruggs through her clenched teeth, there was a knock on the door.

"Sorry for interrupting, but there is a man named Ezra Marsh out here who says he needs to talk with you, Lucy." The receptionist announced.

"Tell him I'm busy now. See if he'll talk with one of the other officers," Lucy answered, though secretly she was glad to have a few more moments to compose herself so that her praise of Agent Scruggs could sound more sincere.

"I tried that," she answered in a shaky voice. "He says he'll only talk with you, and it has to do with the murder of Michael Lake."

"Maybe he was a witness," Scruggs enthused arrogantly. "With the confession and a witness, we can put this thing to bed. Tell him you'll talk to him. We'll watch through the two-way mirror while you speak with him in the interrogation room."

Lucy started to say that she wasn't sure it was going to happen that way, but decided to go along with Scruggs's plan.

She was right: something very different happened.

Chapter 20

Ezra

Lucy took a deep breath and opened the door to the interrogation room. As she was still walking, she smiled.

"Ezra, it's good to see you again. You left the other night before we had a chance to thank you for helping Bobbie. I'm sure you saved her life. We would never have found her in time. We all appreciate you helping her."

Lieutenant Moon, standing outside the interrogation room behind the two-way mirror, looked over his glasses at Ray. Ray looked back. "We haven't had a chance to write a report on that one yet, Sir." Then Ray turned his attention back to the other side of the glass, in an effort to divert the Lieutenant's attention.

"Well, before anyone else gets hurt, I think it's time we end this, I know you're on to me. I'm here to confess to the murder of Michael Lake." His voice was getting softer, almost to a whisper.

This time the Lieutenant looked over his glasses at Agent Scruggs, who pretended not to notice. Like Ray, Scruggs kept his attention focused on the other side of the mirror.

"I'm confused for a lot of reasons. One, because we already have someone who confessed to that murder, and two, what makes you think we even suspect you, much less have a case against you? All you've done is help us," Lucy said as she leaned closer.

"I've heard people talk about you. I know you've lost your children temporarily because of alcohol, just like I almost lost my child. You've been straight for a couple of years. You would never risk losing them because you were a little chilled. You knew when you asked me for that drink that it wasn't whiskey in that bottle."

Now Lieutenant Moon didn't bother to look at anyone; he just rolled his eyes. He'd read Lucy's report, and obviously a few details had been left out.

"Well, I'm glad you have so much confidence in my sobriety, Ezra. I wish I did, but that still doesn't tell me why I should suspect you."

"You can talk with Karen. She'll tell you I used to abuse my daughter and my wife. I never got help for it. I just stopped. When my wife died, I just snapped. I needed to take my rage out on someone. I thought who better than a child nobody wanted and was useless to the world anyway. So I took the baby and beat it to death. Then I burned the body and threw the ashes in the woods where no one would ever find it. I wanted that useless mother and her boyfriend to suffer the way I had suffered," he stated as his eyes began to fill with tears.

"You should have kept your mouth shut, because the boyfriend has already confessed to the murder."

Agent Scruggs walked away from behind the two-way mirror without saying a word. Next anyone saw of him, he was opening the door to the interrogation room. "I'll take over from here, Officer Teller."

"I don't want to talk with you. I want to talk with Lucy," Ezra declared.

"Oh, I'm sorry, but you're a confessed murderer, and we usually don't give them a lot of choices about things. I'm FBI Agent Scruggs, and murder on the reservation is a federal crime, so you'll talk with me." Then he turned to Lucy.

"You need to leave before you end up losing our chance to convict anyone in this case," he told her.

Scruggs turned back to Ezra. "Now let me get this straight. Your wife died so you went to the trouble of kidnapping a child you didn't know in order to get even. Why not just shoot the doctor or the nurses who cared for your wife? How did you even know about this kid anyway?" Scruggs looked at Ezra and waited for an answer, but Ezra just stared back, comfortable in the silence.

Scruggs waited briefly, then he started up again. "You know what I think?" He paused briefly but again got nothing. "I think you're trying to get the boyfriend off the hook, or maybe you're friends with Officer Teller and want to make her look good."

This time Ezra spoke.

"You're just too smart for us, Agent Scruggs. I was trying to help my buddy, but you got the right guy. Sorry I tried to pull the wool over your eyes."

"You know we could charge you with obstructing justice?"

"If you let me go, I'll testify against the boyfriend at trial."

"You got yourself a deal," Scruggs said with a smile.

Lucy, now standing on the other side of the two-way mirror, smiled too. She couldn't let this stand, but it bought her some time, and now it was with the blessing of the FBI.

As Ezra left the interigation room he ran into Bill Blackhalk who was in leg irons and handcuff being escorted to his holding cell. "Now you are going to pay for the lives you've ruined with your chemicals." Ezra barked. Bill looked at him funny, not yet realizing the connection between them. After Scruggs left, Ray and Lucy explained to Lt. Moon with a great deal of trepidation, what they thought was going on, but rather than looking over his glasses at them, he smiled throughout their explanation. Nothing pleased him more than making the FBI look foolish.

Chapter 21

Gabby

Lucy went right to Karen's office. She was feeling energized. She guessed it was partly the excitement of working with Ray and the Lieutenant. Something had definitely changed. She felt, in spite of her blunders as a police officer, that the Lieutenant respected her more, and she wasn't sure how Ray felt, but she knew she felt energy around him she hadn't experienced in years.

She had taken a family sociology class one time, and the instructor had talked about a chemical, abbreviated PEA. It stood for a long chemical name that she couldn't remember and never could pronounce, but it was something your body produced only when you fell in love. It had the combined properties of speed and Hallucinogens. It lasted in the body for only a short while, and no matter what the individual or couple did, the body stopped producing it after three or four years. The instructor's point was that if a couple was going to maintain a relationship, they needed to find other ways to keep their interest in one another. Lucy wasn't ready to admit to love yet, but her body was definitely trying to tell her something about Ray.

She was lucky enough when she reached Karen's office to find her there. Karen smiled when she saw Lucy.

"Where do we start? So much has happened on my end, I don't even know were to begin," Lucy said. "I guess the bottom line is that Dawn's boyfriend confessed to killing Michael, and Ezra tried to confess to killing him, but the FBI didn't want to compromise their case. There's more to it, but I can fill you in as needed as I hear what happened on your end."

"This time Ezra's daughter, Gabby, lived up to her name. I think she was so relieved to be able to talk to someone, she couldn't hold back. She said her father brought the baby over two days after he abducted him. She told her father to return the child, but he would have none of it. She admitted she didn't try too hard to convince him, and within days she began to see a difference in the baby's responsiveness. She promised she wouldn't do anything foolish but admitted it would be hard to give the baby up. She was particularly worried that Dawn would go back to using.

"I assured her that I would do what I could to keep she and Ezra both from getting in trouble, and if Dawn didn't improve, Gabby'd still be the first person I'd choose to care for Michael. What do we do next?"

"Well, the first thing I want to do is let Dawn know her baby's alive, and let Lisa and Dawn see the baby. Then I'll have to spring Dawn's boyfriend, and we may have to pick up Ezra."

"I'd like to go with you to talk with Dawn and to see the baby."

"That's great. I'd like your support."

So Lucy and Karen headed to Shawano. They picked up Lisa from school and met Gabby at her house. She greeted them at the door and offered them coffee and a soft drink for Lisa while Michael was taking a nap. Lisa looked anxious to see her brother, but waited patiently for the baby to wake. Lucy wondered how to bring up what had transpired, but she didn't need to worry. As soon as they were all seated, Gabby started the discussion.

"Have you ever heard of the Berkebinder, Officer Teller?"

"Is that that race they have in Northwest Wisconsin?"

"That's a version of it. Have you ever heard the history of it?"

"No, I can't say as I have," Lucy answered, wondering where this was going.

"The hardest time for my dad after he quit drinking was the winter. The bitter cold days he couldn't get out. He used to ice fish, but that was such a trigger for him to drink, he gave it up. Gradually, he found two things that helped him through. He used to help me with my homework, and he found a great interest in history and geography.

He started reading things, like books and magazines that interested him. When I went off to college near Cable where the Berkebeinder is held, I think my parents followed more to find a bigger library than to be close to me. There my dad found another interest to keep him busy in the winter: cross-country skiing. He could still be out in the nature he loved and allow it to heal him, and he wasn't tempted to drink, because he didn't associate it with alcohol. He'd go out and burn off energy in the day and read till he fell asleep at night.

He got so good, he was even able to complete the 36-mile Birkebinder race. After my mother died, he'd spend the summers cutting narrow paths, too narrow for snowmobilers, through the woods, so he could ski alone on them. One day, I made the mistake of complaining to him about Michael and how his life was in danger and how attached I had become to him.

A few days later, he told me the story of the origin of the Birkebinder. It seems the term came from a group of soldiers in Norway in 1296. They were called that, because they wrapped skins around their legs in the winter and secured them with birch roots. Birkebinder in Norwegian means birch legs.

Anyway, during that time in Norway, there was a civil war being fought between two kings. One of the kings died, and his heir was only two years old. The other king sent soldiers to kill the child, but the birch legs got wind of it and took the boy in a backpack from Lillehammer across the mountains to Rena—36 miles.

The little boy was named Haakon Hakonsson, and he grew up to unite Norway and bring it years of prosperity. They have the race in Norway every year to commemorate the heroism of the birch legs, but in Norway, the 6000 racers must also wear a 3.5 kilo backpack as a symbol of the child that was saved by the birch legs.

"When my father told me that story, I thought he was just relating something he read. I had almost forgotten about it until he showed up at my house in the middle of the night with Michael. To you, my father is a kidnapper, but to him, he's a birch leg soldier saving a young prince from harm."

Lucy was getting ready to answer when she heard a cry from the other room. She looked over at Karen who had tears running down her face.

Lucy had seen her cry only one other time, and that was when Lucy had first entered treatment, and she brought Lucy from treatment to visit her kids for the first time.

Lisa had sat and listened quietly until she heard the baby cry, and then she jumped. Gabby noticed right away and asked Lisa to go with her while she got Michael up from his nap. Lisa smiled and followed her to his bedroom. The three of them came back together just a few minutes later. Lisa couldn't take her eyes off Michael. Lucy was seeing him for the first time and was surprised how responsive he seemed to be for a baby whom everyone thought had so many problems. Karen asked if she could hold him, and her eyes quickly filled with tears again.

His eyes were bright, and he seemed alert. He responded warmly to touch. Lisa was sitting down again but still watching her brother. Gabby asked her if she wanted to hold her brother, and she smiled and shook her head. Perhaps it was coincidence, but Michael put his hand on her cheek in a gesture that looked to all in the room like, "Thanks, Big Sister. You have been my salvation."

"I'd like to take Michael to see his mother in the treatment center," Lucy said, looking compassionately at Gabby. "I promise I'll have him back in a few hours."

Gabby just nodded. "I'll get him dressed. Lisa, come help me."

Lisa followed Gabby into Michael's bedroom.

When they left, Karen just shook her head. "I can't believe the change in that child. Loving people can do miracles," she said.

Little did they know, the real miracle of love was yet to come.

Chapter 22

Michael and Dawn

Michael was a huge hit at the treatment center. The nurses and even Dr. Meany huddled around Dawn when Lucy put Michael in her arms. Dawn started to cry the moment she saw him. "My baby has emerged from a frigid winter with a new soul." She began to speak directly to him. "Yes, Michael, I recognize your body, but your soul is new."

Dr. Wolf, ever mindful of an opportunity for therapeutic intervention, said, "If Michael could talk, I bet he'd say, "Right back at you, Mom." Everyone laughed and applauded for they recognized the truth in that statement. Dawn, too, had been transformed. She had changed perhaps as much as Michael had. Physically, she was so much healthier. Gone were the dark circles under her eyes, the puffmess of her face. Her hair was clean and shiny black, and that's only what you could see. Gone too was the constipation and then diarrhea of withdrawal. Gone were the aches of her muscles and joints. With her kidneys working the way they should, she had lost a lot of water retention, and the exercise she was starting to do was restoring her muscle tone.

That was nothing, however, compared to the changes she was making mentally, emotionally, socially, and spiritually. Gone was the whiny person making everyone else responsible for her pain. She was now out of her room participating in individual and group sessions. She was starting to get out of herself and recognizing and responding to the pain of others, but she was also confronting them with the behaviors she recognized as part of their addiction and becoming increasingly open to her own addictive behavior. She no longer wanted to be alone at other times and was beginning to socialize and laugh with patients and staff. Dr. Wolf told Lucy later that Dawn was the biggest star at the treatment center since Lucy herself had left.

It was as if Dawn and Michael had recognized each other for the first time. The instincts of motherhood had kicked in with Dawn, and Michael responded with the 10-month-old responses of cooing and babbling. He was sitting up without support, and he was aware of his surroundings. Dawn made eye contact with Michael. The two looked at one another for a long moment. Lucy thought that if Michael could talk, he would have said, "You have a new soul, too, Mother."

Dawn then gave the baby to Karen and asked if she would watch him and Lisa, while she talked with Lucy and Dr. Wolf. The three of them went to Dr. Wolf's office. "I wanted to speak to the two of you, before I commit myself, but I'm thinking that maybe I should let Gabby keep Michael. I've seen her with him in the hospital, and she's great. I have my hands full with Lisa, and I need to focus on recovery. Besides, I've had my chance with him, and I blew it. Perhaps Lisa and I could pick him up on the weekends sometimes. When he was missing, I made a deal with God that if he were just alive, I'd find a better home for him. I know I couldn't find a better home than he's in now."

Lucy and Dr. Wolf sat in silence for a while. Partly from shock, partly sorting out all that was said and letting the thoughts flow over them, they gave silence a chance to sort out the magnitude of what was being said. Dr. Wolf spoke first.

"I think the idea is admirable, and I'm even more impressed that you didn't just blurt it out with others around. You truly are getting better. I think it is such an important decision that we should leave it here with the three of us, and we should all continue to think about it. You still have some time in treatment and then months of aftercare and perhaps a half way house. We don't have to decide this today."

"I think that's a great idea, Dr. Wolf," Lucy said. "But on the other hand, the longer that we leave Michael with Gabby, the more attached they will become to one another, and separating them again will be painful. I don't think we should put this off too long."

They agreed to meet again before Dawn left treatment. Lucy also got permission from Dawn to have Lisa see a psychologist. Dawn granted it without hesitation.

On the way back, it was difficult for Lucy not to share Dawn's thoughts with Karen, but Lisa was there, and she knew Karen was wrestling with the same thing. After dropping off Lisa, Karen opened up to Lucy, "After seeing Michael with Gabby, I was convinced I would fight to give her custody, but then I saw Michael with Dawn. Maybe it is time for me to retire. I'm getting to old for this. I am getting too soft for this."

"Maybe we need to let God work it out," Lucy said. "We have some time before we need to make that decision. I'm sure glad that Dawn isn't on an insurance company's plan. She probably would have been moved to outpatient treatment after five days, and that would have been devastating. I think that one reason Dr. Wolf stays on the reservation is that he doesn't have to fight with insurance companies everyday to get people what they need. I think he'll keep her there as long as he can."

After dropping off Karen, Lucy stopped in to see Lieutenant Moon. She told him the news that they had suspected, that Michael was still alive. He took great pleasure in informing Agent Scruggs of that fact, and he and Lucy laughed together at the long pause on the other end when he got the news.

Chapter 23

Bill Blackhawk

Next, Lucy went to talk with Dawn's boyfriend, who was still in custody. His name was Bill Blackhawk and he was father to both Lisa and Michael. Lucy was prepared not to like him since he was responsible for Dawn's addiction to heroin, and the one who kept her supplied with it, but she was surprised. Though she could tell he was still suffering from withdrawal symptoms, the first thing he did was thank Lucy for what she was doing for his family.

"You'll be happy to know that Michael is still alive. Why did you confess to a murder you didn't commit?" Lucy asked.

It took Bill a while to stop crying so he could answer. "Figured that Dawn had somehow done it accidentally and then panicked and dumped the body somewhere. I feel so guilty for what I've done to her and those children, that it was the least I could do to protect her. As for my life, it doesn't amount to anything anyway. So what difference does it make?

"What happened to the baby? And how did you find him?"

"I can't tell you too much about that because it's an ongoing investigation. I can tell you that Michael was kidnapped and taken to a safe place by someone who was concerned for his welfare. You will be happy to know that Michael has done quite well in his new setting and has started to function appropriately for his age level."

"Does this mean I'm free to go?"

"Yes but I have a favor to ask you."

"What's that?"

"I'd like you to either enter treatment the way Dawn did, or leave the area. I think Dawn has a real chance of staying straight, but if you reenter her life, and you are using, you will take her with you. You both will lose everything, even your lives."

Lucy appreciated the fact that Bill thought long and hard about what she had asked. He didn't answer her right away. He sat silently in his cell. Lucy gave him all the time he needed to think.

"I love Dawn and those kids, in spite of what you might think. I don't just use her, although it probably appears that way. But I don't know if I can stop using."

"I'm not asking for promises. You've already gone through the worst of withdrawal. When I let you go, instead of stopping at your dealer, go to treatment. Give it a try."

"Would you take me to treatment center to see Dawn? I know if I leave here now, I don't have the strength to pass up heroin."

Lucy drove him to Maehnowesekiyah. Dawn was surprised to see him and hugged him warmly.

Lucy was hoping he'd stay and allow Dr. Wolf to admit him, but he said he had some business to take care of first. Lucy was sure that meant scoring some heroine but Bill was thinking of another score.

Chapter 24

Lisa

The psychologist thought it would take at least three sessions to gain Lisa's trust and to talk about the losses she had experienced. She allowed Lucy to watch through a two-way mirror after getting Lisa's permission.

Lisa and the psychologist engaged in play therapy. Lucy had told the psychologist of her interest in children and education, so the psychologist explained the process. "It is difficult to get even normal children, especially after a trauma, to just talk. Instead, they often communicate best through play. They gain mastery through their play and they tend to focus on the things that traumatize them. If a child has been in a car accident, they'll crash cars together over and over again. If they've been physically abused, they'll take a doll and hit it again and again. If they've been sexually abused, they'll focus on the genitals of the doll."

What Lucy saw through the two-way mirror surprised her. The room was full of toys, but the psychologist didn't direct her to the cars or the dolls. She said later, "That's like leading the witness," and Lucy understood immediately. Lisa did not go to them on her own. Instead, there was a toy camera in the room, and she was soon taking pictures of everything. After awhile, she focused on a doll as she had done the last time. After taking pictures for a while she dropped the camera and picked up a baby doll. "Would you like me to take the part of the baby" the psychologist asked. "No" Lisa answered "he and his sister are going to sleep now. You be the witch who takes the baby."

So the Psychologist, knowing the story, took some face paint and painted her face and put her brief case on her back held there by a shoulder strap. When she picked up the baby Lisa lifted up the girl doll and speaking for her said "hey where are you going with my brother?"

"I'm going off into the night and you may never see him again. You must stay here and protect your mother I have put her in a deep sleep."

"You are too big and powerful for me witch, I want to help my brother, but what will happen to mother?" Lisa said still speaking through the doll.

"Trust my powerful magic, and maybe you will all be better." The witch answered.

"But I miss my brother." Lisa answered starting to cry.

"I don't want to play anymore." Lisa said though her tears.

Lucy came in from the observation room and held her as she cried.

I think that is enough for today the psychologist said

Great Spirit I could really use some help right now. Lucy began to offer prayers for herself and the wounded child that had been put in her care. Please help me to help her. This was her mantra for the rest of the day. She was exhausted and needed all the help she could get with this one.

Chapter 25

Ezra and Bill

Bill Blackhawk didn't go looking for heroine as Lucy suspected but his mind was still in it's grasp. He had heard from Dawn that Gabby had Michael and she was considering giving her custody. He now put together his brief encounter with Ezra and put two and two together. He decided Ezra would pay for what he had done to his family. His first thought was to take the baby back from Gabby. He got her number from Dawn and called her and asked if he could stop by and see the baby. Gabby agreed, but told him to stop by the next day in the afternoon when her father would be there. Bill waited outside of her house till well after he was suppose to visit and Gabby's husband had arrived home. Soon Ezra left on his snowmobile and Bill stole one from their house and gave chase. Gabby immediately called Lucy and told her what had happened. She wasn't sure it was Bill, but given the circumstances she was pretty sure it was. Lucy called Ray and they put two snowmobiles in her truck along with the skies Hank had left them. They arrived at the fire lane on W just as Bill was crossing it. They unloaded their sleds and skies as quickly as possible, but Bill had a big lead and Ezra would be further ahead, at least they hoped.

Ezra had loaded up with supplies in Shawano while visiting his daughter and after reaching his garage placed them in a sled he pulled behind his skies much like Hank had done with the supplies for the group. He started off on his skies just as Bill arrived. He would have been a sitting duck for Bill, but though many people in Wisconsin were skilled on a snowmobile, Bill wasn't one of them. His recreation for the last several years had come at the end of a needle, plus when he had Ezra dead in his sights he couldn't pull the trigger. Instead Bill swerved and hit a tree. The snowmobile stopped but he didn't. He twisted just enough in the air to keep from hitting the tree head on which would have killed him, but instead left gashes in his face and body that also were life threatening so far from a hospital.

When Ray and Lucy arrived at Ezra's garage, they saw the snowmobile against the tree, and drops of blood near the tree, with a larger amount further away from the tree. It was getting dark and they both turned on their headlamps following drops of blood till it got too dark to see them.

Ray took the lead with his headlamp illuminating the trail and just the edge of the woods. Their skiing had improved dramatically from that first day when they got lessons from Hank. Without the packs they had carried on their first day, and being clear on their destination, they moved at twice the pace they did then, but to Lucy, it was still way too slow.

All Lucy could think of was Bill and Ezra and whether they were alive. There was a lot that Lucy liked about being a cop, but dealing with death was something she hated. She had never gotten used to it, and at times, she was haunted by the finality of it.

They skied silently through the night. Lucy thought of what she had been through just a month or two earlier. She thought about how tired she was, or how her lip had throbbed where Reilly had hit her. She was reminded of the pain in her ribs that were cracked where Kane had hit her, though if she'd been conscious of it, she could have felt the pain increase with each deep breath she took as she exerted herself to move faster down the trail.

What would happen to the kids if they lost both their teacher and his assistant all in one night? What about Kathy's father who still wasn't over the death of his wife, and who had put everything into raising his daughter? What about Brad who finally had the chance to be with the one he had loved from afar for so long?

She could now see a light coming from Ezra's cabin. To Lucy, it was a light of hope burning through the dark woods that surrounded them. It was like the tiny light of life that burns in each of us, that is too often unfairly forced out early by evil. That light that is so fragile and burns for just an instant in comparison to the life of the universe.

To Lucy, Ezra's light didn't seem to get any closer, and occasionally she lost the light when a larger tree would block its view.

Finally, they arrived outside of Ezra's cabin. "Ezra, are you in there?" Lucy shouted.

"Yes, but I'm busy at the moment, so just let yourselves in."

Ray and Lucy skied the additional distance to the cabin and quickly removed their skis. When they entered, they saw Bill lying on his kitchen table. Ezra was bending over him. On the table alongside Bill was some rubbing alcohol and a bottle of whiskey.

"Great," Lucy thought. "Ezra is operating on Bill, and he's drunk on top of it." Though wanting to hold back for fear of what she would see, Lucy rushed over. Ezra never looked up, but as she approached and stood next to him, he spoke softly.

"You guys arrived just in time. I've been looking all over this cabin for a pair of scissors to cut these stitches, and I can't find one. You don't have a Swiss army knife on you, do you?"

Ray pulled one from his pocket and handed it to Lucy.

"Great. When I tell you, cut the thread."

Lucy looked down at Bill and saw that Ezra had removed his coat and sweater and had placed several stitches in a three-inch long gash in his side. Bill looked pale and didn't appear to be conscious. Ray put his arm around Lucy when he noticed she had become pale also. Still not looking up, Ezra said, "I think your friend will be O.K. He's lost some blood, but the tree just grazed his head and his side."

"How did you learn how to do this?" Lucy asked.

"I was a medic in Nam. Ray, why don't you stoke up the fire? He's probably cold without a top on."

Ezra showed Lucy where to cut the thread, and then Ray raised Bill up while Ezra wrapped a bandage made from a pillowcase around his waist. They covered him with one of Ezra's flannel shirts and moved him to Ezra's bed.

"Is he passed out from loss of blood?" Lucy asked.

"I would say he's more likely passed out from the alcohol I gave him."

"Where did you get the whiskey? I can tell it's not the pretend stuff you had the last time we were out here."

"You know, God works in mysterious ways. I haven't had a drink in twenty years, and on the way back with your friend, I found a bottle in a hollow tree that I must have hid during a blackout. Finally, something good has come from those days."

What happened out there? Lucy asked. I had just gotten off my sled, and put on my skies and loaded the provisions on to the sled I pull behind me and hooked it to my waist. I was a sitting duck for Bill to hit me with the snow mobile he was on, but at the last second he veered off and hit a tree. He was laying in the snow and bleeding pretty bad. I told him I'd fix him up if he agreed to get help and be the husband and father he was capable of, or I'd let him bleed to death in the snow. I guess recovery looked like a good alternative to him at the time. I put some snow on his wounds to slow the bleeding, and then I put him on the sled I pull behind my skis, and told him to keep his hand against his side and one at the side of his head. When I found the bottle, I gave him a few good belts to ease the pain. It seemed to start working right away."

"He would come in and out of consciousness and we'd talk on occasion. I suggested he not do it the way I did, that he should get some help. Since I was invested in him now, I'd even go to meetings with him, even be his sponsor if he wanted. You know I've had some amazing discoveries living out here alone. You guys have your cell phones and text messages that I see on TV when I visit my daughter, but I tune into different channels out here. Spiritual ones, but I think it's time for me to connect with the living again and maybe I can help Dawn and Bill and Lisa to survive and find a new life again.

"Could we use that sled to get him to the snow mobiles we have by your garage and get him to a hospital?"

"Sure, I will get my coat and pull him for you."

They bundled Bill up in a coat and blanket. He woke up briefly and smiled when he saw Lucy and Ray. Kathy looked very pale as he drifted off.

"You are about to have a rough ride," Ezra said, and gave him a few more sips of whiskey.

"Careful with that stuff, Ezra. He will need to detox all over again."

"Hell, I would have had it drained ten minutes after I found it. Now I would rather drink battery acid than that stuff. I'm going to die sober."

"Glad to hear you say that, Ezra, but all I say is I'm not going to drink today."

"Well, if you drink tomorrow, I might have to come and take those beautiful children of your's, "Ezra said, smiling.

"They are the reason I will get up tomorrow morning and say I'm not going to drink today."

"Why not get it all out of the way at once like I did?" Ezra asked.

"You will have to come to a meeting with me sometime and I will let the experts explain that."

"Maybe I will do that. I don't think they will influence me much, but I do get lonely out here sometimes, and I could use the fellowship."

Once Bill was safely in the sled, Ezra took off toward the fire lane. Even pulling a sled, Ray and Lucy could barely keep up with Ezra. Once at the fire lane, they attached the sled to one of the snow mobiles and drove to W. When they reached W, there was an ambulance with its dome lights flashing.

Bill opened his eyes and looked at all the commotion with even more confusion. She turned to Lucy and spoke to her for the first time since running into the woods.

"You people in AA, don't you say when your day is going bad that you need a 'do over"?"

Lucy and Ray waited at the hospital nearly an hour while Bill was admitted for observation. Once they got into his room, they all had little to say. Bill had a tube in each arm, one with an antibiotic and the other with blood.

"Do you remember the promise you made to Ezra?" Lucy asked Bill.

"I remember and I plan to keep it. As soon as I get out of here I want to go where Dawn is. I want to get better, and when I get out of there I'm going to drag his ass to a meeting. He's going to pay for every stitch in my head and side. Ray and Lucy looked at one another and smiled.

Chapter 26

Ezra

Lucy was confident that Scruggs would just want this whole case to go away, but to her surprise, he issued a warrant for Ezra's arrest. She was disappointed and wished it could all go away. He listed on the warrant not only kidnapping, but also child endangerment.

Ray and Lucy were given the assignment of serving the warrant and arresting Ezra. They set out the next morning off W in snowmobiles and carrying their skis. Once she was on her skis, Lucy's mind quickly wandered. She began to think about the fact that without Ezra, she may never have started skiing, and now she was quite sure she would continue. She was convinced that Ray enjoyed it too. She was hoping that soon she could get her children to try it.

Both she and Ray had brought their weapons, but she hoped and prayed it wouldn't come to using them. Ezra had been willing to confess once, but that was to protect his daughter and new grandson. She was quite sure Ezra would rather die than go to jail. It was a sunny day with the temperature in the twenties, perfect for skiing. As she looked at the trees, she thought she could see the shadow of spring buds on the branches. The snow sparkled as if saying, "Stay in the moment. Don't wish me away. Appreciate the beauty that I offer."

Ray and Lucy skied in silence. Lucy wondered what Ray's thoughts were as he looked around at the beauty that surrounded them. She felt comfortable with the silence, but she admitted to herself that she wondered what was in his heart. Did he get the same strong feelings when he was around her that she got around him?

Soon they arrived at Ezra's cabin. Lucy saw smoke coming from his chimney and figured he was there.

"Ezra, it's Lucy Teller and Ray Waupause. Can we come and speak with you for a while?" They waited respectfully for him to appear on his porch. It seemed like a long time, but the door finally opened, and he appeared.

"Come in. I'll make some coffee," he shouted and gestured.

Lucy and Ray skied to the porch and took off their skis. They propped them against the side of the house next to Ezra's skis and entered the cabin. Lucy got the impression that Ezra had spent a good part of the morning skiing since there was still snow on his skis, then came back and lit a fire in the stove and lay down to take a nap, when she and Ray interrupted his dreams. The cabin still had a chill to it, and Ezra's bed looked like he had just vacated it. The three of them remained silent while Ezra brewed coffee and then poured three cups.

"So what brings you two out here today?" he asked as he handed them each a cup that steamed excessively in the still chilly air. "It gets so a guy can't get through his daily routine anymore without getting interrupted by the police." This convinced Lucy all the more that Ezra spent his morning skiing and hunting, then lunch followed by a nap. She wondered then if maybe he didn't frequently go to Loon Lake to have dinner with his daughter and family, and then sled and ski back to his cabin in the dark. She felt sad to think what would happen to this man confined to an eight-by-six-foot jail cell.

Lucy saw no way to soften the blow. "I'm afraid we have a warrant for your arrest." Ezra took a deep breath and looked toward heaven and his wife. There was a long silence. Finally, Ezra shook his head.

"I don't understand white man's law. Because of what I did, Michael has a better home and a better life ahead. His mother got the help she needed, and the dad, too. Hank and Bobbie got a chance to relieve some of their grief and guilt. You two had a chance to spend time together and fall in love, whether you know it or not, and I got a chance to work on my grief and loss. For this, I should be punished?

The only thing I did that I should be punished for is scaring Lisa and you guys and Bobbie. That's the only thing I regret."

"I agree." Ray said.

"Then how can you guys do this?" His eyes searched for some answers.

"A person who has higher authority ordered us to bring you in to stand trial," Lucy answered.

"How can there be a higher authority than your own conscience?"

Lucy and Ray looked at each other.

"Just let me put on my skis and head into the woods. Give me a gun with one bullet in it, and I will save the taxpayers the cost of a trial and prison. I will be with Emily and all will be well."

"I would strongly consider that, except for two reasons: one, I have a line of people who are ready to testify on your behalf. White man's justice is blind perhaps, but they sometimes have a heart when it comes to sentencing. I don't think you will get any jail time. Second, you are one of the few men in the world who might be able to say you delivered a baby. I want you to live to enjoy Michael."

Lucy had said the magic words.

"I'll be ready in a minute." Ezra dressed for his trip.

The judge and the district attorney agreed that Ezra was not a flight risk, and a group of people including Hank, Kathy, Ray, and Gabby came up with bail. The trial went as Lucy predicted. Those testifying on Ezra's behalf were Karen, Lucy, Dawn, Bill, Ray, Hank, and Bobbie. Ezra was found guilty of kidnapping, but the judge sentenced him to probation and community service.

He was good to his word and visited Bill in treatment and started attending meetings. He took a group of the alumni from treatment to Garski Flowage between Langlade and Antigo. There they met Hank his family and some friends and spent the day cross-country skiing and picnicking in the warming house there. Just as Lucy suspected Doc Wolf love the skiing he brought his son and daughter who came home for the weekend from college to try it and spend time with him and his wife Gayle. Lucy was surprised that Gayle didn't join them. "She said she didn't want to spend the day freezing her butt off and watching me get addicted to another form of exercise. She decided on the casino instead." Doc said, with a hint of disappointment. "The kids are having a great time though, so maybe this is one I won't have to do alone.

Gayle thought about saying maybe Gayle better worry about her own addictions if she decides on the casino instead of being with her family, but she thought better of it. Still Dr. Wolf didn't seem the same, but she wondered if he was a little uncomfortable playing a different role than he was use to with these people.

Ezra seemed to get along well with the group and talked about attending other functions that the group offered.

The biggest surprise of the day was that agent Scruggs also joined the group. In spite of his stiff external appearance, he was a good athlete and very quickly picked up skiing and even ventured into the expert runs. Lucy sat with him while they warmed up and had some snacks at the warming house. "You know when I was first given this assignment as a new agent right out of the air force I hated it. I thought I'd be wasting my time and talent up here, but I've learned a lot from being here. I've come to appreciate nature and all it has to offer. We would all benefit from spending more time like we are spending it today. But I've learned the most from you officer Teller. There is much more to police work, than you can learn from a book, or the academies. You have a feel for people that no one could teach."

Lucy swallowed and thanked Jim Scruggs sincerely. "That may be true, but I think I miss judged you. I appreciate your coming today so I could get to know you. Not many in your position would do this."

"Maybe that's why so many in my position are out of touch with what really matters in the world."

Chapter 27

Lucy and Kathy

Even though she was going to be in a wedding today, Kathy didn't miss her morning run. It was another fall in full bloom, and Kathy was appreciating every breath which she could see leaving her body like puffs from a steam engine. It was sunny but still cold. The weatherman had predicted a day in the 60's if the sunshine held. Right now, there wasn't a cloud in the sky, but 60's seemed like a stretch.

Still, Kathy wasn't complaining. It was sunny and brilliant. She had parked her car at Lucy's house on Rabbit Ridge Road, as they had planned to dress together. Lucy was excited because getting ready with Kathy was sort of like the prom she had never attended. Kathy followed the path Lucy had told her to follow, up Old South Branch Road and turning off at the sand and gravel road after the hill and the curve. As she continued through a field filled with the gold, brown, and orange of fall, she noticed a familiar figure next to a large tree.

Kathy stopped running and waited respectfully as Lucy completed her smudging ceremony. When the smoke had subsided and Lucy had returned her items to her bag, Kathy spoke.

"I was thinking about some perfume today, too, but I'm thinking of a little different fragrance."

Lucy smiled and stood quickly. The two women hugged.

"I suppose at a wedding you have the right to act like a girly girl."

Lucy and Kathy had remained close since nearly dying together. Lucy had dated Ray Waupuse for several months now. Her children liked him, as did her mother, but Lucy continued to be cautious.

Ray was not demanding. In fact, Lucy thought he was pretty cautious himself about taking on a wife and two children, not to mention a wife one drink away from serious problems. Lucy's program was strong and getting stronger, but the reality of addiction was all around him, particularly in his line of work.

The biggest problem for Lucy was getting used to a man so different from any she had known so intimately. He was kind, gentle, and considerate and even after two years, she found herself doubting he was real. Despite all her experience with men, Lucy couldn't explain why she was attracted to him. But there was no denying she was.

Lucy had continued on in school since the trial and conviction of Kane and Jack Reilly and their accomplices. None of them would see the light of day for a long time, and she hoped Reilly would find every bit of trouble in prison that he was expecting.

She had changed direction in school and now majored in Special Education. She had known it was the right choice from the time she had seen Scott's students at his funeral. She was even helped by a scholarship set up by the Brandt family to which several people who attended the funeral had contributed.

She would never forget the speech Hank Brandt made at the medal ceremony where they presented her with the scholarship.

"You came as close as humanly possible to giving us our son back," he said. Then he added something that perhaps only she fully understood. "We thought our son had died wrapped up in his addiction to snow, but because of your work and the risks you took, we now know our son was involved in protecting the fragile yellow butterflies in his charge. I and my family will always be grateful for that."

"You could still be the maid of honor," Kathy said, as she pulled Lucy back from her thoughts. They had started running back to town together. They had discovered earlier on a run that neither of them had to change their pace for the other.

'You have a maid of honor. Besides, I already have one gown I will never wear again. I don't need two."

"My maid of honor never saved my life, and you can take her place in jeans if you want."

"You still don't get the concept. My stupidity almost cost you your life. I didn't save it. Maybe Ray could be your mister of honor."

"Well, I guess I'll have to settle for the fact that you'll both be there. I'm thankful that you're coming to the wedding and for the friendship we have developed."

Lucy smiled at her, and as their legs continued to move in harmony, she put her arm around Kathy's shoulder for a moment, and no words were necessary.

They finished their run in silence. When they got to Lucy's house, Lucy went inside to pay her respects to Kathy's father, whom Kathy had brought with her. He had been talking with Lucy's mother and children.

"How are you doing, Uncle?" she asked in the traditional greeting toward an elder. "I hear you will be expanding your family soon."

"It helps for me to think of it that way. But I've gotten used to her presence in the house since she moved back home and I sure will miss that." Lucy smiled a sad smile knowing all too well what it was like to have the soul of your house missing. She patted his knee, knowing there were no words.

"Well, I better check on Ray and start getting ready. I don't dress up a lot, so I don't have much practice. Come to think of it, neither does Ray. I'm sure he'll want my help. He doesn't wear a suit very often."

Lucy called Ray and talked with him, then gave the phone to Kathy to talk with Brad who was getting ready at Ray's. They both talked and laughed like kids getting ready for the prom. Lucy began thinking about what it would be like to plan a wedding of her own. After they were all dressed, she walked into the ceremony to see Ray smiling at her. Seeing him with no questions of where she'd been—-just happy to see her—made her planning increase a notch. And her hopes for the future grew even more real.

Chapter 28

Dawn and Bill

Lisa and Michael's parents, Dawn and Bill, had both been straight for over six months now. They both attended AA and aftercare at the treatment center. Lisa stayed with Lucy and her family for a month after Bill finished treatment, to give them all time to adjust to living clean and sober. Michael remained with Gabby. His new Grampa Ezra looked forward to teaching him about the outdoors. Bill and Dawn had given him up for adoption, and with Karen's help, that went smoothly. They visited Gabby and Michael occasionally, and the arrangement seemed to be working well.

Bill asked Dawn to marry him after three months sobriety. Their counselors at the center warned them about making big changes in their lives with less than a year of sobriety, but since they had lived together for years, even the counselors had to admit it wasn't that big a change. Since they didn't have a lot of sober friends after years of using, Dawn asked Lucy, Kathy, and Bobbie to be her bridesmaids.

The whole group had become friends. And Bill asked Ray, Brad, and Tom to be in the wedding party. Lucy, Bobbie, and Kathy drove in Lucy's truck over to All Saints and their families came separately. They would ride around town after the wedding and head for Legend Lake to take photos outside. Lucy hoped to get some pictures with the loons or an eagle in the background. The eagle seemed to be even a more powerful part in her life. Father Mike performed the ceremony. He invited each of the attendants to speak briefly. The group elected Brad to speak for them. Lucy was surprised at Brad. He appeared to be a quiet, shy man, but he seemed comfortable at the pulpit. Brad spoke of wanting them to care for one another. Then he spoke of the three C's— cultivate, commit and communicate.

Father Mike picked right up on the words that Brad spoke.

"In some ways," he said, "words are like the seeds we plant and cultivate. Words can be used to inflict endless damage, or words can be used to heal. Your words can be weeds that choke and destroy life, or your words can nurture and enhance life. Your words can be seeds that create or destroy. Think of the possibility that every word out of your mouth is a seed or a weed.

"Let's each of us choose today, in honor of all the people here today and those that attend in spirit, to plant seeds of life." Father Mike stopped and looked into every face in the church.

"Seeds or weeds, it's your choice. Plant seeds, people. Plant seeds."

Lucy looked over at Ray. This was someone whom she hoped to be planting seeds with on many different levels for a long time to come. She also looked at so many people in the church who were part of her life, and she hoped with all of them she could say and do things that would cultivate and nourish them.

Other Books of Interest
by Robert Bollendorf
From AuthorHouse

Summer Heat

The Challenger

A Rose by Any Other Name

Acknowledgements

Many of the same people were involved in this book that have helped us in each of the books so far. So thank you all for your continued help and support. We would like especially to thank Tom Richardson for his input on cross-country skiing and winter camping. Tom and Rob have been friends for a number of years and have had a number of wilderness adventures together, so his counsel and advise in those areas have been over a number of decades.

Our special thanks also goes to April Hanstad who has worked tirelessly on improving the quality of these books. There are hundreds of details that would have been missed if not for her. Thanks too to Joe Barillari for his efforts to make this a quality product, but also for his faith in us as writers and willingness to take a risk on our behalf.

Printed in the United States
By Bookmasters